Crystal,
Team Cal forever!
XOXO,

Crystal,
Team Cal forever!
XOXO,

LET ME IN
BOOK 4

# Half of My HEART

JESSICA MARIN

For my husband, Matt. Thank you for working so hard to allow me to make my dreams a reality. You've believed in me from day 1 and continue to do so even when I have my own self-doubts.

I love you.

# Blurb

Cal Harrington is an A-list Hollywood Actor who's used to getting any woman he wants. Problem is that he hasn't seen the woman he wants in four years.

Meeting Jenna Pruitt on a first-class flight to Las Vegas led to the best week of his life. The beautiful divorcée rocked Cal's world in a whirlwind fling, leaving him wanting more. But she made it clear they could be nothing more since her heart was still battered from her divorce. Being the "British Gentleman" that his reputation calls him, he let her go with only her email address as a point of contact.

Now he's done being a gentleman.

Cal's convinced that after all this time, Jenna was the one that got away and he's determined to do everything in his power to make her his.

But Jenna has been keeping a secret and a tale of lies, deceit, and miscommunication is uncovered. Will Cal's love and devotion for Jenna be able to heal the mistrust between them?

****Half of My Heart is the hero's POV from Heartbreak Warfare. While some scenes overlap, this book contains brand new content never released!*****

# A Note From The Author

When I wrote Heartbreak Warfare in 2018, the only point of view that was speaking to me was the voice of the heroine, Jenna Pruitt. I had this story in my head for about five years before I physically typed it out and published it. Every book since then has had a dual point of view with the hero and heroine except for Heartbreak Warfare. It was time that Cal's voice was heard and I'm beyond excited to finally share with you his side of the story in Half of My Heart.

Cal and Jenna are just one of those couples that always come to my mind. I don't know if it's because they were the couple that started it all for me or what, but I love bringing them back to life in other stories whenever I can. I hope you fall in love with them as much as I have.

If you are a new to me reader and are wondering which book you should read first, I would hope that each book could be read as a standalone. Heartbreak Warfare is in Jenna's POV and starts from the very beginning of when and how they met. Half of My Heart is Cal's POV and it picks up during a gap where they were not together anymore. You would be fine reading this book first, but if you want the full experience of the Let Me In series, then I recommend starting with Heartbreak Warfare, Half of My Heart, Perfectly Lonely and then Edge of Desire.

Thank you so much for being here and taking the time out of your busy lives to read my words.

XOXO,

Jessica

LET ME IN
BOOK 4

# Half of My HEART

# Prologue

I STORM THROUGH the entrance of my hotel room, slamming the door shut behind me, and toss my keycard down on the console table. My cell phone in my pants pocket keeps vibrating with calls and messages from my agent and friends asking, *Where are you* and *Is everything okay?*

If they only knew what was wrong with me, they'd think I was crazy. My mood is as black as the tuxedo I'm wearing and it's all because my mind keeps playing tricks on me, making me see the one woman who's been haunting me for years.

Jenna Pruitt.

It's award season here in Hollywood, and tonight I was on the red-carpet doing press when a petite brunette caught my attention. From behind, she looked exactly like Jenna with the same hair color, build, and height. My heart hammered in my chest with hope that it was her and all rational thoughts disappeared from my brain. I rudely walked away from the reporter who was interviewing me and roughly grabbed the woman's arm to turn her around to face me. Of course she wasn't Jenna, and I should've known better. There's no reason for Jenna to be here. She's not involved in my industry and when I met her all those years ago, she made it crystal clear that she wasn't interested in dating a Hollywood actor.

After apologizing to the woman I grabbed, I turned around and saw that my actions were caught on camera by the paparazzi. I smiled and played it off the best I could, but on the inside, I felt like I was suffocating. I had to get away—no, I *needed* to get away. Away from the fake smiles, the blinding lights of the cameras flashes watching my every move, and most importantly, I needed to get away from the people acting as if they give a fuck about me.

That was the thing I admired most about Jenna. She didn't care who I was.

I take off my jacket and toss it over the back of the sofa. My fingers roughly tug at the bowtie around my neck before I'm able to free it from my shirt. I walk over to the wet bar, pour myself a shot of whiskey, and down it in a single gulp. The burning sensation from the liquid fire briefly distracts me from my thoughts of Jenna. I take a couple deep breaths, willing myself to calm down.

*How can I be this obsessed over someone I barely knew?*

Anytime I see someone who remotely resembles Jenna, a wave of memories of our time together comes crashing across my mind. So many emotions are coursing through me, causing me to pace from my high energy. My mother always told me that if I can't express myself verbally, then writing words down would be the next best thing. I walk over to the desk and rummage through the drawers until I find a pad of paper with the hotel's name on it along with a pen. I sit down on the couch to think of what I want to say. I start to mentally craft a letter to Jenna and start writing.

*Fuck, does this feel stupid*, I momentarily think and pause but what does it matter? She'll never read it. This is for my benefit only to finally admit my true feelings for her. I close my eyes and take a deep breath before continuing.

*Dear Jenna,*

*I can only imagine the look of surprise that would cross your beautiful face if you ever saw this letter. Considering it's been over four years since we last saw each other and I have no way of getting in touch with you, I'm confident you'll never read this. My last email to you bounced back. Why? What the hell happened? I don't recall seeing any warning signs from you. Your emails were the only thing that kept me sane during my grueling work schedule. I told my assistant to let you know that I would write you back as soon as I could. I'm sorry if you felt neglected by my lack of communication. I realize now that I completely fed into your fears of dating an actor by not making you a priority.*

*Why am I asking these questions after all this time? Because I can't stop thinking of you. Lately, my mind seems to conjure you up everywhere I go. You would've thought it would have been bad in the beginning, but my need to see you has only gotten worse. After I stopped hearing from you and finished the movie I was working on when we met, I kept myself busy. I threw myself into work, accepting back-to-back movie roles until I was mentally and physically worn out. I kept telling myself that I just needed to move on, and I tried, Jenna, fuck did I try, but no other woman has compared to you. I knew from our first date that you were something special and I should've never let you go.*

*I was a damn fucking fool for only accepting your email address after our incredible week together in Las Vegas. I should've demanded your phone number and not have been so respectful of your hesitation to give it to me. But I knew your scars from your divorce were fresh and deep. I was determined that our emails were going to prove you wrong–that we weren't just going to be a fling. But for whatever reason, I stopped hearing from you and that isn't fucking acceptable anymore. I need a reason why, Jenna, because I can now admit to myself that being your rebound fling wasn't going to be enough for me.*

*I want to be your forever.*

*How in the hell do I fix this, Jenna? Have you even thought about me at all these past four years? Because you haven't left me. It's like your scent has made a bubble around me, making me take deep breaths of an illusion that you're somewhere nearby. Your smile pops into my head at any given time and I can still hear your sexy voice.*

*Fuck, I'm getting hard just remembering what you looked like when I made you come.*

*It's time, Jenna. I'm done chasing after ghosts. I refuse to believe that the bond between us was just my imagination. I pray to God that you aren't married again, because if you're not–NO ONE will be standing in the way of making you mine.*

*I'm coming for you, Jenna.*

*Yours,*

*Cal*

I put the pen down and smile at how fucking right this feels. I'm going to find Jenna and fate just handed me the perfect opportunity with my next movie filming in her last known location—Chicago. Finding her is going to require some help though. I grab my cell phone and dial my agent's phone number.

"Cal, what the fuck? Where'd you go? I have some unhappy people here demanding you come back," Philip yells as soon as he picks up my call.

"I need to hire a private investigator, Philip."

"A private investigator? Cal, can't this wait until the morning? You need to get your ass back here *now!*"

"Accept the fucking fact that I'm not coming back there tonight until I talk to a private investigator," I growl at him.

"Shit, Cal," he mutters in defeat, knowing full well he won't win this argument. “I know someone that I can call for you, but what is so damn important that it has to be done right now?”

“I need to find Jenna Pruitt and I need to find her ASAP.”

# Chapter 1

"SO, LET ME make sure I'm understanding you correctly. You left one of the biggest awards shows in our industry because you assaulted some strange woman you didn't know, stormed off back to your hotel before the show even began, and made our agent hire a private investigator to find the girl you banged for one week years ago?"

I grit my teeth in annoyance at the sarcasm in my best friend's voice and how crazy he makes me sound. I knew he wouldn't understand, and I was dreading this conversation. "I didn't assault the woman, I just surprised her by grabbing her arm and turning her around to face me."

Sean stares at me in silence, blinks a couple of times before laughing uncontrollably. I growl out in frustration and go back to doing my workout, willing myself to ignore his mockery. After Philip got me in touch with his private investigator, I flew back home to London, which is where I live in between filming. I'm eager to hear back from the P.I., but he warned me that it might take him a week or two before he can get started since he was already in the middle of another job and was doing this as a favor for Phillip. I've been trying to keep myself distracted with reading scripts, working out, and spending time with my family and friends. I hadn't talked to Sean since my appearance on the red carpet, so I invited him to workout with me today.

What a stupid idea that was.

Sean Lindsey is one of my best mates from boarding school and also a Hollywood actor. Our families have gone on holidays with one another and we've now made multiple movies together. Sean has found his fame with romantic comedies whereas I prefer roles that have more drama and suspense. Calling him my best friend is an understatement.

He's more like the brother I never had.

He met Jenna when we were in Las Vegas because we were working on the same movie together. He knew I was trying to pursue something deeper with her after she had left and was there to get me drunk numerous times when I was down about her cutting me out of her life. I was expecting his support in my pursuit of finding her—not him making me feel like a damn fool.

His laughter starts to subside, and I take a peek at him while mentally counting my reps of chest presses. He stares at me with a smile and shakes his head.

"Mate, I love you like a brother, but this shit is crazy talk. Every time you're in between movies, you wonder about that lass. You know what I think?"

I really don't want to, but he's going to indulge me anyway.

"You need to fuck her out of your system and what better way than to get inside someone else?"

I glare at him while putting my bar back in its holder. I ignore his comment and stand up to go to the punching bag. Maybe picturing the bag as his head will make me feel better.

He follows me to the bag, determination set in his eyes. "When was the last time you had a taste of some succulent cherry pie, eh?" He looks around quickly to see if anyone heard him and then winks at me.

"Shut up," I growl in disgust, trying to stay focused on my

boxing and not on the direction this conversation is going.

"I'm serious, Cal. This broody asshole you play on screen might be killing it at the box office and creaming women's panties all over the world, but it's getting tiresome amongst your friends and family."

I stop the bag and hold it with my hands before raising an eyebrow at him in question. "Really? I didn't realize you had become the new press secretary for the Harrington Clan." I resume punching the bag, forcing Sean to take a step back. "And as far as my friends go, you're the only person I consider to be a friend. Anyone else claiming they are can go piss off."

"What about Cora? You used to consider her a friend." His expression turns serious as it does most of the time when talking about Cora. "She's worried about you too."

"I bet she is," I sarcastically respond, refusing to say more. Sean gets the hint and turns around to go run on the treadmill.

Sean and I met Cora Gregory when we all were at boarding school together. Cora came from a rough homelife, so we always felt the need to protect her from the bullies at school. All three of us got discovered at the same time by an agent while we were on a holiday break. Having all of us start this journey together at the same time made it easier and reassured us that we had someone we could trust going through the same process. I always viewed Cora like a sister but as the years moved on, she started developing feelings for me. Cora turned into a stunning woman, but I never felt the same way for her as she did for me. Not to mention, I saw the way Sean looked at her from the moment he met her at school. I knew he was in love with her, and I did my best to never lead her on. I tried to make it clear—I didn't want more than just a friendship with her.

But Cora never took the hint and even managed to get me to kiss her one night while I was absolutely blitzed out of my mind. All three of us were at a friend's party and I had just broken up with a girl I was dating because I had lost interest in her, sizing her up to the memory of Jenna. I thought getting drunk would be the temporary amnesia of Jenna I needed, and Cora was game in feeding into that. She was by my side the whole night, helping me get drunk and when she saw I was past the point of oblivion, she took me to a bathroom and locked us in. I was in no condition to fight off her advances and the alcohol convinced my mind that Cora was actually Jenna. Thinking I was with Jenna, I accepted and participated in Cora's advances and if it wasn't for Sean banging on the door and discovering us, I shudder to think how far it would've gone.

Since that night, I've tried to keep my distance from Cora. I felt like an asshole for betraying Sean and his feelings for her. Even though he knew I wasn't myself, he was hurt by my actions. I apologized to him and vowed I would never let myself be alone with Cora again. I saw a different side to her that evening—a side that was calculated and manipulative.

A side that felt evil.

She knows exactly how Sean feels about her. He's made it perfectly clear that he wants to be with her, but she continues to dangle him on a rope, using him when it's only convenient for herself. I wish he would move on and realize he deserves better, but for some reason, he just can't shake off her toxic claws.

My cell phone ringing breaks me out of my memories and back to the present. I sprint over to my gym bag to retrieve it. Thomas Matthews, the name of the private investigator, flashes across my screen and I immediately answer it.

"I've got some news on Jenna Pruitt, Mr. Harrington," Thomas tells me after we exchange pleasantries. "She's still living in Chicago and continues to run her event planning business. In fact, she seems to be one of the most sought-after event planners in Chicago. Even has a TV segment on one of the local news channels."

My pulse races in excitement at the news that she's still in Chicago and is thriving with her career. But he still hasn't answered the most important question. "Has she remarried?" I cut him off impatiently, needing to know the answer.

"No, sir, she has not remarried but she is currently in a relationship with Mr. Jax Morrow, a defensive forward for the local professional hockey team." My mood immediately blackens, and I didn't realize I'd growled until I felt Sean's grip on my bicep. I look up to see him watching me with concern.

"How long?" I demand, squashing my disappointment that she's taken and praying that it's not serious.

"According to my calculations of the earliest report of them seen together, it's been almost a year. Hard to say because he spent his summer back in Canada where he's from to be with his daughter from a previous marriage. He did fly to Chicago three times to see Ms. Pruitt during that time frame."

*Fuck.* Him flying to see Jenna while he was back home for the off-season means it could be serious—at least on his part. "Did she go see him in Canada?"

"Not sure. I have contacts in his city and they've never seen her there, but if they stayed secluded in his house, then no one would really know."

I can't handle the thought of Jenna being secluded with any other man so I chose to ignore that part of his conversation. I pray his contacts are accurate because if Jenna hasn't visited his hometown she might not be as invested in the relationship as he is.

"I want confirmation on how long they've been together and if it's serious. Is that possible?"

"I'll try, Mr. Harrington. I've scheduled my flight to Chicago and will have more information for you within the next two weeks."

"Excellent. Safe travels and I look forward to hearing from

you soon."

I end the call and take a deep breath of satisfaction, knowing that I'm one step closer in finding Jenna.

"I'm assuming your guy found her and she's not married?" I nod my head at Sean's question and a glimmer of hope starts to form in my chest.

"Not married, but in a relationship with some hockey bloke."

"So, you're saying there's a chance…" Sean jokes with an evil smile and glint in his eye. I've never been one to pursue someone who's already in a relationship, but when it comes to Jenna, everything is off limits. If she's happy and she tells me herself that he's the one for her, then I will back down.

Until that happens…game fucking on.

"Oh, there's definitely a chance."

# Chapter 2

I STARE OUT the window of my office, my mind a million miles away from the present. My sister, who also happens to be my personal assistant, is here going over the schedule for the next couple of months. I should be paying attention to this important information, but I'm distracted by the fact that it's been three weeks since I've heard from Thomas and I'm growing restless. While he never told me the exact date of when he was traveling to Chicago, I automatically assumed it would be sooner rather than later.

"Wanker!"

That jolts me out of my thoughts, and I look at my sister in surprise.

"Excuse me?"

"So, you hear that loud and clear but you're a daft cow before then?" I blink at her, not confirming or denying her claim. "That's exactly what I thought, so yes, you're a wanker."

"I'm sorry, Bridget." I exhale out my apology because there are no good excuses that would be acceptable for ignoring her. "I have a lot on my mind."

"Yeah, well I have a lot on my mind and my plate, so I don't need to be wasting my time or my breath if it's only going to fall on deaf ears," she scolds, and I feel like we're children again and I'm getting into trouble for something I didn't do.

Bridget has been my personal assistant now for two years when I could no longer trust my former assistant, Valerie. Valerie almost cost me a job due to her jealousy of other women. I never knew she had feelings for me—our relationship was strictly professional on my end. It's been a breath of fresh air not having to question my sister's loyalty or trust like I had to with Valerie.

"Again, I'm sorry. I promise you have my full attention this time."

"No, I don't think so. I think you need to tell me what's going on that has your focus somewhere else."

I narrow my eyes at her, trying to gauge if she's genuinely concerned or just wants something to gossip about with my other sister and parents. Bridget is notorious for not keeping secrets and would always rat me out when growing up. But since she's now my personal assistant, I feel it might be best to tell her what's going on, especially so she won't be surprised when getting the invoice from Thomas.

"I've hired a private investigator and I'm waiting to hear back from him."

Now it's her turn to narrow her eyes at me. "Why did you hire a private investigator?"

"To find somebody."

"Well, no bloody shit. *Who* are you trying to find, Cal?"

"A person from my past."

She rolls her eyes and sighs before gathering her papers off my desk and standing up to leave. "Ring me when you're not distracted anymore and *maybe* I'll be available."

"Sit down, Bridget." I sigh in frustration. We have a staring contest for about ten seconds before she reluctantly sits down again. "I'm sorry for being a prick."

"Thank you, but you're not forgiven until you give me more

specific details."

I shake my head, grab the bridge of my nose, and silently count to ten before continuing. "I'm trying to find a woman I met over four years ago. She lives in Chicago, and I would like to get in touch with her to see if we can meet up when I arrive."

She tilts her head to the side, her eyes burning with questions. "Why do you want to meet up with her?"

"Just to catch up and see how she's doing."

"Is she young or old?"

"She's in our age range," I answer, not understanding the point of the question. "Why does that even matter?"

"Because you don't just casually want to see people unless they serve a purpose," she says in exasperation.

"That's not true."

"Is so. What's her name?"

"Jenna."

Her mouth drops open in shock at my answer. "Oi! Is this the chick you shagged for a week and after a month of long distance dating, she ghosted you?"

"How in the bloody hell do you know about that?" I question in anger, knowing full well I never told my family about Jenna.

Bridget smirks and I instantly know my answer. "Who do you think?"

"Fucking Sean."

I shouldn't be surprised that Sean told my sister, but somehow, I am. He's very close with my family and they treat him as if he's their other son

"Don't be mad at him—he was worried about you. He said he's never seen you act like that over a woman before."

"It wasn't his business to tell you."

"If you would've told us, he wouldn't have had to," she counters back, and I don't disagree with her. "So, are you trying to find her so you can have a fuck buddy while in Chicago?"

"She's more than just a fuck," I growl, not liking how casual Bridget is making her sound.

Bridget's eyes widen in surprise. "How so, Cal? If she's something more, then why are you now trying to get in touch with all these years later?"

"When I met Jenna, she was still hurt from her divorce. She wasn't looking to date again, especially to someone like me, someone who was never rooted in one place very long due to my grueling schedule…and because of the obvious. My profession. She didn't think a long-distance relationship was worth pursuing. I was hoping I could change her mind, but it was hard to stay on top of emailing her back while shooting a movie."

"What do you mean, emailing her back? Why didn't you just pick up the phone and call her?"

"She refused to give me her phone number." I smile sadly at Bridget's shocked expression. "When we parted, she was too scared to give it to me. I was lucky to even get her email."

"If you liked her so much, why didn't you demand she give you her number or she couldn't leave?"

I give my sister an exasperated look, wondering if she's really as crazy as she sounds. "I can't hold someone against their will, Bridget." I scowl at the devilish grin that spreads on her face. "Furthermore, I was trying to be a gentleman and give her time. I was hoping that after we corresponded for a while, she would miss me and see how ridiculous emailing was."

"Wow," Bridget drawls out, seeming impressed with my response. "I bet it was a test on her part. It's harder to keep up with email, so if you were consistently keeping in touch with her that way, then that would've shown her you were serious about her."

"Maybe." I shrug, pondering her thoughts on the matter. "But I did give her my phone number to call me and she never did… or so I think."

"What do you mean?"

"When I was at the cast party once the movie was done shooting, I remember my cell phone ringing with an unknown number. I handed my phone to Valerie to answer since I don't answer unknown numbers and I was busy in the middle of a conversation with someone else. But I could've sworn I overheard her say Jenna's name when greeting whoever was on the phone. But I'll never know because Valerie dropped my phone by accident and it conveniently broke."

"Do you really think that was an accident?" Bridget asks with a pointed look.

"Valerie said it was an accident and when I questioned who it was, she claims she didn't hear their name before the phone fell out of her hand." I clench my fists in anger at the memory. I was slightly drunk at that party, so I believed every word Valerie said to me because at the time, I didn't know what a liar and manipulator she was. "We'll never know the real truth."

"And that's when you changed your number, right?"

"Yes, but I would've had to change it regardless because some random fan got a hold of that number and wouldn't leave me alone. It's why I have two separate cell phones now—one for work and one just for family and close friends. So even if Jenna did try to call me again, that number is no longer in service."

"Hmm, true. Did you email her asking if she tried calling you?"

"Yes, and the email went unanswered. I emailed her multiple times before finally giving up."

"Why didn't you try to find her then?"

"Because as soon as I was done shooting that movie, I had to scramble back to Norway to continue shooting 'Wrath of the Vikings.' That TV show catapulted my career, and we were shooting the third season. I couldn't ask the director to hold up production so I could go looking for someone who 'seemed' to be avoiding me.

We sit in comfortable silence for a moment, both of us dissecting the situation.

"Here's the thing, Cal, and I'm not saying this to be a bitch or anything," Bridget starts, and I brace myself to not like what I'm about to hear. "You're my baby brother and I'll always tell you the truth, but if she really wanted to try to do the long distance thing, she would've given you her phone number the day she left Las Vegas."

I nod my head curtly knowing that this could be the case. It's crossed my mind plenty of times. Not to mention, Sean said the same thing all those years ago when Jenna stopped emailing me back. Hell, it's why I haven't put an effort into trying to find her sooner.

"You might be right, but I won't know until I find her again."

"But why are you going to spend so much money trying to find someone who might not want to be found?"

"Because *I* need closure, Bridget," I say in frustration and get out of my chair so swiftly that the movement causes it to slide back into the wall. I start pacing, the restless energy of me needing answers making me feel like a caged tiger. "I can't stop thinking of her. I felt things with her that no woman has ever come close to making me feel since then and I could've sworn I made her feel that way too." I stop pacing and rake my hands through my hair. I look up at the ceiling and sigh, letting all of my emotions out in one whoosh of a breath.

"I've just got to know, Bridget. I must find her and see for myself. If the chemistry isn't still there for her…if she's moved on, I'll let her go. Then maybe I can finally stop having regrets about letting her walk out of my life four years ago."

I look back down at Bridget to see her blinking rapidly to try to keep her tears at bay. "Sean was right. I've never seen you this way before." She stops and gulps before continuing, "She must be special for you to go through all this trouble to find her."

"She is, Bridget. She's this petite little lass, but she's so strong. And I don't just mean physically. She's mentally strong and was building her business while going through a divorce. She's brilliant and quick-witted, kind, and respectful of others." I smile as the cascade of memories of my time with Jenna starts spilling through me. "She always tried to pay for everything and would get angry when I wouldn't let her at least split the bills." I chuckle at the image of Jenna's beautiful, disgruntled face when I had paid for our last dinner together without her knowing. "I felt like myself with her, Bridget. She wasn't impressed with me being an actor. If anything, that was the turn off. She liked me for me. Or so I presumed."

"I'm sure she did, Cal," she says with a small smile playing on her lips. "She sounds lovely. What does she look like?"

"To me, she's gorgeous. She has hair the color of milk chocolate that always smelled like peaches. Her eyes are the color of amber that tends to hypnotize you sometimes." I leave out the fact of how they would darken in desire and how I crave to see them turn that color again one day very soon.

"Damn it, Cal," Bridget groans and grabs a tissue from the Kleenex box on my desk to dab her eyes with. "You're right. You've got to find her, and I pray to God, Jesus, Zeus, Allah, Buddha—whomever we need to pray to—that she's yours for the keeping." Bridget stands up and gives me a tight hug.

"Thanks, Sister." I squeeze her tightly before letting her go. I know she's going to tell the other members of the family everything, but I realize that I don't care anymore. Maybe giving her version and seeing how serious I am will help them welcome Jenna with open arms when they finally do get to meet her.

Because they will meet her when I make her mine.

"What can I do to help?" she asks before taking her seat again.

"When I hear back from the private investigator about her

physical location, I want you to book my hotel as close to her as possible. I don't care if it is far from the movie set."

Bridget slowly smiles, the evil glint of my childhood nightmares twinkling in her eyes. "Oh, I can definitely do that."

# Chapter 3

THE SOUNDS OF laughter fill the air as my family and I enjoy my nephew Jack telling us about his day at school. While being home in England during my time off, I try to make as many family dinners as possible since they're one of my favorite parts about being home. My sisters and their families live within thirty minutes of my parents and every Friday night they have dinner together. It's the best time to try to catch up with everyone's daily schedules and helps me not feel so left out. Since I'll be leaving again for the States in a couple of days, each minute with my family is special. I look around the table with a smile on my face, hoping that one day I will have a family of my own at this dinner table.

Jenna would fit right in here. Her bubbly personality and eagerness to talk to anyone will make her a family favorite. *But what about children?* My smile turns down into a frown. *Does Jenna even want kids?* Memories from our time in Las Vegas together remind me that Jenna said she didn't think she could have children due to an abnormal uterus she discovered when trying with her ex-husband. *We could always adopt.* I shake my head at getting ahead of myself at the thoughts of Jenna becoming mine. Besides, it doesn't matter to me if Jenna wants kids or not.

All I want is her.

The vibration of my cell phone brings me out of my thoughts. I retrieve it out of my pocket to see Philip calling. I ignore his call and put it back, not wanting to talk during family dinner. Not ten seconds later, Bridget is pulling her phone out of her pocket and giving me a questionable look.

"Philip is calling me. Should I answer?" she inquires, and I shake my head no, especially with my mother giving us the evil eye for even looking at our phones. She has a strict no phone rule at family dinners and I try to be respectful of her request.

But then I get a text from Philip, saying it's an emergency and I need to call him back as soon as possible. "I need to take this call. Seems there is some sort of emergency," I tell my family before leaving the dining room. I walk through the living room and head toward my father's study. I'm just about to shut the door when I see Bridget down the hall, coming my way. I leave the door ajar for her and immediately call Philip back.

"What's wrong?" I demand when he picks up. I've never had Philip text me with an emergency before and my heart is racing with adrenaline. My immediate thoughts go to Sean, wondering if he's hurt, but I've gotten zero notifications from him or his family.

"Hold on while I conference in Thomas."

Before I can ask why, Philip puts me on hold. Dread starts slithering into my veins because this call can only be about one person: Jenna.

"Thomas, I finally got a hold of him." Philip announces, alerting me that they're back on the line. "Go ahead and tell him what you've uncovered."

"Is something wrong with Jenna, Thomas?" I interrupt, needing to know if she's all right.

"Mr. Harrington, have you seen any articles about yourself

today?"

"No, Thomas, I try to avoid any news about myself," I tell him dryly. "You didn't answer my question about Jenna."

"Ms. Pruitt seems to be just fine, sir."

"So what is this about?"

"An article has started circulating about you. And sir, it seems to be picking up traction."

"Okay," I respond slowly, still not understanding why Thomas is involved. I don't give the tabloids the time of day with all the misinformation they report, so something must be wrong if both Philip and Thomas are calling me about this. "What is the article about?"

"The article is about you and your lack of involvement in your child's life."

I stop dead in my tracks, not realizing that I was pacing. "What did you just say?" Surely, I couldn't have heard him correctly. *A child?* "You know damn fucking well I don't have a child. Someone better explain to me what the hell is going on," I growl in a low, menacing voice, not believing what I just heard.

"Are you near a computer, Cal?" Philip asks and I answer yes while rounding the corner of my father's desk. "I just emailed you the link to one of the articles."

I sit down in his chair and start typing out my father's password that I created for him. I go to the internet and log into my email. I open the email from Philip and click on the link. The link takes me to the National Mail, a British tabloid website, and the headline in big, bold letters reads **"CAL HARRINGTON IS A DEADBEAT DAD!"**

What. The. Fuck.

I scroll down and my eyes don't focus on the article or the picture of me, but on the photo of Jenna carrying a small child. Jenna is smiling at the girl and I'm momentarily hypnotized. I drink that photo in for a minute before clicking on it to see if I can get a better look at the child. I zoom in on her face, but it's only a side view. I minimize the photo and go back to the article. I scroll down some more and that's when I discover another photo in the article. This time the child is holding onto Jenna's neck, her face looking directly at the camera. I click on the photo and when it enlarges on my screen, I suck in my breath.

She looks just like me.

"Is it possible, Cal?" Philip must have heard my gasp and I try to focus on his question, but my mind is reeling.

"Thomas, tell me who this is," I demand because my gut is telling me that Thomas has done some research before alerting Philip to the article.

"Birth records are not public in the state of Illinois, Cal, so I don't have all the answers for you. I called the news agency where this article originated from and couldn't get much information. The only thing my source was able to tell me is that these photos were taken last week, and the photographer and source are anonymous. They wouldn't reveal where they got the information from. I'm in Chicago and just followed Ms. Pruitt. She dropped off the same little girl at this pre-school that is near her condo. The girl looks to be around three or four years old, which is close to the timeline of when you were with Ms. Pruitt in Las Vegas."

"How do we know this?" I question my mind on autopilot while I try to digest that Jenna has a child.

*I* might have a child.

"Read the article, Cal," Philip instructs quietly. I scroll back up to the start of the article and close my eyes, trying to give myself a moment before continuing.

"Cal, is everything okay?" I hear Bridget's voice before opening my eyes to acknowledge her. I shake my head no before my gaze reverts to the article.

**Cal Harrington Is A Deadbeat Dad!**

**The British Gentleman refuses to take care of his own daughter.**

**Seems like The British Gentleman is not so gentlemanly after all. The Hollywood A-Lister is apparently a daddy, having a child with American event planner Jenna Pruitt. The two met over four years ago on a business trip to Las Vegas where they had a weeklong tryst. According to our anonymous source, Jenna discovered she was pregnant three months later and when she told the British heartthrob of her news, he told her he wanted nothing to do with her or the baby.**

**"Cal Harrington not only refused to financially take care of his daughter, but he won't even see her," our source has confirmed.**

**Ms. Pruitt has been raising their daughter all by herself while being one of the most sought-after event planners in Chicago. So why is this scandalous news suddenly seeing the light of day now?**

**"It's time the world knows what Cal Harrington is really like."**

"What the bloody hell is this, Cal? This can't be true!" Bridget whispers next to my ear. I didn't even realize she walked around me to read over my shoulder.

"I don't know what this is, but I do know that I was never told I had a child, nor would I ever fucking say any of those things."

I'm shell-shocked and momentarily speechless because I don't want to believe this is true.

*This can't fucking be true.*

Jenna wouldn't keep something this big from me. She's not evil or conniving. I would've seen if she was. She isn't capable of this kind of deceit.

*Is she?*

My whole world just spun off its axis and I can't even think straight.

My sister, sensing my despair and struggle to regain some sort of control, grabs my phone out of my hand, places it on the desk and hits the speakerphone button. "Philip, what do we do? These are some serious allegations."

"Cal, can any of this be true?" Philip asks again and I start to shake my head as if he can physically see me.

"We used protection the whole time."

"Condoms can break, Cal."

"I know this, but she told me she couldn't get pregnant. Something about an abnormal uterus."

"Miracles can happen every day, Cal. There are plenty of women who've been told that by their doctors and then they get pregnant," Bridget informs me gently.

"I think she lied. She made it up in hopes you would stop using condoms so she could trap you," Philip concludes, causing me to shake my head again in denial. I can't believe Jenna would lie about that. I *refuse* to believe it.

"No, she wouldn't deceive me like that."

"Cal, f*or the millionth fucking time*, you barely knew this girl!" Philip sneers in annoyance, frustrated that he has to remind me once again that I don't really know Jenna as well as I think I do. "You don't know what ulterior motives she may have had."

"If that's true, why would she wait until now?"

"Either her business is not as successful as it seems, and she needs money or just the opposite. Her business is so successful that she sees this as another opportunity to make more money by being associated with you." His reasoning makes me sick, especially because they're valid arguments as to what her motives would be for revealing this now. "You're at the height of your career, Cal. You're making twenty million dollars per film. This would be the perfect opportunity for a scandal like this to come forward."

"*No!*" I shout, slamming my palms down on the desk with such force that everything on it rattles. I stand up and start to pace again, refusing to believe that Jenna is capable of what Philip is insinuating.

Even though there might be some truth to his words.

"What's going on in here?" My father questions from the doorway. I look up to see the rest of my family standing behind him, concern written all over their faces. Bridget shakes her head at him, giving them a silent warning to stay quiet.

"Why wouldn't she try to contact me privately?" I question, my glimmer of hope fading as time goes on.

"Because she'll get the outcome she's hoping for if she makes it a public scandal for you." I close my eyes as Philip's words sink in. Doubt slowly slides into my brain like fog rolling in, hazing my judgment and leaving me cold with bitterness.

"I suggest you don't respond to these allegations yet until we have some more facts," Thomas advises, breaking his silence. I nod my head in agreement because the thought of making a statement right now without knowing the truth would be a stupid mistake. I squeeze my eyes to clear my thoughts and will myself to come up with a game plan.

"I agree with Thomas. Let's keep quiet for right now. Philip, I need you to get me in touch with the best family attorney in Chicago *tonight.* Secure a phone call with them—I don't care what time of the night it is. It must be done within the next couple of hours."

"Not a problem, Cal. I know plenty of lawyers here in California that would know someone there."

"Then I need you to secure a plane for me. I want to be in Chicago by tomorrow and have this lawyer meet up with me right away. I want them to lay out all my options if a paternity test concludes she's mine."

"Thomas, can you be available to meet with me after my meeting with the lawyer?" I ask, switching the subject now to him.

"Absolutely, just let me know what time your meeting is and I'll be available."

"Excellent. In the meantime, keep following Jenna and securing as much information as you can. I want to know about all the people who are in her everyday life and what her daily routine is."

"Not a problem, Mr. Harrington."

I hang up with Thomas and look over at my family in a daze of confusion as to how my life just changed in a blink of an eye.

"What is your plan after meeting with Thomas, Cal?" Bridget asks gently.

"It will be time to find Jenna and learn the truth."

# CHAPTER 4

I RUB MY eyes with the palm of my hands, exhausted beyond belief. I was never good at sleeping on planes, but with everything that's happening, I thought it would be a good idea to try. Too bad my brain refuses to shut off. Too much adrenaline coursing through me and for once, I wished I was already in America when the news story broke. But I wasn't and here we are, on a plane to Chicago. I open the window shade and look down to see we are finally across the Atlantic and over land. It's hard to distinguish what part of the United States we're over, but it doesn't matter since we'll probably be landing soon.

I sit back in my seat and sigh, trying to digest how the course of my life vastly changed within twenty-four hours. David, the lawyer Philip secured for me, suggested that when I meet with Jenna, I voluntarily ask first for a paternity test. If she refuses, then we will immediately go to court and request one to be ordered. If the paternity test comes out positive, I need to fill out and file a voluntary acknowledgement of paternity.

*If* the test comes back positive.

If the test comes back negative, then I can take legal action against Jenna or wash my hands of her forever and walk away, which won't be hard to do. If she is behind all of this, then there's no way she's the woman I thought she was.

The thought makes me completely sick to my stomach.

Thomas emailed over more information on Jenna's business, which included YouTube links to her news segments. I spent most of the plane ride mesmerized by those videos and seeing the progression of Jenna's pregnancy play out on television. Her beautiful face became fuller, her clothes baggier as the segments progressed over months and then finally, she would hide behind the table and props she brought along to share.

*But why did she hide her pregnancy? And if the baby is mine, why did she hide it from me?*

Her business is thriving, and this kind of publicity will only make people more intrigued about her. People will book her just to say they booked the girl who was associated with Cal Harrington. I close my eyes, still not wanting to believe the possibility that Jenna is being an opportunist. My gut is telling me that it can't be true, but what other explanation could there be? The Jenna I thought I knew would never hide something like this from me.

So many fucking questions that I need answers to. I feel like I'm spiraling out of control and I hate that feeling. I'm always in control of my life, my circumstances, and my situations. I have to be in this industry, but this has completely derailed me.

"Mr. Harrington?" I open my eyes to see one of the flight attendants standing next to me. "We will be landing in one hour. Is it okay if I wake up Mrs. Harrington?" My mother was adamant about coming with me and refused to take no for an answer. I'm relieved that she's here with me because I need someone to keep me level-headed when I see Jenna for the first time.

"Yes, that's fine," I respond and watch her walk toward the back of the plane where the bedroom is located. I decide to stand up and utilize the bathroom in the front of the plane to wash my face and brush my teeth.

When I'm finished, I come out to find my mother awake and seated with tea being served to her.

"Hello darling, did you get any sleep?" she asks before thanking the flight attendant. I request a cup for myself before responding back to her.

"No, I was doing more research." Basically, stalking Jenna for the majority of the flight.

"So, what is the plan when we land in Chicago?"

I look at my watch and calculate the time in my head. "With the time change, it will be around 9:00 a.m. when we land. A driver should be waiting for us and will take us straight to the hotel. We will then meet with the lawyer and Thomas. After that we will have lunch and then head to Jenna's."

"Have you called Jenna to let her know you're coming?" My mother raises an eyebrow at me, knowing full well that I have not personally called her.

"David has been trying and told me that her phone line is continuously busy." My lawyer called Jenna's business line to try to reach her, but either the mailbox is not activated or off the hook to avoid being picked up.

"I don't think it would be wise for us to just show up without giving her some sort of proper notice."

"I don't particularly care for courtesy notices at this point, Mother. We're here for a reason and the sooner we get answers, the better. Besides, it's not our fault we can't get a hold of her."

"Cal," she says in her warning voice. "You sound like your mind's made up that Jenna is guilty. What if she's not? What are you going to do?"

"Mother, please." I scrub my hands up and down my face, my brain and body beyond tired from this whirlwind. "I don't know who or what to believe, but right now the evidence is pointing at Jenna and unfortunately, she's the only one who knows the truth."

“Okay, son,” my mother says softly and now I feel like an asshole for being stern with her. The flight attendant brings me my tea and we sit in silence until I can’t take the guilt eating at me for being snappy with my mother.

“Sorry for being so pissy, Mum. Let’s just wait and see what happens before making any decisions.” I offer her a small smile and am rewarded back with one of her own.

“You are under a lot of pressure, my boy. No need to apologize.”

“Thanks for coming, Mum,” I tell her with sincerity.

“There’s nowhere else I rather be, especially if there’s a possibility of meeting another one of my grandchildren.”

I swallow down the rest of my drink and nod at her, still not wanting to believe the possibility that I’ve had a daughter whom I’ve never known about.

*We’ll find out soon enough.*

Forty-five minutes later, we have landed safely and are being driven to the Ritz-Carlton in downtown Chicago. We check into our residential suite and within thirty minutes, David arrives. I pre-sign some documents and we go over our strategy one more time regarding Jenna.

“Call me as soon as you’re done meeting with her. If you are the father, we need to get the ball rolling on claiming paternity.”

*Father.* Fuck if that word doesn’t give me goosebumps. I shake his hand while thanking him and walk him to the door. Next meeting is with Thomas and I ask my mother to order us all lunch from room service. He gives me a USB drive of his files on Jenna and we continue our conversation about her over lunch.

“The story is circulating, and paparazzi have already arrived in swarms. You’re going to need someone on the inside. I trust a guy named Chase Wilson. He’s one of the best in the business but has a conscience. Here’s his card.” Thomas hands me Chase’s card and I briefly glance at it before putting it into my pocket. "I recommend googling him before call so you know his backstory. At this point in time, he'll be better suited for you than I will be."

"Why is that?" I question, not understanding how paparazzi is better than a private investigator.

"Paparazzi are like smaller versions of P.I.s. He'll be following her and you during all hours to get the money shots. I advise you to hire him to follow Jenna and have him report back to you what his fellow peers are saying and doing."

"I like the way you operate, Thomas," I tell him in appreciation because I never even thought about that.

"Unless you need me for something else, I believe my job here is done. When will you be meeting with Ms. Pruitt?"

"As soon as you leave," I confirm, nodding over to my mother who looks up at me in surprise.

"Then let me not keep you waiting." He puts down his napkin on the table and stands up to leave. I thank him again and walk him to the door. As soon as he leaves, I turn around to look at my mother.

"I'm going to take a quick shower. Can you be ready to leave within the hour?"

"Did David get in touch with her?"

"No, and it doesn't matter at this point. We're here, I know where she lives, and we're going. So please get ready."

I don't give my mother time to respond back. I walk to my bedroom, close the door and head quickly to the shower.

*It's time, Jenna.*

# CHAPTER 5

2201

The numbers are in gold and the door is painted black. There's a tiny peep hole indicating the occupants inside can see who's outside their door. I blink a couple of times at the numbers, frozen in my spot because I'm still having a hard time coming to terms over why I'm here today. A couple of days ago, I was hoping to be standing outside of this door, praying for a second chance with the woman who I've been missing—not standing here, about to see if she's been hiding my own daughter from me.

*Fuck, how is this my life right now?*

"Cal?" my mother questions softly. I don't know why I'm stalling the inevitable. Maybe because there's nothing happy about the circumstances. Either the child is mine and has been kept from me all these years or she's not mine and this is all a publicity stunt. Either way, I was lied to, and all signs are pointing at Jenna being the culprit.

It makes me fucking furious.

I close my eyes and try to tone down my anger. Needing to get this over with, I silently count to ten. When I'm done, I nod my head at my mother and then knock on the door.

No one answers right away, but we can hear whispering on the other side of it. Jenna knows it's me standing out here because she had to give the front desk security guard permission to let us upstairs. Impatience rears its ugly head and I'm about to pound the living shit out of the door when it finally swings open and a pair of whiskey-colored eyes—the same ones that I've been dreaming about—stare back at me.

I drink her in, not caring that she sees my gaze wandering from her head down to her toes. Jenna looks as beautiful as ever, even with no makeup on and her hair in a ponytail. Her body is encased in workout clothes, and I notice that she seems thinner than before. I stare at her legs, briefly remembering a time when they were wrapped around my hips in only high heels as I deliciously pounded into her, the screams of her orgasms echoing through my mind.

Fuck, have I missed her.

"Hello, Jenna," I murmur, my voice huskier than I intend it to be. Seeing her for the first time since Las Vegas opens the floodgates of memories of how incredible our time together was. Her eyes are sizing me up as well and I briefly wonder if she's remembering the same things I am.

"Cal," she nods curtly, her voice cool and her eyes cold when they finally meet mine. "How kind of you to show up without calling."

Her sarcastic demeanor washes away our steamy memories and my defenses are now on high alert. I'm not used to this version of Jenna, and it makes my blood pressure rise at the animosity radiating from her stare. "My lawyer did try to call your work line, but no one answered." I equally match her cool tone, telling myself that I'm here for business because this sure as fuck is not going to be the happy reunion I was hoping for.

"We've been bombarded with calls from reporters, so that line goes straight to voicemail. Nice to see that you're finally doing your own dirty work for once by showing up in person though."

I'm immediately taken back by her words. I frown in confusion at her jab, not understanding what she means or why she's so angry. If anyone should be angry, it should be me. My eyes narrow at her, trying to figure out what her game is, but her attention is now directed at my mum.

"Hello, I'm Jenna. I'm assuming you are Cal's mother?"

"Oh yes, Rosalind Harrington, but please call me Rose," she responds to Jenna, thrusting out her hand for her to shake. "Thank you for accepting to see us on such short notice, Jenna. I've seen so many pictures of you the last two days, and I must say that you are even prettier in person."

Of course my mother would compliment her, being the proper British woman that she is. But I'm done with the pleasantries. I'm done with any games, and I want the answers I came here for.

"You were wondering if you were going to hear from me? Cut the bullshit, Jenna, how could you *not* hear from me? This story is everywhere, and your timing of planting it is brilliant. I brought my mother here to be a witness for the paternity test and then we will be leaving. My lawyer will be in touch with you once the results are in."

Her mouth drops open and she stares at me as if I just physically slapped her. "Excuse me, but did you just accuse me of selling this story to the media?" she questions in disbelief.

If she's acting right now, she's a fucking brilliant actress because she actually looks shocked. *Stay focused, Cal.* "Bloody right I am and don't lie about it! I know your business has been doing well, and that this piece of information can bring your company into the spotlight you have been hoping for." The rage inside of me is mounting and I can't keep my disgust at the situation buried any longer. "One week together never brought out your calculating, manipulative, bitch side."

"Calvin! There's no need to be rude until we get the facts straight," my mother chides, looking appalled at my behavior, and a part of me is disappointed with myself, but I can't take back what I just said. Her attitude toward me is insulting and I refuse to be played.

"How dare you!" Jenna hisses at me, her fists balled up at her sides. Her eyes are wild, and she looks like she's holding herself back from raking my eyes out with her nails. "How dare you come to my house, accuse me of lying and planting this story to boost my business! I would never use an innocent child like that! Unlike *you*, I don't want the spotlight and I never wanted the story to be made public. Once you refused to be part of her life, I was done with you and your games. I never wanted to hear or see you ever again!"

"What the *fuck* are you talking about?" I growl out in frustration, not understanding again what in the hell she's accusing me of. "I never knew about a baby until you went to the tabloids. I would never refuse to see my own child!"

"Look who is lying now!" She yells in my face, stunning me speechless at her fury. "How convenient that you have forgotten the email you wrote me stating that if the baby was yours, you have no time in your life for it. You even copied your assistant on it."

"Valerie? When did you talk to Valerie?" I question in confusion, a knot of uneasiness forming in the pit of my stomach at the mere mention of her name. It had to be Valerie because my sister was not my assistant during my time with Jenna.

*Something feels terribly wrong about this if Valerie was involved.*

"When did I not talk with Valerie? I was always talking with Valerie because you never picked up the phone yourself. Did you forget that you told me that she handles your phone calls when you are on set working? Every single time I called you, she picked up the phone. She even started to respond to my emails when you stopped. You were too much of a coward to talk to me," she spits out furiously and points her finger in my face. "Never again, Cal! I'm done with your bullshit and lies! You can talk with my lawyers." She's about to shut the door in my face, but I quickly react and place my foot in between the door and the frame, blocking her from shutting it.

I feel the color draining from my face as her words sink in. *Valerie*. Valerie was involved with this? So, Jenna did call me. This whole time I thought Jenna never called. I hear my mother gasp and I briefly glance at her, her eyes telling me she's thinking the same thing I am. *That fucking bitch. What has she done?*

"Jenna, there seems to be a misunderstanding," is all I can mutter out in shock at this new development in an already fucked up situation.

"You bet there's been a huge misunderstanding, and it's that you think you can waltz into our lives four years later just because the story has been made public, and now everyone knows you are a deadbeat dad!" I flinch at her words, because fuck they hurt, but I see the torment in her eyes. I see the pent-up anger and pain she's had to endure because of me, and I know I just need to let her have her moment of getting it all out, right here, right now. No matter how hard it's going to be for me to hear it.

"I will not let you take my child away from me. I have been doing just fine without any help from you! I don't want your money or you in our lives. It's one thing to not want me, but to not want your own child? And then to finally show up only when the story will affect your career? *You're disgusting!*" she yells out, her eyes overflowing with hatred for me. "I would never have slept with you if I would have known what a despicable human being you are. I want you to get the hell out of my life, you fucking asshole!"

Her chest is heaving and she's sucking in air as if she can't breathe anymore, but I've stopped paying attention to her. A small, tiny hand appeared on Jenna's thigh and that is all I can concentrate on. I couldn't tear my eyes away from that little hand until I saw Jenna's fingers entwine it into hers. My gaze slowly travels to a small chin, adorable pouty pink lips, beautiful brown hair and then right to her eyes.

Blue eyes—the exact color as mine—staring right at me.

Staring right into my soul.

I hold my breath, my eyes sucking all of her in at once because I know without a shadow of a doubt this child is mine.

I have a daughter.

A daughter whom I haven't met in four years.

# Chapter 6

FOUR. FUCKING. YEARS.

My daughter is mesmerized with me as I'm with her and I almost forget to breathe. Her eyes are watery as if she's about to cry. She looks up at Jenna, who gives her a reassuring smile. She returns her attention to me, briefly looking at my mother, her gaze turning curious as to who I am—the stranger that her mother is yelling at.

*Could she understand what we were saying? Does she know I'm her father? Does she call someone else Daddy?* My heart starts to hurt at that thought.

"I'm sorry, Jenna, I tried to keep her in her room, but she heard the yelling and got upset." I look behind her to see a man approaching us. I recognize him from photos Thomas sent me and identified him as Jenna's assistant, Robert.

"Mommy, you need to get ready for swimming," she tells Jenna and starts to tug her inside the apartment. Her sweet, whimsical voice is one of the best sounds I've ever heard in my whole entire life. "Let's go have some tea first since it makes you feel better." She stops pulling at Jenna and places her little fists on her hips. She looks straight at me and suddenly her eyes change. Her blue eyes turn stormy, and she looks at me in anger and screams, "Stop yelling at my mommy you fucking asshole!"

I have to bite the insides of my cheek to not laugh out loud at how hilarious it is to hear a four-year-old try to curse at me. I raise a teasing eyebrow at Jenna, who looks completely mortified while she is tugging at her bottom lip and shaking her head in resignation. Our child is adorable and my heart aches in need. I just want to pick her up in my arms and hold her to me. I want to tell her I *am* a fucking asshole for not knowing she was alive. I want to know everything about her. What she smells like. What she likes to eat. Who her friends are. What she likes to play with.

Everything. I want to know everything.

"Avery," Jenna says, kneeling to her level and looking in her eyes. "Mommy didn't mean to call her friend that bad name that you just said. Please don't repeat after me, okay?"

*Avery. My daughter's name is Avery.* The name is beautiful, just like she is.

"What bad words, Mommy?" Avery asks her mother in confusion. Clearly, Avery didn't understand what she said, but I see Jenna's need to explain so she doesn't repeat those words in public. Although it would be brilliantly funny if she did.

"The bad words that Mommy just said that you repeated," Jenna gently tells her, using a soothing voice.

"Silly Mommy, I didn't say any bad words! I was just calling him by his name. You said his name was fucking asshole," Avery says with a smile, as if she's proud of herself for remembering my "name." I chuckle at her astuteness and look over at my mother, who's covering her mouth to try to stifle her giggle and fails.

"That's not really his name, Avery."

"You called your friend a bad word, Mommy?" Avery whispers with a shocked look on her face, not believing that her mother could do something wrong.

"Yes, I did. Mommy was a little upset and should not have

said those bad words. It was an accident, and I will try very hard not to do it again."

"Mommy, you need to say you're sorry to your friend."

I look over at Jenna, who looks revolted at the idea. I can't help but smirk at her, thoroughly enjoying the fact that Jenna will have to eat her own words.

"Yes, Avery, Mommy will apologize to her friend," Jenna says with an annoyed sigh. She reluctantly stands up, turns around and looks at me with a scowl. I can't contain my amusement at the utter look of disgust on her face for having to apologize to me. "Cal, I'm sorry for calling you those bad words," she mutters, not even looking me in the eye. If this was any other time, any other moment, I would pick her up, kiss the shit out of her until she was begging me for more. But instead, she hates me, and I somehow have to get to the bottom of this, because I've realized that having Jenna hating me is a feeling I don't handle well.

"Apology accepted," I tell Jenna with a small smile. I gulp down everything I want to say to her because now is not the time. Not in front of Avery. I look down at my daughter and decide to kneel so we are on the same level. It's time I introduce myself to her, but I tread with caution. Jenna and I need to strategize together how we are going to reveal that I'm her father and right now is not that time. So instead, I will go along with Jenna's idea of me being a new friend.

"Hello Avery, my name is Cal, and this is my mother, Rose."

"Rose? That's my middle name, Avery Rose Pruitt!" she announces with excitement. My mother inhales sharply and I turn my head and look at Jenna in shock, my eyes questioning if her middle name was to honor my mother. She nods in confirmation, and I'm even more taken aback that she remembers me telling her. I vividly recall it—we were laying in each other's arms after a night full of passion. It was the wee hours of the morning on our last day together, and we were cramming in as much information about each other as we could because we knew we were racing against the clock before Jenna's flight to go home.

Little did we know the direction our lives were going to go.

I blink back the memories and turn my attention back to my daughter. "Your name is beautiful, Avery. We came all the way from London to play with you."

"London? Do you know Wendy, John, and Michael? They live in London. Do you see Peter Pan flying to their house?" she quizzes us, and I smile down at her rapid questioning. I love how curious she is and the fact that she adores Peter Pan.

"Yes, Avery, I know all about Peter Pan," my mother answers for us. "Can I join you for tea and tell you all about them?"

"Yes, you can. Mommy, let's go!" she squeals in excitement and resumes pulling Jenna back into the condo.

"Avery, your mommy and Cal need to talk about some things. Is it okay if you show me your room and you and I have tea together?" Rose looks over at Jenna, who nods her head in approval.

"Go ahead and have fun with Rose, Avery. She flew a long way just to have some alone time with you. Mommy will be in her office talking with Cal." Jenna looks over at me and I nod in confirmation. I'm dying to hear what Valerie told Jenna because I'm seething inside, and my rage is barely hanging on by a thread. I still don't understand how or why Valerie kept Jenna and my daughter from my life.

"Okay, Mommy. Let's go, Rose!" Avery grabs Rose's hand to take her to her room and stops to introduce her to Robert. "Uncle Robert, this is Rose. She knows Peter Pan!" she tells him with enthusiasm. "C'mon Rose, c'mon Uncle Robert, I will race you." She takes off toward her room ahead of them.

Jenna turns her attention back to me and we briefly size each other up one more time. Her gaze is filled with confusion and doubt, and it kills me. She gives me a polite smile, turns to her side and gestures for me to come inside. I walk past her into the hallway of her condo. I hear her shut the door behind me and I walk further in, taking in my surroundings. I'm slightly taken aback at the incredible views of Lake Michigan and how nice this condo is. As I admire my surroundings, I notice Robert staring at me.

"And you must be Jenna's assistant, the infamous Robert?" I smile, extending out my hand in greeting.

Robert blushes and shakes my hand back. "That's me! Can I get you anything to drink or eat, Mr. Harrington?" he asks shyly, not directly meeting my gaze. Jenna told me all about Robert and how he was her rock when she was going through her divorce. Seeing that he's still here working for her, I have no doubt that means he's been a big part of Avery's life too.

"Please call me Cal and water would be great, thank you." I take off my coat and before I can put it down, Robert grabs it from me and retreats to the kitchen. I watch Jenna follow him and more whispering ensues. I hear the word "enemy" come out of Jenna's mouth and I have to bite back my annoyance. Jenna thinking I wanted nothing to do with her and Avery means her hatred for me runs deep. I frown at this, disappointed that she believed Valerie, then again what other choice did she have?

*How the hell am I going to fix this?*

I hear her footsteps coming toward me and she returns from the kitchen with my water. I nod my thanks before taking a big gulp.

"Why don't we go into my office?" she asks and before I can say anything, turns on her heel and leads the way. I follow her to a room with French doors and once I'm inside, she shuts them behind me for privacy.

"This place is nice. How long have you lived here?" I ask, trying to make small talk to help relieve the tension that's permeating the air.

"Ten years," she responds while walking around me. I'm surprised by her answer because the condo looks brand new and modern. "My grandmother left it to me." I nod my head in acknowledgement, silently watching her uneasiness with my presence. She rubs her palms against her legs and refuses to look me in the eye. Seeming unsure what to do with herself, she turns her back on me and looks out the window. "So, help me understand how this has all been a big misunderstanding?"

I let the words hang in the air because for once, I'm speechless and don't know how to proceed. When she finally looks over her shoulder at me, I rake my hands through my hair and sigh, trying to figure out where to begin. I take another sip of water and start our journey back through memory lane.

"Do you remember the story of how Valerie and I first met?" She nods at my question, and I continue on. "I really didn't think anything of it when she told me she should handle my phone calls and emails while I was on set. She made it sound like it was the professional thing to do and that all assistants did that. I never bothered to ask my fellow actors if this was normal, nor did I ever notice any missed calls or emails. Fast forward to when I met you. I told her we were emailing and that hopefully you would soon be calling as well. I told her that you were a priority in my life, and to please make sure I knew about any missed emails or phone calls that she might see before I did." She looks over at me and this time, she stares into my eyes, and I can see the battle she is having with herself on deciding if she believes me. "She never in the past acted jealous over anyone, so I had no reason to be suspicious of her. I believed her when she told me you hadn't emailed or called, especially with how reluctant you were with keeping in touch when we went our separate ways. One time I thought I caught her talking to you, but she denied it, saying she would have told me if you called.

Then my phone conveniently broke and she got me a new phone with a new phone number. All of my contacts were in the old phone, so I again had no reason to be suspicious. She said my emails had been hacked into, which is very common for people in my industry. I asked her to send you my new email address and she told me she did."

I pause for a moment, letting my words sink in so she understands that she was a priority to me and I did make it clear to Valerie that she was. "When time went on and I didn't hear from you, I resigned myself to the fact that you thought it should only be a fling and had moved on. Again, I had zero reasons to think anything was amiss." I walk toward her, stopping right next to her and looking down at her. I watch her swallow and she seems uncomfortable with my closeness. But I need to be close to her for what I'm about to tell her next.

"In order to prepare for one of my movies, I had to be in a certain kind of shape, so the studio hired a trainer for me. The trainer happened to be a female named Geri Roberts. Valerie was on vacation when I had my first meeting with Geri. She was gone for one week and had not met or known about Geri. The only detail she knew was that I was going to be working out with a different trainer other than my own. When Geri called wanting to talk with me, Valerie told her I would call her back, but never gave me the message because she had no idea of Geri's relevance—just that it was a female that she had never heard about. This went on for almost two weeks. Geri finally complained to the studio about how I never returned her calls, when I had been waiting to hear from her. I thought Geri was the unprofessional one. When I found out that Geri had been calling me all along, I questioned Valerie, who in turn confessed that she was in love with me. I fired her and had a restraining order placed against her." I pause a moment and then tell her, "That was two years ago."

She closes her eyes and wraps her arms around her waist. I ball my fists in helplessness as I watch the emotional rollercoaster ride she's currently on riding out while digesting this information. I know with every fiber of my being that Jenna is innocent. No one can fake the hurt, anger, and mistrust that is playing like a slow movie across her face.

I can't handle watching her in such turmoil and despair. I move to stand in front of her and grab her arms. She inhales at my touch and opens her eyes to look at me. I stare intently into those brown orbs, needing her to see that I never knew of her emails or phone calls. "Jenna, you've got to believe me when I tell you that I had no idea that you were still trying to contact me."

"So you were not the one who wrote that email saying you didn't want to be in Avery's life?" Skepticism laces her voice and a part of me hates that she still doesn't believe me but if the roles were reversed, I would probably feel the same way she does.

"No, I stopped seeing emails from you before I left for Hong Kong."

"What?" she gasps in shock. "There were more emails after that. She must have deleted them before you logged on to see them and obviously, your account wasn't hacked at all. She probably changed the login information so you wouldn't check for yourself." She shakes her head in disbelief. "I have every single email correspondence in a file that I can give you if you want to read them."

I let go of her arms and instead, run my hands through my hair, gripping it to try to hold on to my composure. I can't handle seeing those emails right now. I'll eventually need to see them, but right now my focus is trying to slowly regain Jenna's trust back. "I don't need to see them. I believe you, Jenna. Do you believe me though?" I let go of my hair and reach for her again but stop myself. "I know we don't know each other that well, but you've got to believe me when I say I would never have abandoned you both if I had known the truth."

She doesn't answer right away and I can't blame her. All this time she believed it was me who didn't want to be part of their life and to now learn that was all untrue is a lot to take in. I know I need to give her time to think through everything, but I feel desperate for her to believe me.

"I don't know what to believe, Cal," she whispers, and I hate that fucking answer. I hate it because I should've never let this happen. I should've never put all my trust in Valerie. I should've fought harder to maintain my relationship with Jenna. I should've never listened to people when they said I need to let her go and not try to find her.

This is all *my* fault.

I start to pace around her office, my fury at the situation starting to bubble up and boil over. "I can't fucking believe this! I can't believe I've had a child for the last four years and had no idea about it. That fucking, conniving bitch!" I spit out in disbelief. "She's lucky I already have a restraining order against her." A thought occurs to me, and I suddenly stop pacing to look at Jenna. *If Jenna never told the press about Avery, then who did?* "How did the press find out about Avery if you didn't tell them?"

She looks down at her hands and starts fidgeting with her nails, uneasiness creeping into her voice. "Long story short, Layla told the wrong person at the wrong time."

Layla is Jenna's best friend who I met while in Las Vegas. From my small amount of interaction with Layla, they seemed to be as close as Sean and I are.

"Why would Layla tell someone?"

She sighs and looks back up at me. "Does it even matter at this point? It was an accident."

*An accident? What does that even mean?* I ponder this information and the gravity of it. "So, if she hadn't accidentally told the person that went to the press, I still wouldn't know about Avery?" She gives me a look that confirms I wouldn't be standing here today and my jaw clenches tightly. My guess is Layla must've been drunk when revealing that information because she would've never betrayed Jenna by willingly going to the press.

Avery's voice pulls me out of my thoughts, and I turn to watch her and my mother coming out of her bedroom through the glass of the French doors. We watch in silence as she shows my mum her shopping cart of fake food and her little kitchen that is close to the real kitchen. The look on my mother's face is pure joy while she sits and watches her new granddaughter.

Guilt and longing stream through me. I look back at Jenna with remorse. "I'm sorry, Jenna," I tell her with regret. "I'm very sorry for all the lies that were told to you. I'm sorry for not being there for you when you were all alone dealing with this." Without thinking, I grab her in my arms and crush her to me. I hold her tightly, hoping she can feel every emotion that is radiating from my body. Every regret, every sorrow. I inhale her intoxicating scent and my grip tightens on her because she feels like home. She fits perfectly in my arms, and it makes me realize what an uphill battle I have to climb to win hers and Avery's trust.

"Please let go of me," she begs while being muffled against my chest. Her hands are trying to push me away, but my grip on her is too much. I know she's someone else's right now, but I just can't seem to let her go. *You touching her is the last thing she wants*, I remind myself and release her. I back away from her and grumble, "Sorry," even though I'm not fucking sorry at all for holding her.

I want to be holding her forever.

She tries to put some distance between us and clears her

throat "When do you want to do the paternity test?" she asks, changing the subject and not at all acknowledging my apology.

I know I will need to do one for legality purposes, but in order to regain Jenna's trust, I need her to see that I trust and believe her. For now, I will let her see that the courts mandate it and that it isn't coming from me. "It isn't necessary. She looks just like me," I tell her with a smile and damn if I'm not feeling full of pride at the fact that Avery looks like a Harrington.

"Yeah… she does," Jenna sighs out, giving me a small smile.

That small glimmer of a smile reminds me of the past, where smiles and laughter between us were infectious. Jenna must be feeling the nostalgia as well because we stare at each other, both caught up in a time long ago. But reality comes slithering back to me and I realize so much time has been lost. I've missed out on so much of my daughter's life that now I need to play catch up. I can't seem to stop the anger that is simmering like a beast inside of me and it's taking all my willpower to control it while I'm in front of Jenna.

I swallow down my emotions and clear my throat. "I would like to come back tomorrow with my lawyer to discuss legalities. I need all her vital information so that I can add her to my will and create some bank accounts for her. We also need to discuss my visitation rights when I permanently move to Chicago." My mind is racing with all the things I need to do that I almost miss Jenna's sharp intake of breath.

"Wait, what? You're moving to Chicago?"

"Of course I'm going to move to Chicago. We're starting to shoot my new movie here in a couple of weeks, so I'll be in a hotel at first, but then I'll find a place to buy." She looks at me with such shock that I wonder what she was expecting. "This is where you live. I would never imagine uprooting Avery when I can be flexible. Visitation needs to be situated because I would like for her to visit my family in England with me as well."

"She's never been on a plane before." Her voice is filled with anxiety, and she rubs her forehead as if she has a headache. "This is all going too fast. I can't deal with this right now," she says and shakes her head.

"I want a relationship with my daughter, Jenna, and I will need your help with that," I tell her in a firm tone. I know this is a lot of information to handle and I'm confident that Jenna wouldn't deny me my daughter, but her response to my moving to Chicago bothers me.

"These things are going to take time, Cal. She doesn't even know you exist!"

I narrow my eyes at her, not liking her answer. "What do you mean? You told her she doesn't have a father?"

"She knows she has a father, but I didn't tell her who her father was. All she was told is that her daddy does not live with us and works all the time," she explains and I feel relieved that she somewhat told her the truth and didn't lie.

"Well, thanks for not telling her I was dead," I say with a sheepish smile because she easily could have.

"There's no reason to lie to her. I knew one day she would want to know about her real father."

"Does she currently have some sort of father figure?" I ask, straightening up my spine as if that's going to shield me from the answer I'm dreading to hear from her.

"Just my dad and Robert. I'm dating someone, but he isn't present much in her life right now."

*Thank you, God.* "Ah yes, the hockey player."

She nods her head at me and is about to speak but gets distracted by the presence of Robert outside the office doors. "Will you excuse me for one moment, please?" she asks, but leaves without waiting for a response from me.

I briefly close my eyes and take a deep breath to calm me down. I need to call Philip and figure out what can be done about Valerie. The bitch needs to pay and I need to figure out my retribution. I open my eyes when I hear Jenna's footsteps coming closer.

"My lawyer can meet tomorrow at 9:00 a.m. Is that too early for you and your lawyer?"

"That should work," I tell her and see her demeanor has changed to all business. I think this is the perfect time to make our exit. I need to call my lawyer and Philip. "We need to get going. Oh, and this time, I will need your phone number," I request with a satisfied smirk. There's no way in hell I'm leaving here without her number. She frowns but nods her head in agreement.

I follow her out to the living room where she retrieves her phone from the kitchen counter and we exchange numbers. Once that is done, I turn to my mother and nod at her. "I hate to announce this, but it's time for us to go, Avery."

"Thank you for playing with me, Rose. I had so much fun!" Avery throws her little arms around my mother's legs and squeezes. She responds by kneeling and hugging Avery back, her eyes closed, but her face beaming in happiness. Pride fills me with my daughter's sweet gesture, and I can see my mother is trying to keep her composure and not cry in front of Avery.

"Thank you so much for letting me play with you, Avery," she tells her. I walk over to them and help my mother back to her feet. To my surprise, she walks over to Jenna and embraces her. "Thank you!" I hear her whisper to Jenna, who stands there in awkward silence. When my mother pulls away, Jenna nods at her and it seems she's fighting to keep her emotions at bay as well. I know once these two get to know each other, my mother will love Jenna as if she's another one of her daughters. I see my mother look at Avery with longing and an idea springs to mind.

"Will it be okay if my mother spends time with Avery tomorrow while we have our meeting?" I ask Jenna, my eyes pleading with her to say yes. My mother looks at Jenna with hope while Avery jumps up and down in excitement, screaming her approval.

"Avery's usually in school by then," Jenna responds, but I can see she's thinking. She suddenly looks at Robert, who nods his head as if he's read her mind, "But since this is a special occasion, I can keep her home in the morning for you to spend time together."

"Thank you very much," I tell her with sincerity, grateful that she's giving my mother more time with Avery.

We all walk toward her door, and I open it with dread, not wanting to leave but knowing I need to. I motion for my mother to walk in front of me and when we are through the door, I turn around one more time to look at Avery and then at Jenna. I briefly stare at them watching me and remind myself that this will be my new normal.

"Until tomorrow." I nod goodbye and it takes every ounce of strength in me to put one foot in front of the other.

# CHAPTER 7

THIS FEELS SO damn wrong.

Leaving Jenna's condo after I just found them isn't sitting right and it's just adding more fuel to the fire that's building inside of me. None of this would be happening if I was told the truth from day one.

I stalk toward the elevator and once I reach it, I punch at the down button. Not being able to stand still, I start to pace while we wait. My mother remains silent, but she watches me with concern. She knows I'm like a volcano ready to erupt.

The ding of the elevator alerts us to its arrival, and we walk inside when the doors open. As soon as they close, I can't hold myself back any longer.

"*Fuck!*" I roar out before turning toward the wall and kicking the shit out of the wood paneling. "Fuck, fuck, fuck!"

I kick the wall harder, the hole that has formed growing larger with each kick.

"Cal, please stop!" My mother pleads and I stop long enough for her to throw her arms around me, holding me as tightly as she can. I will myself to calm down and try to take deep breaths to regain my composure. Before I'm ready, we've reached the lobby of the building and the doors to the elevator open. Needing to get out of the confined space, I don't even bother looking at the damage and instead, head straight to the front desk to report it.

"My name is Cal Harrington and I've damaged your elevator," I tell the front desk concierge bluntly without any greeting. I take my calling card out of my coat pocket and hand it to him. "This is my assistant's phone number. Please let her know how much it costs for repairs and I will pay for it."

"I know who you are, sir, and if this behavior happens again, you will be banned from entering the building. Do you understand?" He barely glances at me while reaching for the phone and dialing what I presume to be the maintenance department.

"Noted," I nod at him, liking the fact that he isn't accepting my bullshit just because I'm a celebrity.

I turn and walk toward the front entrance, my mother following behind. As soon as we get outside, we walk to our awaiting car. I open the door for my mother, my anger subsiding enough for me to remember my manners. I shut her door once she's in and move around the back of the car to my side, where the driver is holding the door open for me. I get in and once he shuts the door, I stare out the window. I can't handle small talk right now and my mother must sense it because she gives me about five minutes of silence before speaking.

"Talk to me, Cal." Her soft voice cuts through my thoughts, but my eyes remain locked on the outside world as it passes by.

"All this time. All this fucking time they've been out here without me." I shake my head because I just don't have the words for how lost I feel about everything.

"I'm so terribly sorry this has happened to you, Cal." She reaches over and grabs my hand, giving it a squeeze of encouragement. "You have every right to be angry, but now that you know the truth, you need to regroup and focus on the future.

You have a lot of decisions to make."

"The only decision I need to figure out right now is how I'm going to make my ex-assistant pay for what she did. Everything else is decided. I'm moving to Chicago and being a part of my daughter's life. There's no discussion needed on that."

"Revenge isn't going to take away the past and the time you've lost with your daughter. Let that go, Cal. You need to put all your energy in building back Jenna's trust. You and Jenna need to have an amicable relationship in order to co-parent without issues."

"Oh, I plan on having more than just an amicable relationship with Jenna, Mother."

"Cal…" she warns but before she can go any further, my cell phone rings. I grab it out of my coat pocket, hoping it's Jenna, but disappointed to see that it's Philip.

"Can you talk because the suspense is killing me!"

"Valerie," I spit out in disgust. "Valerie was the mastermind behind all of this. She deleted emails from me, never told me when Jenna called and when Jenna told her that she was pregnant, Valerie pretended to be me in an email and told Jenna I wanted nothing to do with the baby."

"Shut the fuck up!" Philip says in astonishment. "Are you serious?"

"When she said my email account was hacked and she 'accidentally' broke my phone and got me a new number…all lies so Jenna would have no way of contacting me anymore."

"But didn't you have Jenna's email address on a card?" Philip asks.

"Yes, but apparently Jenna changed her email address when she thought I didn't want to be in their lives."

"Wow, Cal, I'm in shock right now," Philip mutters. "I just can't get over what a crazy bitch Valerie is."

"She needs to pay for this, Phillip."

"What do you mean? We're not killing anybody over this, Cal," he says with a nervous laugh.

"I want to ruin her for what she's done to me… *to us*."

"Cal," my mother starts but I raise my finger up to signal for her to stop so I can finish my phone call.

"Unless there's concrete proof showing she's behind this, there's nothing we can do now, Cal."

"Jenna has saved all the emails."

"Yes, but Valerie isn't going to admit that she was portraying you. It's hearsay."

"She needs to fucking pay, Philip," I shout into the phone, not caring how crazy I might sound to my mother or my driver.

"Cal, I understand that you're hurt and upset, but listen to me…she's not worth ruining your career over. She isn't even working in the industry anymore. She's married to some rich Italian producer who has mob connections. She isn't worth your time."

"Philip…I need something done," I demand in a deadly tone.

He lets out a long breath and I can picture him running his hands through his hair. "Let me think, Cal. Right now, the only thing I can come up with is getting a permanent restraining order but even that might be hard without proof."

"Figure it out and call me tomorrow." I hang up after saying goodbye and turn my attention back to the window.

"Revenge is not the answer, Cal. Please, I beg you to let this go," my mother pleads, worry tingeing in her voice. I briefly look over at her before an idea pops into my head.

"Marco," I call out to the driver, who looks at me in his rearview mirror. "Can you please take us to the nearest toy store?" Marco nods and reroutes his navigation.

I turn to my mother and look at her. "I don't want to discuss Valerie anymore tonight, Mother. Can you do that for me, please?" She nods and I ignore the look of disappointment in her eyes. “We are heading to the toy store where we will pick up gifts for Avery from both of us to bring to her tomorrow. I need your expertise on what to pick out.” She gives me a small smile and shakes her head.

“Fine but remember to not buy out the entire store. Jenna’s condo is already snug with all of Avery’s toys.”

“Yes, we will need to remedy that in the future as well.”

My mother narrows her eyes at me. “What do you mean by that?”

“Jenna needs a bigger place.” I shrug my shoulders, trying to look innocent, but my mother sees right through me.

“Listen to me, Cal. From what I saw today, Jenna is not some docile, wallflower that is going to let you walk into her life and take it over for her. She’s an independent woman who has been a single mother these last four years doing just fine on her own.” I tighten my jaw, feeling my blood pressure rise at the reminder.

“Jenna is not your property or your concern. She’s not going to accept you making decisions for both her and Avery.”

“She’s the mother of my child. Of course she’s going to be my concern.”

“I’m not doubting that you want what’s best for Jenna, especially since if she’s happy, then Avery will be happy. But son, you might not be the best choice for Jenna.”

I snap my eyes up to hers and stare at her. “What’s that supposed to mean?”

“She’s already in a relationship, Cal. One that doesn’t need you meddling into because you feel you know what’s best,” she scolds, shooting me a knowing look.

“I don’t plan on meddling into her relationship, Mother, even though I know I am the best one for her. Jenna will come to that conclusion on her own.” I will not be a third party in someone’s relationship, but I’m confident there’s still chemistry between us. I just have to figure out a way for Jenna to realize that. “Trust me, Mother. Jenna will be mine. It might take time, but she will be."

"Oh really? She won't if you keep sounding like an arrogant arsehole like you do now." She lets her words hang in the air a few seconds before breathing out a sigh and grabbing my hand. "While I would like nothing more than to see you happy and settled down, I beg of you to tread carefully, Cal. She's been through a lot and it's going to get worse. She hasn't lived your lifestyle and what it's like to be in the public eye. She doesn't know how to handle the paparazzi and now she has to share her child with someone who is a complete stranger." I'm about to comment that I'm not a stranger, but my mother is having none of it.

"You *are* a complete stranger, Cal, and you need to realize that." She slices her hand through the air, hushing me. "It's going to take her a long time to trust you as a person and as Avery's father. I know you like to be in control of everything, but please Cal, be slow and cautious with Jenna. This must be a partnership with open communication between the two. Not you wanting to handle everything."

I absorb my mother's words, knowing there is a lot of truth in what she says. "I'll try my best, Mother." I take a deep breath, close my eyes and lean my head back against the headrest. "I just want to fix everything and move forward."

"I know you do, but this is a delicate situation. There's nothing to fix—you just need to show them the real Cal and be the best father to Avery that you can be. And forget the revenge, Cal." I open my eyes and just stare at her. I'm too tired to argue with her at this point as exhaustion is finally settling in from the lack of sleep and emotions from the day.

We pull up to the curb in front of the toy shop and come to a stop. We both just sit and stare at it for a moment, neither one of us attempting to exit the car.

"Maybe this isn't a good idea," I murmur, not knowing what the hell I'm doing. "Afterall, I have no idea what she likes."

"Well, we know she likes Peter Pan and tea parties, so that's a start." My mother pats my hand in encouragement. "Come now, son. This is the part when grandmothers know best. Just follow me and give me your credit card when I'm ready." She winks at me, and I chuckle, grateful for my mum being here with me.

A warm feeling of happiness slowly starts to wash over me at the thought of seeing my daughter tomorrow and her beautiful smile as she opens her first present that comes from me.

Her father.

# Chapter 8

A SENSE OF déjà vu washes over me as we approach Jenna's door the following morning. We're arriving earlier than expected for our meeting with the lawyers, but I wanted to bring the girls breakfast and Avery her toys that we bought. With my hands full carrying bags, my mother knocks on the door.

A few moments later, Jenna opens it with a surprised look on her face. "Oh, I'm sorry, I wasn't expecting you so soon." Her hair and makeup are done, but she's not dressed yet and I'm transfixed, watching her hands clutch the lapels of her baby blue satin robe together, careful not to reveal anything. But I know exactly what her body looks like and my mind immediately envisions what's underneath. I remember running my hands over her silky, smooth body, salivating over her curves that are in all the right places. I lick my lips remembering how her rosy nipples on those luscious breasts of hers would pucker underneath my touch. Remembering her sweet little moans every time I kissed her makes my dick instantly harden.

I shift uncomfortably on my feet and will myself to focus on her face and not the memory of her body. "I'm sorry for not giving you any warning, but we wanted to surprise you both with treats."

“Treats? What kind of treats?” Avery’s voice comes from behind Jenna, the pitter-patter of her feet echoing off the wood floors.

“Good morning, Avery.” I greet my daughter with a big smile. Jenna motions for us to enter and we step into the condo. “Do you like hot chocolate?” I ask.

Avery gives me a cheeky lopsided grin, revealing tiny dimples in those cheeks that I just want to kiss. “Yes!” Her eyes light up and she stands on her tippy toes as she answers.

“Do you also like strawberry donuts?”

“Those are my favorite,” she whispers in awe, and I’m pleased to know that we share the same affection for donut flavors.

“Anything with sugar is your favorite,” Jenna replies with a smirk.

“Then I have the perfect breakfast for you,” I tell her with a wink. I put the bags I was holding on the kitchen counter while my mother sets down the drinks she was carrying and retrieves the box of donuts out of one of the bags.

“But I’ve already had breakfast this morning,” Avery announces and looks at her mother with a frown. Her lips start to quiver into a pout, and I can already predict that I will have zero willpower telling this child no for anything she wants. I look at Jenna for help and she chuckles at my helplessness.

“You can have two breakfasts for today, Avery. But just this once.” Jenna has to shout above Avery’s scream of delight.

“Thank you,” I softly tell Jenna. “And if memory serves me correctly, do you still drink a hazelnut latte in the mornings?” I question with a raised eyebrow, praying I got it right.

I watch her swallow and slowly nod. “You are correct. Thank you.” She gives me a hesitant smile before reaching for the coffee I bought her. Our fingers touch when I hand her the drink and I fucking love the cute blush that stains her cheeks.

“Um, if you will excuse me for a moment, I’m going to finish getting ready," she says, her eyes not meeting my gaze. She turns and asks Robert, "Do you mind entertaining our guests with Avery?"

"Only if I'm allowed to have a donut," Robert responds, and I hand him the box so he can choose one.

"Thank you," she says to him, and I watch her walk into her bedroom. She turns around and briefly meets my eyes before shutting her door. I stare at that door for a moment longer, hopeful that soon there will be no more barriers between us. I focus my attention back to Avery, but not before I catch Robert looking at me with a wicked glint in his eye and a knowing grin on his face.

"Avery, who's that on your jammies?" I ask her just as she takes a huge bite out of her donut.

"Cinderwelly," she mutters, a big glob of strawberry gooeyness falling out of her mouth and onto her plate.

"Avery, you know your mother always tells you not to talk with food in your mouth," Robert warns her, giving me a knowing look.

"Is Cinderella your favorite Disney Princess?" My mother asks her when she is done chewing.

"Yes. And Jasmine, and Ariel, and Merida." She stops to think if she has left anyone out. "And Olaf."

We all laugh at her answer, and I make a mental note to ask Jenna if Avery's been to Disney World yet. It would be the perfect first trip together—hopefully as a family.

My mother politely asks Robert about his background while we watch Avery eat. As I'm listening to him recall how he came to work for Jenna, my phone vibrates in my pocket. I pull it out to see I've missed Bridget's call.

"Robert, is there a room I can take a call in?"

"You can use Jenna's office." He nods toward the French doors, and I give him a thumbs up before excusing myself. Once inside, I shut the doors and call my sister back.

"I was able to coordinate both yours and mother's plane to depart around the same time, so don't be late," she says as soon as I greet her.

"My plane? I'm not coming back to London."

"No shit, you're going to Los Angeles for the Oscars."

"Fuck," I growl, completely forgetting that I'm a presenter this year.

"Can you tell Philip—"

"One hundred percent no, I will not tell Philip you're not going!" Bridget interrupts, reading my mind completely on what I was going to ask her to do. "You know this is a big deal for you to show up, do pre-interviews for your upcoming movie and present."

She's right. It will look bad if I back out, not to mention Philip and the studio would be livid. One week away from my girls doesn't seem like a lot, but it's going to be torture, especially with the uphill battle I have to fight to gain Jenna's trust.

"Fine," I sigh in resolve. "What time are our planes?"

"Both depart at 8:00 p.m. at the same private hub where you landed before. I already sent Marco your information."

"Thanks, Bridget."

"How's it going?"

"It's going. I'm at Jenna's right now and we're about to leave for the lawyer's office."

"Does Avery know yet?" Bridget asks with hope in her voice.

"No, and we haven't talked about when we will tell her. For now, she thinks I'm a family friend."

"Bummer."

"It's only been twenty-four hours, Bridget. These things take time." I chuckle at her impatience because I feel the exact same way, but I know it's for the best to tell Avery when the time is right. "Listen, I need to go," I tell her as I spot Jenna through the windows of the French doors. "I'll call you later."

I end the call and exit Jenna's office. I stop short at the sight of her and inwardly groan. She has that whole hot, professional looking vibe going on dressed in a white silk blouse, gray pencil skirt that is molded to those sexy hips of hers, and black heels. My mind conjures up all the dirty little things I could do to her while she's dressed like that. My dick stirs and I can already tell it's going to take every ounce of strength to keep my hands to myself.

"Mommy, you look pretty!" Avery tells her and I couldn't agree more. Feeling my intense stare on her, Jenna glances at me and a blush creeps back up those cheeks. She quickly looks away and clears her throat.

*I still affect her like she does me,* I think and smile.

"Thank you, honey. Now Avery, I need you to make good decisions and listen to Robert and Rose while Mommy is gone, okay?"

"Yes, Mommy, I will be so very good that you will want to buy me a present for my good behavior."

Jenna grins at Avery and bends down to give her a hug and a kiss. "Maybe I will. We'll see."

"Jenna, I rearranged your schedule today so you don't have anything planned until 5:00 p.m.," Robert mentions when he hands her sunglasses and hugs her goodbye.

"Why would I have something planned at 5:00 p.m.?" She questions with a confused look on her face.

"Hair and make-up for the Blackhawks' charity gala."

The Blackhawks are the local hockey team, which means Jenna will be with her boyfriend tonight. My smile falters and I'm completely irritated that I won't be around to keep her from seeing him.

"Oh crap! I forgot," she says with a guilty look on her face.

"It's okay, Jenna. I've got you covered. Go focus on your

meeting," he tells her.

"I have a car waiting for us if you're ready to go?" I interrupt their conversation, wanting her to forget the subject of Jax Morrow and focus on the task at hand.

We say our goodbyes and head to the elevator in silence. Once it arrives and we enter it, I notice she stands as far away from me as she possibly can. I smile as I push the lobby button and wonder if she remembers the last time we were alone in an elevator together. I know I can't dwell on those memories, otherwise I'll be hard as a rock and standing at attention, so instead I tell her about the circus act that is currently waiting for us outside.

"Just to warn you, there are a lot of paparazzi downstairs. As soon as the elevator doors open, put your sunglasses on. Follow my lead to the car and don't say anything to them. Understand?"

"Can't wait!" she replies sarcastically and reaches in her purse to grab her sunglasses.

I abhor this aspect of fame and feel guilty for bringing this into her life, but unfortunately, it comes with the territory. I try my hardest not to bring attention to myself outside of my career, but this "scandal" was the perfect excuse for paparazzi all over the world to descend upon Chicago. Some of these guys will make millions of dollars off the perfect photo of us. I don't quite understand the insatiable need for celebrity gossip but it's a billion-dollar industry.

The doors open and I hear her gasp in shock to see close to twenty camera lenses being pointed in our direction outside of the main lobby windows. I want to grab her hand so badly, but that will only add more speculation to the gossip.

The clicking of the cameras and questions come flying at us once we make our way out of the comfort of her building. We quickly make our way to my parked car and I don't think we take a breath until we are safely inside. I watch Jenna turn around to look behind us and she's transfixed by all of them scattering like ants to jump into their cars and taxis to follow us.

"Jenna," I say in a stern voice and her gaze reverts to me, but not before I see the fear in her eyes. "I need you to let the driver know the address of where we are going."

"Yes, sorry, that would really be helpful, wouldn't it?" she nervously giggles and gives Marco the address to her lawyer's office. He starts to drive away, but soon the paparazzi have caught up with us in their own cars.

"How do you get used to this?" she questions with a dazed look on her face.

"It will die down, Jenna. These paps don't like being outside in the cold weather," I tell her, hoping my answer will make her feel better, but instead she just looks even more confused.

"Winter isn't for another couple of months—they'll stay here that whole time?"

*Shit, maybe I shouldn't have told her that.*

"Afraid so. Just always keep your head down, let them get their shot, and don't tell them anything." She nods at me and turns to continue looking out the window. I don't think my answer was to her liking, but I don't want to lie to her either. I want her to be fully prepared during the times I'm not able to be around and protect her.

We pull up in front of her lawyer's building and our car is immediately boxed in with paparazzi.

"Jenna, let me get out first and then come out on my side instead so I can help you navigate through them, okay?" She nods her head and I get out of the car.

I smile and wave at them to divert the attention from Jenna to me. I turn around and extend my hand to help Jenna out of the car. As soon as she's out, she lets go of my hand and I lead her ahead of me by placing my hand on the small of her back. We reach the doors that security is holding open for us and proceed to be greeted by our lawyers who are waiting to escort us upstairs. We exchange introductions to our respective lawyers and follow them to the meeting room to start the proceedings of making Avery officially mine.

# Chapter 9

"WHY ARE WE going to Jenna's again? Is everything okay with her and Avery?" My mother asks with concern after she hears me tell Marco to make a detour to Jenna's place before going to the airport.

"I just want to make sure she's okay after our meeting with the lawyers this morning."

I wasn't expecting our meeting to be emotional for Jenna, but it turns out it was. It started off fine at first. She signed off on the paperwork for voluntary declaration of paternity. We then crafted a joint statement to put out to the press asking them to respect our privacy while we deal with this situation as a family. We agreed that Jenna should have primary physical custody of Avery, but we'll share joint legal custody so I can be involved in all decision making that impacts her. When the discussion turned to holiday sharing, her demeanor started to change. She smiled less and was snappier.

"Why wouldn't she be okay? You said today went well."

"I think it did, but she seemed to get upset when we started to discuss money."

"Did she feel what you were offering was too low?" my mother asks, looking perplexed.

"On the contrary, she felt it was too high."

Jenna was adamant about not accepting alimony from me, arguing that she does just fine on her own and doesn't want or need my money. Her lawyer had to pull her out of the room to try to convince her otherwise. When they returned, she still refused my offer and instead, reluctantly agreed on me retroactively paying for her expenses these past four years after she produces receipts. I have a feeling Jenna plans on conveniently *not* turning any in.

When my mother gives me a questioning look, I continue to explain. "She basically refused alimony and thinks the amount of money I want to pay for child support is exuberant. When she found out how much Avery plans on gaining when she turns twenty-five, she went ballistic and said our child will not become a spoiled rich kid who does not know the value of money."

"That makes me like Jenna even more," my mother comments with a smile.

I nod my head in agreement because Jenna is extraordinary. I couldn't have picked a better woman and role model to be the mother of my child. "She's pretty special, Mum, but also very stubborn." I smile as I recall her eyes flashing with anger at me. It was sexy as fuck and I wanted to pound that anger right out of her. Although I don't enjoy her being mad at me, at least it was for the good of our daughter.

"Well, that explains why she was a little distant earlier, but does she even know we are stopping by again?"

"No, because if I asked, she would've said no." I give her a boyish smile, one I know usually melts her heart.

"Calvin," she scolds using my full name. "This isn't a good idea."

"Why not?" I ask in mock innocence. "I'm concerned for her well-being and just want to check in on her." The car conveniently pulls up in front of Jenna's building at the exact same time. "We're here already and it won't take us long. Besides, don't you want to get one more goodbye hug from your granddaughter?" I give her a victorious smile because of course she isn't going to say no to that.

"Fine," she groans, already reaching for the door handle. "But we must be quick about it. I don't want to intrude on Jenna's privacy."

I tell Marco to stay here since we won't be long, and we exit the car and go into the building. We make our way to the front desk to sign in where a tall man with blond hair is waiting with his back to us. As we approach, the concierge sees us and nods his acknowledgment while on the phone. "I have Cal Harrington *and* Jax Morrow here for Ms. Pruitt."

I turn to look at the blond man standing next to me, his expression mirroring my surprise as we stare at each other. I completely forgot about Robert and Jenna's earlier conversation about her seeing him tonight and I especially wasn't aware of what time. I knew Jax Morrow was a good-looking bastard from the photos Thomas had sent me, but it pisses me off that he looks better in person. I wasn't anticipating meeting him so quickly. In fact, I was hoping to *not* be meeting him at all. My mood darkens at the realization that I will have to watch him interact with Avery and even worse, watch him put his hands on Jenna.

"You're both free to go up after you sign in."

We take turns signing in and he gets a head start on us for the elevator. I watch him walk swiftly ahead and notice he's just as tall as I am, but leaner in build. We stop beside him to wait for the elevator and the air is thick with tension. He decides to break the ice by turning toward us and introducing himself.

"I'm Jax Morrow, Jenna's boyfriend."

I clench my jaw at his words and notice he holds out his hand for my mother to shake, but only nods in my direction.

"I'm Cal Harrington and this is my mother, Rose."

The elevator doors open, and we walk in together. He pushes the button for Jenna's floor and then turns his attention to my mother.

"Ah, you're Avery's grandmother," he acknowledges in her direction with a smile on his face. "Avery is a wonderful child. I enjoy every moment I get to spend with her. How long will you be in town for?"

I see the game this man is starting to play, and it makes me want to punch his fucking face in. Although his question was directed to my mother, I answer for her. "My mother is leaving tonight to go back to London, but I will be moving here permanently as soon as possible."

His smile falters but he quickly masks his surprise. "How wonderful for Avery," he responds with fake enthusiasm and says nothing more.

My mother decides to fill the awkward silence by asking questions on where Jax is from and what he does for a living. He answers her questions politely while we get off the elevator and walk down the hall to Jenna's door. I don't contribute to the conversation because everything he's telling her are things I already knew and quite honestly…I don't give two shits about this bloke and prefer him out of our lives.

Unfortunately, none of that is up to me.

Robert welcomes us into Jenna's condo and the first person Avery sees is Jax. She screams out his name and runs into his open arms. I watch in jealousy as he picks up my child, holds her high and then proceeds to give her a tight hug before holding her on his hip. My anger seethes that I'm not close enough with her yet to get that same reaction out of her and I can't mask my hatred for him at this moment.

"Cal and Rose, you're back!" She waves at us but stays in his arms. I'm about to extract her from him when the site of Jenna snags all my attention.

She appears from her bedroom in a long, navy, beaded lace cocktail dress that hugs her hips and bodice with a V-neckline that shows off the top of her breasts. Her hair is pulled down into a whimsical low bun at the base of her neck with tendrils of hair curled around her face. She's wearing heavy eye make-up with fake eyelashes but with nude lipstick that I want to kiss right off those lips. She looks stunning, momentarily rendering me speechless with her beauty. She gives me a hesitant smile and nods in my direction, but stays rooted in her spot, seemingly indecisive on who she should go to first.

I make my way further into the hallway to go to her when I notice out of the corner of my eye movement coming from Avery's bedroom. I turn to my right to see Layla, Jenna's best friend, coming out of the room, a weary expression on her face as she acknowledges me.

"It's nice to see you again, Layla. May I introduce you to my mother?" I make the introductions and I try to give Layla a hug hello, but she stops me from doing so.

"Sorry, Cal, but I've hated your guts these past four years and really don't know how I feel about seeing you. No offense, Mrs. Harrington," she says, giving my mom a genuine smile, but for me, one that is a little bit more reserved.

"Seems to be the consensus in this place," I tease and look in Jenna's direction to see her smirk at my answer.

"Well, can you blame us?" Layla demands and I shake my head at her because their feelings were one hundred percent valid.

"No, I can't. And even though I'm sure at the time you thought it was devastating, I'm forever grateful to you for telling whoever you told about Avery." Despite her feelings toward me, I grab her and give her a tight hug even though she doesn't return it.

I like to believe that I would've found out about Avery from

Thomas, but what if I never hired him? If it wasn't for Layla, the truth would've been kept from me underneath the umbrella of lies that were spun. I meant what I said about my gratitude towards her. She gives me an awkward smile when I let her go and just pats my arm, her uncomfortableness with the situation clearly on display.

"Wow, Avery, look at your mommy. Isn't she gorgeous?" Jax's statement diverts my attention and I watch Jenna beam at him. Her smile is a punch to my gut because that's exactly how I want her to be looking at me.

Jax carries Avery over to Jenna and they engulf her in a group hug. They look like a picture-perfect happy family and when he whispers something in her ear and kisses her full on the lips, my vision turns red. I feel my mother's hand on my arm, and she squeezes. I look over at her and her eyes are begging me not to do anything. I nod and mentally count to ten. I will not physically harm Jax Morrow, but I will gladly beat him at his mental mind fuck.

Jenna is the first one to pull away, glancing at me with an uncomfortable smile. "Has everyone been introduced?" she asks, looking around the room at each of us.

"Yes, we rode the elevator up and Jax introduced himself to us then," I respond, and then purposely proceed to eye fuck her in such a way that I see Jax's grip tighten around her waist. It doesn't matter that he's here or not—the way Jenna looks tonight would have the same reaction out of me. I watch her swallow and shuffle on her feet, and I know she could feel the heat from my stare. I want Jenna and I will gladly let the whole world know my intentions for her.

"Yes, but I wasn't expecting to be introduced to Mr. Harrington tonight. Better now than never!" Jax declares with the fakest of smiles. I would've preferred never, and I bet he feels the same way.

"That's my fault for this surprise visit. We're leaving tonight and I just wanted to say goodbye to Avery one more time," my mother says as she steps forward. I look at her in surprise because she did not have to say that since it was my idea to visit in the first place.

"Leaving tonight?" Jenna looks at me for an explanation.

"My mother needs to get back to London and I have to be in Los Angeles this week for business. I'll be back next Monday to discuss our future," I tell her with a flirtatious smile, ignoring Jax when he clears his throat. Jenna's eyes widen and she looks over at Robert, who has a shit-eating grin on his face.

"Will I ever get to see you again, Rose?" Avery asks and my heart aches when I see my daughter's expression when she looks at my mother.

"I hope so, Avery. Maybe this summer?" I see Jenna tense at my mother's words, and I slightly shake my head, my eyes telling her that my mother will not say anything out loud about our agreement of Avery spending summers in England.

"Oh Mommy, can we?" Avery asks with excitement and Jenna gives her a hesitant smile.

"We'll see, Avery. Mommy has to go. Give me a hug and a kiss." Jenna grabs her out of Jax's arms and gives her a hug and a kiss. Avery starts to get upset at the idea of Jenna leaving and starts to beg her not to go. I take a step toward her, but Layla beats me to it and takes Avery from Jenna and starts playing with her as a distraction.

I watch Jenna hug everyone goodbye—even my mother—and I'm her last obstacle before she can reach the door. I quickly look up to see Jax saying goodbye to Robert and I make my move. I lean in and quickly kiss Jenna on the cheek before moving to her ear.

"You look beautiful," I whisper gruffly, causing Jenna to shiver. She takes a step back from me and rewards me with a sexy glare that makes me chuckle. "I'll call you when I'm back," I tell her loud enough for Jax to hear, who is now at her side shooting daggers at me with his eyes. I thrust out my hand for him to shake, which he does and squeezes as hard as he can. If Jenna wasn't around, he would probably try to break every bone in my hand.

"Good to meet you, Cal. I'll see you when you get back," Jax says with a slimy smile, and I pray to God I never see this bastard again.

I nod my head at them and will myself to not turn around and watch them walk out the door. I hear the door click behind me and know they are gone.

"Oooh wee, it was getting hot in here," Robert jokes as he walks up next to me. I shoot him a warning look, which only makes him laugh. Robert feeling comfortable enough with me to joke around sparks a thought. I'm going to need help when it pertains to both Avery and Jenna and Robert's the best man for that job.

"Robert, I think we should exchange numbers for emergency purposes." I take my cell phone out of my pocket and raise an eyebrow at him when he just stares at me.

"O-okay," he stammers and looks at Layla for help, who responds by shrugging her shoulders.

"You too, Layla," I request of her and even though I know Layla won't be as helpful as Robert, it's still a good idea to have hers as well. I expect resistance, but she surprises me by giving it to me without hesitation.

"Avery, we have to get going, but I promise you that I will talk to you every day while I'm gone." I kneel in front of her and to my delight, she throws her arms around my neck and gives me a hug. I breathe in her sweet scent and realize her hair smells like peaches—just like her mother's.

"Be safe and have fun, Cal," she tells me and I laugh because it's such an odd thing for a four year old to say.

"Is that what your mother says to you?" I ask.

She nods her head and smiles, "Every day after she leaves me at school, but she always comes back to get me. Will you come back, Cal?"

The question guts me, especially seeing the worry in her little blue eyes. I tell her without conviction, "I will always come back, Avery."

"YOU'RE QUIET, WHAT are you thinking?" My mother asks, breaking our comfortable silence while on our journey to the airport.

"Just strategizing about my time here."

"I hope that doesn't include how to break up her relationship." Her comments make me look over at her with a questioning look. "Your behavior up there was incorrigible. Let me remind you yet again that her relationship is not your business, Cal," she scolds, knowing me well enough to see through my bullshit.

"Of course it's my business, Mother. Anyone in my daughter's life is my business."

"Cal, don't do anything stupid that will make Jenna continue to hate you. She has years of pent-up anger toward you. You need to tread lightly and adjust your life to theirs."

"I have no intention of breaking up her relationship if that's what you're implying. She will do that on her own when she realizes that he's the wrong man for her."

She throws up her arms and snorts. "How arrogant of you! You don't even know if *you* are the right man for her. You barely even know her."

"I firmly believe there's a reason we are here now, all these years later. There's a reason why I haven't stopped thinking about her since the day I met her. There's a reason why the chemistry between us is still electric. So yes, Mother, I *am* the right man for her. I'm hers and she's fucking mine," I growl, tired of this subject and why people are questioning my feelings. I've never felt this certain; this strongly about someone in my entire life.

"But she's not, Cal!" she says with a raised voice, her eyes flashing with anger. "Cal, you need to accept the possibility that Jenna might not feel the same way you do. She might be in love with her boyfriend. She has more history with him than she does with you. You were a weeklong fling that ended in lies and a baby she has spent the last four years raising all by herself."

"That was not my fault," I roar, still seething from the fact that someone fucked with my life and denied me my child's first formative years.

"I understand that, but you can't swoop in and make decisions for them."

"Mother," I sigh in frustration, not wanting to be disrespectful to her but also wanting to end this conversation. "I need you to trust me on this, please. Give me six months to prove you wrong."

"This is not a game, Cal. I hope you do prove me wrong. I want nothing more than to see you happy with the woman you love and if that woman happens to be the mother of your child, even better. I'm asking you not to be the other man in someone else's relationship. I'm asking you to place yourself in someone else's shoes and view things from Jenna's point of view. I'm asking you to go slowly with both Jenna and Avery because this is going to be a huge adjustment for both of them."

"I will, Mother," I assure her.

"And I'm asking you to prepare yourself in case you're not the man for Jenna. Being amicable co-parents should be the number one priority, Cal, so if she rejects you, don't hold it against her."

That isn't even an option for me, so I pacify her with a quick "Yes, Mum." She rolls her eyes at me, knowing my antics and sits back against her seat.

Jax Morrow might be my current obstacle, but I've no doubt that Jenna is my future.

Now it's just a matter of time—and some work on my part—to show Jenna that we've been given a second chance.

# Chapter 10

*I'VE GOT TO get out of this place.*

I glance at my watch to see that I still have another two hours to go before I can leave and board my plane back to Chicago. It's been a long week of doing press and having meetings and quite honestly, my mind just hasn't been into it. Usually, I love talking about my upcoming movies and meeting with directors for potential future projects, but I realized that the only place I want to be right now is back with my girls, getting myself acclimated into their lives and vice versa.

I've talked with Avery multiple times since I've been away, each time my heart aching when it was time to hang up with her. I can tell she's starting to get used to talking with me, each conversation getting easier and less awkward, which gives me hope that the transition of her spending time alone with me will feel natural for her.

Jenna, on the other hand, is a different story. Each time I try to engage in conversation with her, she rushes off the phone or quickly hands the phone to Avery. It's obvious that it's going to take her a whole lot longer to get used to me than it will for our daughter. I've started texting more with Robert, hoping he can provide insight on how to better understand Jenna and learn ways to support her when she refuses my help. I can tell he's hesitant about talking to me, as if he's betraying Jenna, but I think once he sees my intentions are good, he'll come around.

"Cal, did you hear me?"

I look over at my publicist and give her an apologetic smile. "I'm sorry, Liz. Can you please repeat what you said?"

"You and Cora will exit the car at the same time and take photos together and then separately."

"Why do we need to take photos together?" I question, not wanting to put any more speculation out there than there already is about us being a couple.

"What's the matter, Cal? Am I cramping your style?" Cora laughs in jest but I'm pretty sure she can sense the change in me. I had completely forgotten that I agreed to attend the Oscars with her, because it has been almost a year since Philip brought it up and requested I attend. I didn't think twice back then about Cora coming with me because as a friend, she has accompanied me to many premieres and events. But Cora has changed and I'm realizing that the friendship has always been one-sided. I need to shield my daughter from the ugliness of Hollywood and that may even include Cora.

I don't bother answering Cora's question and instead, give her a quick smile before turning my attention back to Liz, who makes it no secret that she can't stand Cora. She proceeds to give us our instructions about tonight's events and tells me what time I need to leave my seat to go backstage to get in the presenters' line.

"Once you are done presenting, mingle a little bit backstage, take photos with any other actors who are back there and then proceed back to your seat."

"I won't be returning once I'm done presenting. I have a plane ready to take me back to Chicago tonight," I tell Liz, who quickly whips out her phone and starts texting someone.

"What?" Cora questions, a surprise look on her face. "Since when did this happen? You can't just leave me, Cal."

"You'll be fine, Cora. I'm sure Liz can arrange for some handsome bloke to be my seat filler."

Liz rolls her eyes while Cora shakes her head.

"Well, that's pretty shitty of you to inform us now," Cora says, her voice laced with irritation. "Why do you need to get back to Chicago so quickly anyway? I thought your new movie hadn't started pre-production yet."

I stare at her, wondering if she's really forgotten all about my daughter or just doesn't give a shit.

My guess is the latter considering she hasn't asked me once about Avery.

"I want to get back to my daughter, Cora. I have a lot of catching up to do with her."

"You have a lifetime with her, Cal. The Oscars are a rare opportunity if you don't get consistently invited."

I clench my jaw and give her a death glare at her insensitivity. This has always been what matters most to Cora. Not friendships, not love, but fame, power, and money. She's one of the most beautiful women in the world and could have such an incredible life with Sean if she would just open her eyes and her heart to him, but instead she is filled with malice. She has a giant chip on her shoulder and thinks the world owes her for her shitty childhood but yet, she gives nothing in return.

I'm relieved to see we have pulled up to the Dolby Theatre and have entered the receiving line. The air in the limo has become hostile and I want nothing more than to get the fuck out of here.

"I'd rather spend every waking moment with my daughter then one minute in a room with fake fucks who pretend to be my friend but only want me for my name and what I can get them." I lift my chin up at Cora and without waiting for her response, I open the door and exit the car.

EIGHT HOURS LATER, I'm standing in front of Jenna's door, running on adrenaline to see my girls. I'm just about to knock when the door swings open and Jenna starts to step out but screams, not anticipating seeing anyone at her doorstep.

"*Ah!*" She places a hand over her heart and grips the doorway. "You scared me!" I reach out to steady her and am about to ask if she's okay when Avery's voice interrupts me.

"Cal!" She yells in excitement as she runs past her mother and jumps into my awaiting arms. I give her a bear hug and inhale her delicious scent. She lets me hold her for a few seconds before she pulls back and gives me one of her gorgeous smiles, making my heart mush in her hands.

Fuck if this is not the best feeling in the world.

I look over at Jenna to see her staring at us in awe and it gives me a chance to check her out. She's decked out in workout clothes again and I must say, Jenna in workout clothes is just as sexy as Jenna in a formal gown. I clear away my salacious thoughts and remind myself to behave.

"I'm sorry to have scared you, Jenna. Security let me right in and you opened the door before I could knock."

"Yeah, I put you and Jax on the approved guest list." I hate hearing that bastard has access anytime he wants, but it was probably only fair that she put both of our names on the list. She gives her head a little shake, but then looks at me with confusion. "Wait, how are you even here? We just saw you on TV last night in Los Angeles."

I chuckle and am happy to know they were watching me. "I took the red eye back. It's time to start getting settled here."

I give her a knowing look, which causes her to blush, and she looks anywhere but at me. I glance at Avery and tap her cute button nose before asking, “Where are you ladies going?”

“I’m taking Avery to school and then working out,” Jenna responds but I keep my gaze on Avery.

“Can I go to school with you?” I ask Avery while tickling her stomach. She giggles and tries to swat my hand away.

“Sure, you can come. It probably would be good for you to see where she goes. Oh, and the principal wants to talk with me today about the paparazzi. She and the rest of the parents aren’t happy with the attention they bring.”

I draw in my eyebrows and frown at this. *Fucking paps*. Children are supposed to be off-limits, but some of these bastards don’t care. “Yes, let’s meet with her so we can discuss some solutions.”

Jenna grabs Avery’s bag off the floor from where she dropped it and closes the door behind her. I put Avery down, give her a mischievous smile and say, “Race you to the elevators, Avery.” I give her a head start before lightly jogging to keep up with her. Her laughter is infectious and before long, she beats me to the elevator buttons.

“Carry me, Cal. I’m tired,” she complains dramatically, pretending to pant out little breaths. Jenna shakes her head and laughs while we enter the elevator. I do as I’m commanded and pick Avery up.

“Another man wrapped around her little pinky. We are in serious trouble with her,” Jenna shares and I don’t even want to think about my daughter getting older, let alone dating, or any other men she has wrapped around her fingers.

“No boyfriends allowed,” I tell Avery with a stern voice.

“Right,” Jenna says sarcastically while rolling her eyes.

“I already have a boyfriend, Cal.”

I pretend to be shocked, which makes Avery laugh. “Who is

this boy, because I must meet him."

"Well, he lives on a boat and only comes to visit me at nighttime."

I raise my eyebrow at Jenna, who shrugs while exiting the elevator. "Is your boyfriend a pirate?" I ask, following behind Jenna so she can lead the way.

"No, he's a prince!" Avery says with excitement. "I'm going to be a princess!" She claps her hands and I chuckle.

"Has he asked you to marry him yet? You know he must ask me—I mean, your mum first." I catch Jenna's eye and the little minx actually smirks at me.

"He will once he gets rid of his other girlfriend," Avery says so casually that I start to choke on my laughter. We stop in front of a black Land Rover and I watch Jenna unlock the car and open the back door for our daughter.

"I understand your dilemma, Avery," I tell her, giving Jenna a wicked grin. She pretends not to notice, but the blush on her cheeks says otherwise.

"Let me show you how to strap her into her car seat," Jenna murmurs as I watch her strap Avery in. She closes the door and walks around to the other side while I get into the car.

"Nice ride," I say, admiring the interior of her car. My mind can't help but wonder if she bought this with her own money or if it was a gift from Jax.

"Thanks. It was the only thing my ex-husband gave me that I decided to keep," she answers, as if she was reading my mind. Her revelation surprises me since the car looks brand new. From how she previously expressed her distaste for her ex-husband, I wasn't expecting her to still have anything from him. She obviously takes care of the car and when I glance over at the dashboard, her mileage confirms that she barely drives.

"How was last night?" she asks, deliberately changing the subject. We pull out of the garage and are immediately bombarded with paparazzi. They enclose both sides of the car, trying to get our attention with questions while they snap our photo.

"Exhausting, but good," I tell her, trying to hide the irritation by focusing on her question. "Nice to see some people I haven't seen in a while and a lot of great movies won."

"Cal, was that girl in the green dress your girlfriend?" Avery asks, and I quickly glance at Jenna to see her reaction at the question. Her eyes are hiding behind sunglasses, so it's hard for me to tell.

"That is my friend Cora and no, she's not my girlfriend," I tell her, continuing to watch Jenna while I answer. "You'll get to meet her and my friend, Sean, very soon."

"Yeah! I love meeting new people!" Avery says and we laugh at how cute she sounds.

No more than five minutes later, Jenna makes a left into the parking lot of an office building and pulls into a space. "Wow, we're here already?" I ask in surprise. My shock quickly turns into anger as I watch a swarm of paparazzi get out of their cars and move closer to the entrance of the building. It seems they figured out Jenna's morning routine quickly.

"Yes, normally we walk to school, but they've been making it difficult to do so." She nods her head toward the paparazzi. "Avery, put your sunglasses on. You can say hi to these men if you want too, but let's keep the sunglasses on, okay?" She slides on her sunglasses and is ready to go.

I prefer Avery not to talk to anyone, but my reasoning if she asks why might scare her. Jenna and I make a plan that I will quickly grab Avery out of the car while Jenna makes her way to the front entrance first to divert the paparazzi into two directions. As soon as we get out of the car, they start taking pictures and calling out our names. With my strides longer than Jenna's, I quickly catch up to her and we walk inside together. Once through the front door, I put Avery down as Jenna checks us in at the front desk and introduces me to the receptionist. She has me fill out a form and scans my ID so I can have access to pick up Avery by myself without Jenna. Once the paperwork is filled out and done, Avery takes my hand and practically pulls me toward her classroom.

We get inside and she proceeds to introduce me as her friend to her teachers and classmates. The two teachers look between me and Jenna, confusion written all over their faces.

"I will fill you in later," Jenna tells them, and they nod in agreement.

"Will you be picking me up too, Cal?" Avery looks up at me with hope in her eyes.

"Absolutely, sweetheart."

I can feel Jenna's questioning glare, so I meet her eyes and grin at her, which doesn't bode well. She narrows her eyes at me, her lips forming a thin line. I return my attention to Avery, kiss her cheek goodbye, and tell her I will see her later.

We walk in silence to the principal's office, where we are greeted by her assistant who escorts us inside.

The principal looks up from her paperwork and surprise registers on her face at seeing me. Jenna makes the introductions, and we sit down.

"Mr. Harrington, what a nice surprise to see you today. Thanks for coming as well. As I told Ms. Pruitt, the photographers have been very disruptive to our environment and myself and a lot of other parents are very concerned about safety. If this doesn't stop soon, we're going to need Avery to find another school."

"I completely understand, Principal Hayes, and am very sorry for the disruption. I will provide a full-time officer at the door until things calm down, as well as make a sizable donation to the school. We're appreciative of all the hard work you and your staff do for our children. Again, I apologize for the inconvenience of everything and hope this solution will work for you?"

"That sounds wonderful, Mr. Harrington. Please take my card and call me when the officer is secured and I will give you information on how to make that generous donation," she tells me, seeming quite satisfied with my answer.

I smile over at Jenna, who stares at the principal with her mouth hanging open in shock. She regains her composure when the principal stands up and shakes our hands. I give her Bridget's phone number and email for her to discuss the payment of the officer. We say our goodbyes and proceed to leave the building.

"Does money always get you out of trouble?" Jenna asks when we are back in the privacy of her car after maneuvering our way through the paparazzi.

I think about her question for a moment, remembering how she refused my child support. "Not with everyone." I give her a pointed look and she bursts out laughing. The sound is music to my ears and I feel I just gained a huge victory with her. She's laughing with me, just the two of us, and I almost forgot how amazing her laugh was. She catches me staring at her and the emotions on my face must scare her because she stops laughing and quickly becomes serious again.

"Um, where am I going?" She asks while turning the car on and I hate that she's back to acting awkward with me. She's putting up her protective walls one by one and I just want to fucking smash them all away. I need her to remember how comfortable she used to be with me.

"I thought we were going to work out?" I tease and she gives me a surprised look since she was the one who talked about working out, not "we".

She looks me up and down, eyeing my jeans and t-shirt with skepticism. "How are you going to work out in that?"

I look down at my clothes, knowing full well I will work out in anything if it gets me more time with her. "I can manage to do weights. Where's your gym?"

"I was going to work out in my building's gym," she answers while driving us out of the school's parking lot.

"Okay, I'll just work out with you."

"Why do you want to work out with me?" she questions with suspicion, and I'm surprised she doesn't already know that answer. Unless she's testing me, which I'm beginning to learn that Jenna likes to test people as part of her defense mechanism.

"Because for one thing, I need to get a workout in, and secondly, I think it's important that you and I spend as much time together as possible so we get to know each other better. I think that'll help my progress with Avery if I know and understand her mother better." Everything I said is true, but my ulterior motive is for Jenna to realize that we belong together, and she won't if I don't get some alone time with her.

She ponders my reasoning for a few minutes and my intuition is telling me she's going to turn me down.

"I don't think that's a good idea, Cal," she finally responds. "People will talk and the next thing we know, there will be a story out saying you are living with me. Even though we know the truth, that isn't fair to Jax."

"While I disagree with you, I'm in no mood to argue. Why don't you and I discuss this over dinner?" I try to act serious but the flabbergasted look on her face makes me grin.

"We can't have dinner out together!" she exclaims with exasperation.

"Why not? People need to eat," I tell her matter-of-factly.

"Because it will be labeled as a date by the paparazzi, and I can't have that."

"Robert told me there's a restaurant at the top of your building. We can go there and the paparazzi will never know," I suggest while trying to give her my most charming smile. I haven't told her where my hotel is yet and I noticed we've been going in circles, but I don't care. I'm enjoying teasing her and don't want our time to end.

"Of course Robert would tell you that," she mutters in annoyance. I don't want to get Robert in trouble, but I do want her to know that he and I communicate.

"I've been talking quite a bit to Robert now that I have his number."

"I bet you have." Her voice is filled with so much sarcasm that I laugh.

"You still haven't told me what hotel to drop you off at," she reminds me, and I give her a suggestive smile because she knows damn well why I haven't told her where to go.

"Yes, I know," I slowly admit. "I've been enjoying our car ride together." She briefly stares at me before turning her gaze back to the road. I watch her swallow her emotions and I know without a single doubt she can still feel that sizzling electricity between us. I want nothing more than for her to park the car so I can take her in my arms and ravish her. I'm not a patient man by any means, but I know to have Jenna in my life forever, things need to go at her pace.

Not to mention the one big problem standing in my way: her boyfriend.

"I have work to do today, so please, what hotel are you staying at?" Her voice is filled with tired resignation, and I can tell it's time for this to end.

"I'm staying at the Ritz-Carlton." She nods and steers the car in that direction.

"Please consider having dinner with me because we need to talk about my schedule. Filming doesn't start for another two weeks, so I would like to spend as much time with Avery as possible. I want to take her to school, pick her up, go sight-seeing with her, and eat meals with her. Everything that normal families do with each other, I want to do. I need you to be there with us for the time being so she gets comfortable with me, and then eventually, start doing things with just her and me."

Despite my focus on winning Jenna back, it's true that she's an intricate part of helping Avery transition full time into my life. I need her to realize the importance of this and her being a willing participant will only make things smoother.

"I also would like for you to go house hunting with me so you can feel comfortable in the home I pick out for her." She gives me a raised eyebrow but doesn't say anything, so I continue. "Once filming begins, my schedule is going to be limited for the next three months. I'm going to try to work with the director to see if we can shoot more night scenes, but I don't know if he'll agree to that. This is another reason why I'll need your help."

She remains silent and I give her time to marinate on what I've asked of her. We stay that way when she pulls up to the curb of the hotel and puts the car in park. She looks out the window at all the paparazzi taking our photo and sighs.

"I'll work on trying to be accessible for you," she says softly and my heart soars with gratitude.

And victory.

"Thank you, Jenna. You truly don't know what this means to me. I'll see you later for school pick up." I don't try to steal a kiss on the cheek this time, not with so many paps taking our photo. I swiftly exit the car and shut the door. I watch her pull away with regret, hating these circumstances that we are under. Hating that we are not under the same roof together.

*Patience, Cal*, I remind myself. *It will happen one day.*

I make my way into the hotel and wonder what her plans are for tonight. Is she seeing him? The thought makes me grind my teeth together in jealousy and then I remember the conversation I had with Thomas and the card he gave me for someone who I can hire to follow Jenna. I take the elevator to my suite and once I arrive, I rummage through the stacks of paper that are on my desk until I find the business card for Chase Wilson. I dial his number.

"Chase Wilson here." He identifies himself on the third ring, his voice deep and crisp.

"Chase, this is Cal Harrington. I received your name and number from Thomas Black."

He's silent for a moment, as if he's deciding whether he believes who I am. "What can I do for you?" he finally asks with hesitancy.

"I have a business proposition for you that I would like to discuss in person. Do you have time to meet with me today?"

"I can meet you right now," he says, his voice still sounding skeptical.

"Brilliant. I'm staying at the Ritz-Carlton. Check in at the front desk and I will approve you to be escorted up."

"See you in twenty minutes," he says and hangs up.

I put down my phone and make my way to my bedroom to freshen up and change. Having Jenna followed might not be the ethical thing to do, but it will give me peace of mind knowing she's always being watched and kept safe.

# Chapter 11

THERE'S SOMETHING ABOUT Chase Wilson that doesn't add up.

Why is a guy, who is heir to a once billion-dollar company, now working as a paparazzi? From my quick research, the man is one of Canada's most eligible bachelors and previously worked for his father's company, Wilson Enterprises. With model good looks and making millions of dollars, he seemed to have the dream life. But something happened when his father died because it's now reported that Chase refused to claim his right to the company and instead, left it to his brother, Rhys, who had to quit being a professional hockey player in order to save it.

*Why would he not take over the company himself?*

*Why did the company need saving?*

*Why become a photographer?*

I study him as he takes a seat in front of my desk after we shake hands and exchange greetings. He seems familiar to me, yet I can't remember when I would've met him.

"Have we met before?" I inquire, hoping he remembers if we have.

"Yeah, way back when. Before you became…you" He lifts his chin at me and smirks.

"What's that supposed to mean?" I narrow my eyes at him, not liking his tone and what he's insinuating.

"Back when you made paid appearances." His smile is bitter and never reaches his eyes. *What the fuck is this guy's problem?*

"Have I done something to offend you, Mr. Wilson?" I ask. Not that I give two shits about this bloke, but his hostility is starting to irritate me.

"Not taking responsibility for your own child offends me," he responds, his tone dead serious and his eyes never wavering from mine.

"As we said in our joint statement, it's a misunderstanding that's being dealt with privately," I grit out, my jaw clenched in anger at his audacity.

"Right…the bullshit excuse for paying your baby momma off now that the news affects your reputation."

"I don't give two shits about my reputation and my private life is none of your goddamn business," I growl at him. My temper flares as this was not how I planned for this meeting to go.

"If that's the case, then why am I here, Mr. Harrington?"

"Before I tell you why, I need you to sign an NDA and that once you sign it, you understand that everything discussed is confidential." I slide across the desk my standard non-disclosure agreement that I make everyone sign. He stares at it, blinks, then looks up at me. Questions are swirling through those hazel eyes of his and I can tell his curiosity is eating at him. He glances back down and starts reading the disclosure. Once I see he's close to the end, I strategically place a pen near the signature line.

He finishes reading, sits back and folds his arms across his chest. "Why should I agree to this?"

"Because I will pay you six figures for a couple months' worth of work."

His eyebrows shoot up and I know he's interested now. "What kind of work?"

I tap my finger on the form and shake my head. "That doesn't get revealed until after you sign."

His eyes bounce between me and the agreement. "Why should I trust you?"

"I could ask you the exact same question. But everything in life is a gamble, even trust." I lean back in my seat and regard him coolly. "So Mr. Wilson, do you like to gamble?"

Despite him being a prick since the moment he's stepped foot into my space, I'm impressed that the mere mention of a six-figure payout didn't make him sign right away. I trust Thomas, so if he's recommending this guy, there must be something to him regardless of his shitty disposition.

He sits quietly for a minute and seems to have an internal battle with himself over whether to sign. He rubs his hands back and forth against the fabric of his jeans. I'm fascinated that he's actually debating this. If it was anyone else, the deal would've been done. Something else is definitely going on with him and if he signs on, I'll be hiring Thomas to find out what.

After a couple more minutes of brooding, he grabs the pen, scribbles his signature, and throws the pen down. "No more games. Now what are you hiring me for?"

I tilt my head and give him a perplexed smile at his choice of words. "I'm hiring you to follow Jenna. I need eyes and ears on her at all times. Her whereabouts, who she's with, etc."

He narrows his eyes at me. "Why? You don't trust her?"

"I trust her completely. It's other people I don't trust." I rake my hands through my hair, deciding I need to be more upfront with him. "I was unaware I had a child because someone in my close circle lied and kept that news hidden. Therefore, my capability to trust people is limited."

"You had no idea you had a kid?" he asks with skepticism.

"None," I tell him with a shake of my head. "I still don't even know who told the press."

He seems surprised by that but quickly masks his shock. "So, what exactly are you wanting me to do when I follow her?"

"I want you to follow her to make sure she's safe and listen to any chatter amongst your peers."

"I'm not a bodyguard, Mr. Harrington. If you want protection, hire someone who's qualified. As far as the other guys, you do need to watch out for some of them. One in particular is named Danny Salari. He's ruthless and doesn't care how he gets his money-making shots. Most of the guys are respectful, but he's far from it. Some of the newbies will follow his lead but they're not as seasoned as he is. I actually warned Ms. Pruitt about him a couple of weeks ago when she caught me taking photos of her walking down the street."

I write down Danny Salari's name to send to Thomas to investigate. "Do you really think Jenna needs a bodyguard?" I inquire because I've been toying with the idea of hiring one for her, but not sure how she will react.

"I don't see this story dying down anytime soon, especially with you in town shooting a movie and spending time with your daughter. With people like Salari, I just wouldn't take the chance. Hire one temporarily and once things die down, then re-evaluate."

I nod my head while grabbing my phone and texting my sister to inquire into one.

"I can follow her and let you know if I see any trouble brewing, but the best I can do in that situation is call the cops."

"And me." I look him straight in the eyes to see how serious I am. "Here's my card with my cell phone on it. Do not hesitate to call if you see she needs help. In the meantime, I expect daily emails of her whereabouts. If you know the people she is meeting, even better. If you hear any alarming comments from the other guys, call me."

He nods and takes the card. "When do I start?"

"Now," I demand, raising an eyebrow to see if he argues. He just smiles and shakes his head at me.

"What's your endgame with all of this, Harrington?"

I pause before answering, wanting to craft my words wisely without revealing too much information. "To protect my daughter and her mother."

Chase Wilson doesn't need to know that my true intentions are to win my family back.

# CHAPTER 12

THERE ARE KIDS running and screaming around me like crazy little banshees.

Parents are chasing after them, yelling at them with exasperated voices and tired eyes. And then there's my daughter, who's laughing like a lunatic due to the sugar high from the cotton candy I bought her. I've never been in this type of environment before and even though it's chaotic and at an ungodly decimal level, I'm having the time of my life.

Mainly because I've never seen my daughter this happy.

This week has been a learning curve with observing the girls' routines and Jenna keeps Avery on a tight schedule. During the weekday, Avery goes to preschool from 9:00 a.m. to 4:00 p.m. so Jenna can work. From 4:30 to 5:30 p.m., Jenna then takes her to the indoor pool in her building or to the park, but due to the paparazzi, they've been staying at the pool. After that is dinner, play games, then a bath and a couple of books before bed. Jenna has let me take the lead on story time this week and Avery seems to love when I get into character.

Friday nights Jenna takes her ice skating, a ritual from when she was a little girl. I love how she is passing down traditions from her childhood to Avery and I can't wait to start incorporating some of mine. I've never ice skated before, so there was lots of laughter watching me wipe out. Not being steady on my feet gave me a good excuse to hold Jenna's hand while she helped me balance on my skates. Did I milk it for as long as I could? Yes, yes I did. Once she saw I got the hang of it, she let go and kept her distance.

Today Jenna is letting us play hooky from preschool and I took Avery by myself to the Children's Museum while she and Robert went to a business appointment. She's supposed to meet us at any moment and from here, we will grab lunch and take the water taxi around the city. I'm hoping to persuade Jenna to take the rest of the week off so we can keep Avery home from school and do more fun things together. I only have one more week left before production starts on my movie and with that will come a crazy schedule. Although I'll try to spend every hour I'm not working with Avery, I know there'll be a lot of nighttime shoots and some twelve-hour days coming.

Avery has gotten completely comfortable with me now, but Jenna is still guarded. She treats me as a client, acting cool and professional no matter how hard I put on the charm. I believe her attitude toward me is because of Jax. Per my daily reports from Chase, she has met with Jax for lunch a couple times before he left for his away games. It guts me that she's freely giving him her time, giving him her smiles…her kisses. And while I can't let my mind go to the thoughts of him touching her, I'm almost certain that she goes to bed alone each night. Chase still watches Jenna's building long after I leave, and he has not seen Jax come over once.

Trouble must be brewing because Chase said they were arguing outside of the restaurant they were eating at yesterday and even though he couldn't hear the conversation clearly, he thinks it has something to do with me.

Jax's insecurities will only push Jenna straight into my

awaiting arms—exactly what I'm hoping will happen. It's only a matter of time before his jealousy gets the best of him and be the demise of their relationship.

I smile at the thought and focus my attention back to the present and my daughter. I'm about to lead her to another section of the museum when I see Jenna a couple feet away, looking around for us. She seems anxious and frustrated. Her gaze finally locks on mine, and she smiles, but it doesn't reach her eyes.

Something is wrong.

"Hey baby girl," she greets Avery, who screams in excitement and practically tackles Jenna.

"Whoa," Jenna nervously giggles as she catches her. "Seems like you're having fun."

"Mommy! Cal bought me cotton candy and it's so yummy. How come you haven't given it to me before?"

Jenna looks over at me and I realize I should have texted her first about it.

*Shit!*

I look at her with wide eyes, ready to plead my case about not knowing she wasn't allowed cotton candy when she bursts out laughing.

"Your face," she sputters, trying to catch her breath. "You looked like a little boy who just got in trouble with the principal at school."

Avery starts giggling with her mother and I join them, warmth spreading through my heart as I hear their whimsical laughter.

"Ah, I needed that," Jenna says after she stops giggling. She puts Avery down and wipes underneath her eyes to make sure her mascara hasn't run. She looks back up at me and smiles, this time it's genuine.

"Bad day?" I ask as we follow Avery to another learning station.

She nods. "Our meeting didn't go as planned."

"What happened?"

She grimaces and doesn't answer right away. Her facial expressions give away that she's debating whether to tell me.

"Let's just say their intentions when setting up the meeting weren't honest."

"What did they want?"

She sighs and turns to watch Avery play before looking back at me. "They wanted you."

Dread starts seeping into my veins at her answer. "What do you mean?"

"Basically, they were hoping a meeting with me would get them an in with you." She smiles sadly before continuing. "Unfortunately, this has been happening more frequently since the story broke."

"Jenna, I'm so sorry." I reach out to take her in my arms but catch myself before making contact.

"It's okay. It's not like you are intentionally making people do this. I guess it just comes with the territory of being associated with someone famous."

"It does but it shouldn't have to be," I mutter, disgusted with people.

"It is what it is. At least I'm growing thick skin," she responds before walking over to help Avery.

Jenna already has walls guarding her heart. I don't need her to become hard and bitter as well.

We spend another hour exploring the museum and then stop at a pizzeria so I can experience what true Chicago deep dish pizza tastes like. After that, we had some time to kill before our water taxi, so I took the girls on the Centennial Wheel at Navy Pier.

"Look Mommy, there's our building." Avery points out the window as we reach the top, giving us a 360-degree view of Chicago and Lake Michigan. Jenna's views from her condo are magnificent and I make a mental note to try to find a house on the lake if I can. I've been pleasantly surprised by what I've seen so far of Chicago, and I'm convinced that the permanent transition here from London will be easier than anticipated.

Once the ride is done, we make our way through Navy Pier to the dock for our water taxi. A manager is waiting by the entrance to greet us and escorts us to our boat. After we board, Jenna looks around the empty vessel before asking, "Where's everyone else?"

I smile sheepishly at her and give her a boyish smile. "I might've called ahead of time and reserved a private boat for us."

She shakes her head, a small smile playing on her lips. "Of course you did," she mutters but her smile fades, and she looks around once more. "Actually, it will be nice to not have people filming us for once while out and about, so thank you. That was a really thoughtful thing to do."

"I would do anything for you, Jenna. You just say the word." I stare into her eyes, holding her gaze for a moment before she swallows, nods and looks down at Avery, asking where she wants to sit.

"Cal's lap!" she exclaims, and I can't stop the big, satisfied smile that spreads across my face. Jenna chuckles and tells Avery to pick our seats. We get settled and the captain proceeds to steer the boat away from the dock.

For forty-minutes, we get enraptured with the captain talking about the city's history and pointing out landmark buildings. As the boat circles back to Navy Pier, I feel Avery's arms go limp and I tighten my hold around her.

"She's asleep," Jenna whispers and looks up at me with a smile. I grin back at her and put a kiss on top of Avery's head.

"This has been one of the best weeks of my life, Jenna. Thank you for that."

"You don't need to thank me, Cal. I'm happy to see you want to be involved."

"Of course I want to be involved. I wish I could spend every waking moment with her…and you." A gust of wind whips off the lake, causing Jenna's hair to blow in her face. I move my hand, grabbing the hair between my fingers while I caress her cheek before gently pushing her hair behind her ear.

"Cal," she whispers in a small warning. I drop my hand and give her a sad smile, hating this barrier between us. I take a deep breath, figuring this is the perfect moment for me to ask about next week.

"I want to ask a huge favor from you. Can I keep Avery home from school all next week as well?"

She doesn't say anything at first. Just bites her lip and looks down at Avery, contemplating my request. "What do you have in mind?"

"I can come get her before your first appointment in the mornings and take her to the Aquarium, the Zoo...basically all her favorite places that I can experience with her. We would be back in time to meet you for dinner. Unless you want to join us and take the whole week off as well? I know Robert can run everything with his eyes closed." I give her a mischievous grin that would rival The Grinch's and she laughs. Watching Jenna laugh makes my fingers twitch with the urge to tangle them in her hair and crush her pretty little mouth to mine.

She shakes her head at me with a smile. "While I can't take the whole week off, I might be able to make it a long weekend and take Thursday and Friday off. Let me just check my schedule and confirm with Robert first."

I'm fucking ecstatic to see that Jenna is willing to take any time off to be alone with us. I nod at her with satisfaction and know that with a little bit of time, Jenna will start trusting me completely.

# Chapter 13

It's my last free day with Avery and Jenna before the pre-production of my movie starts. I've always enjoyed the start of a new movie, but this time the excitement isn't there. I've been making so much headway with both girls in the last two weeks that I know me being gone is going to be a setback. I keep reminding myself it's only for a couple of months and then I'll take a break to get settled here. I need to be more strategic now with what projects I decide to sign onto. I'm committed to one more movie after this one and that's it for now. I've made enough money in my career that I don't have to ever work again, but that's not my nature. I'll take on some projects, but they need to be convenient for my daughter and her schedule. I refuse to not be part of her everyday life. She hasn't questioned why she's spending so much alone time with me, and I feel that soon we can reveal my true identity to her.

Tonight, I have a surprise mermaid party planned for her at my hotel. After we went to the zoo, Jenna took Avery home for a nap. While the girls were resting, Robert came by with their event planning staff and decorated the living room to make it a temporary enchanted underwater playroom. I hope both Avery and Jenna enjoy the surprise, even though Jenna isn't planning on staying. I know she plans on seeing Jax while I'm with Avery, which pisses me off. My patience is thinning, but I still have a lot to prove to her.

"Wow, you guys are good," I tell Robert as I survey the room. "So, this is what you and Jenna do all day?"

"No, not all day," Robert laughs. "We don't do as many children's parties as we used to. The money is in large corporate events and that's what we have moved onto throughout the years. Jenna will still do blog posts about children's parties, and we still sell the party supplies. I think she only does it because that is how she got her start, so she'll always have a soft spot for it."

"I can see why. It truly feels magical in here." I glance at my watch to see I only have a little time left before Jenna shows up. "Listen, I need to talk to you about something. Can you spare five minutes in my office?"

He nods and tells one of the employees he'll be back. We enter my office and I shut the door behind us. I motion for him to take a seat and I sit on the edge of my desk.

"Jenna and Avery's safety is my number one priority. Because the paparazzi hasn't died down, I think it would be best to secure a bodyguard for them."

Robert looks at me in surprise. "Jenna agreed to one? It must be worse than what she's telling me."

"She doesn't know yet and I would like to keep it that way until I can talk to her about it."

Robert starts to laugh, and I stare at him, not understanding what's so funny about the situation. "Oh Cal," he answers when he's regained his composure. "She'll never agree to a bodyguard."

"I figured, but she has no choice in the matter. I have to be able to find some way of keeping her and Avery safe when I'm not around."

"Hire one without talking to her and she's going to be angry with you," he warns.

"That's the price I might have to pay if she refuses and won't be reasonable about this."

"Is it really *that* serious? I know they still follow her everywhere, but would they physically harm her?"

"You just never know. One of them called her a bitch yesterday for not smiling at them."

"What?" Robert jumps up from his chair in outrage. "Jenna never told me about that."

"She didn't tell me either," I reveal and know what's coming next.

"Then how did you find out?" he asks with narrowed eyes.

"I've hired one of the paparazzi to follow her at all times."

"Cal," Robert slowly exhales out and I hold up my hand for him to stop talking. He sits back down and raises an eyebrow at me.

"This is where I need your help, Robert. I need you to be his point person when I'm on set because cell phones aren't allowed to be in use when we're doing our scenes. He will need her daily schedule from you so he can always make sure he's with her."

"No." Robert shakes his head back and forth. "I'm not betraying Jenna's trust."

"You aren't betraying her—you're helping me protect her," I growl, needing his cooperation. "I just need your help until the bodyguard is secured. Once the bodyguard is hired, I won't need Jenna followed any longer."

He closes his eyes and squeezes the bridge of his nose while contemplating. "I have a terrible feeling about this."

"Don't be dramatic. Once Jenna realizes that it's for hers and Avery's safety, she'll come around."

He opens his eyes and huffs at me. "You obviously still don't know Jenna very well because she won't see it that way at all. She will think you're taking away her freedom and trying to control her. Trust me when I tell you that if you don't talk to her about this before the bodyguard arrives, you can kiss any chance with her you have goodbye."

"So, I have a chance?" I inquire with a sly smile, not meaning to change the subject, but wanting to hear his thoughts.

"Oh, dear lord." He rolls his eyes and shakes his head as if I just said the dumbest thing in the world. "You look at her as if you're a dog in heat, ready to pounce and claim your territory. The only thing standing in your way is Jax and we'll see how much longer that will be."

"Don't leave me hanging with that," I demand in frustration when he doesn't elaborate. "Tell me what's happening."

"No, because that *would* betray Jenna's trust," he emphasizes and I scowl at him, not happy that he won't tell me. "All I will tell you is he's not happy that you're in her life and she's not happy with how he's handling it, but she feels guilty for never telling him about you in the first place."

"Why do you think she didn't?"

"Because she never thought you would be in her life again," he comments softly, giving me a pointed look.

"Right." I nod, wanting to change the subject because the thought of *not* being in hers and Avery's lives makes my chest ache. "There's one other item I need your help with."

"Oh dear lord, what is it? I still haven't agreed to your first request, you know?"

I smile and ignore that because I need him to help me. I have no other option. "The tabloids are publishing some false stories about Jenna that are affecting her reputation."

"Yeah, we've seen them and they're awful." He scowls and shakes his head. "How can they get away with saying some of that stuff?"

"First Amendment rights. But here's what I think we need to do—any negative stories we find about Jenna, we're going to counteract with one that sheds a more positive light on her. I will need you to do that and be the 'anonymous source.'"

He looks at me as if I've grown two heads. "I don't know how to do any of that shit!"

"My publicist will teach you."

He blinks a couple of times and just stares at me. "Wow. Does this kind of stuff happen frequently?"

"All the time."

"Hollywood is weird." His face scrunches up in disgust and I chuckle because he's exactly right on how 'weird' it actually gets in Hollywood.

"So, will you help me, Robert?"

"Fine," he says with a sigh, not looking happy at all. "But this bodyguard better get here soon."

"I'm working on it. I've interviewed a couple, but the problem is how quickly I need them here. Most of them have to serve out the rest of their contracts and that can take months."

"I'm not going behind her back like this for months, Cal."

"No, we won't be," I confirm just as there's a knock on the door and my assigned butler pops his head in.

"Ms. Pruitt is on her way up, sir."

"Thank you, Randall." Robert gets up from his chair and we walk out of my office and to the front door. We step outside and close the door, not wanting the girls to see my surprise yet.

They round the corner and as soon as Avery sees me, she runs down the hallway and hugs my legs. I lift her up and hold her in my arms while we watch Jenna walk toward us. She's wearing Jax's team's jersey with tight jeans that hug every inch of her legs and open toe booties. I bite the inside of my cheek to not show my displeasure because I would like nothing more than to rip that jersey off her body and burn it.

"Why are you waiting outside for us and Robert, what are you doing here? You told me you were going for a site inspection."

"Yeah, I lied," Robert confirms nonchalantly with a shrug of his shoulders. "Cal arranged a surprise for Avery that he needed my help with."

"A surprise? For me?" Avery giggles in excitement.

"That's right, but before we can go in, you need to close your eyes. Do you think you can do that without opening them or do you need a sparkly eye mask?" I ask, wanting to see which she chooses.

"Eye mask because Mommy says I cheat sometimes when we play games so I would cheat and open my eyes." We laugh at her honesty, and I set her back down on her feet.

"Well, since Avery chose the mask, that means Mommy has to wear one too." Robert produces two sparkling masks and hands one to Jenna and one to Avery.

"Ooh, this is exciting," Jenna exclaims, intrigued by the surprise. She helps Avery with her mask before putting on her own. When we know the masks are secured, I take Avery's hand and Robert takes Jenna's and we carefully walk them inside.

We move about two feet in before we stop. "All right girls, on the count of three you can take off your blindfold. One, two… three!"

They rip off their masks and Avery starts to scream in delight. She runs toward the pile of treasures and starts bouncing around from the turquoise balloon wall to the arts and crafts table to the themed food table complete with gummy sharks and mermaid tail cookies, and then continues through the seashell teepee dining "room".

I smile in satisfaction at seeing how happy she is and turn to get a glimpse of Jenna. Her mouth is open in awe while she drinks the scenery in.

"What do you think?" I ask, hoping that she's as happy as our daughter is.

"This is incredible," she murmurs and looks at Robert.

"Amazing job, Robert." He nods his thanks at her before following Avery to show her the snacks. Jenna turns toward me, and I can see the appreciation in her eyes. "You didn't have to do this, Cal."

"I wanted to do something memorable before our days together become inconsistent."

"Every day she's had with you so far has been memorable." Her words leave me speechless, and I realize that's exactly the affirmation that I needed to hear, and this coming from her makes my heart race. She glances over at Avery when we hear her laugh at something Robert says to her as she looks down at her watch.

"I better get going." She smiles politely at me and is about to say goodbye when I quickly grab her hands and grasp them tightly, fearing she will pull away from me.

"Stay," I whisper to her, my eyes staring into hers, begging her not to leave. I need her to be here with us. I need her to see the family we can be.

*Stay with me forever,* my heart silently screams.

"I can't," she whispers back with a sad smile and my heart deflates like a balloon losing all of its air. "I promised Jax I would be at his game tonight."

I simply nod and let go of her hands before turning away from her because it hurts too much to look at her. I watch silently as she says goodbye to Avery and Robert, and I barely acknowledge when she confirms what time she will be back to pick Avery up.

When the door shuts after her, it feels like half of my heart just disappeared. I play Robert's words from earlier over in my head to try to remain hopeful that soon Jax Morrow will be out of our lives.

# Chapter 14

I SLOWLY MAKE my way back to my trailer, exhaustion settling into my muscles from the grueling shoot we had today. We've hit the ground running these last couple of weeks on production and so far, the schedule has been manageable. I'm able to join Jenna in taking Avery to school in the mornings, but nights are sporadic. The evenings I do have off, I join the girls at their place for dinner and partake in their nighttime rituals. Sometimes Robert and Layla are both there, other times just Robert, but it's nice to get to know those two better as well. It makes me worry less to know that Jenna did have a support system without me, but it still doesn't replace the fact that I should have been here from day one.

A couple of the nights I've been there, I've fallen asleep with Avery. Jenna usually wakes me up, but one night, she let me stay and woke me up at five in the morning to go back to my place to shower and get ready for the day. I still can't get the memory of Jenna out of my mind that morning, waking me up and seeing her sleepy eyed in her pajamas. I immediately remembered what she looked like underneath that layer of clothing, what she felt like. My hands were burning to roam that beautiful body of hers and bury myself deep inside of her. And as I stared at her, trying to talk myself out of grabbing her and taking her back to the bedroom to devour her, I could see in her eyes that she remembered what it was like for us too. It took every ounce of strength to keep my hands to myself and walk out that door.

Being a good guy has never felt so fucking wrong.

I know she feels the same way I do and the tension between us has gotten even more strained with want. Jenna's as loyal as they come and because of her commitment to her boyfriend, she's back to treating me as a stranger. She's always polite and cordial, but she never lets me catch her gaze for more than a second and she makes sure we're never alone together anymore.

Tonight, she's going to one of Jax's home games and I'm supposed to take over babysitting duties from Robert as soon as I get off. The plan is to take a quick shower and then head straight to Jenna's condo. I reach my trailer, unlock the door, and grab my phone off the counter. My stomach drops when I see I have five missed calls from Robert and a text saying I need to call him ASAP.

"We have a serious situation, Cal," he states as soon as he picks up my call. His voice is filled with tension and immediately my heart starts to pound in panic.

"What's wrong? Are the girls okay?"

"I just opened the mail and there is a death threat against Jenna and Avery," he whispers in anger, his voice laced with urgency.

"*Fuck*," I groan and quickly rummage through my trailer to find a bag to pack some clothes. "Did Jenna see it?"

"No, she's already gone and I'm at her place with Avery. They sent it to our work P.O. Box and I was opening our mail. I quickly hid it so Avery didn't see it."

"Good, keep it hidden until I get there and whatever you do, do not tell Jenna yet."

"Cal, I don't like this."

"I have a plan and we'll strategize when I arrive."

I hang up without saying another word, stuff clothes into a bag so I can take a shower at Jenna's and race out of my trailer to my awaiting car. Fortunately, I'm not far from her condo and it only takes me twenty minutes to get there.

Robert and I feed Avery and take turns playing with her. When it's time for bed, I read her two stories and stay with her until she falls asleep. Once I hear her steady breathing, I creep out of her room and silently shut the door.

When he sees that I'm back, Robert motions for me to meet him in Jenna's office. I leave the door ajar so I can hear if Avery wakes up.and turn back to face him. He hands me a manilla envelope. I reach inside and take out a Ziplock bag that contains a photo inside. As soon as I flip it over and see what it is, my insides turn cold. It's a black-and-white photo zoomed in on Jenna holding Avery. Both of their eyes have been cut out and there is a gooey red substance all over the photo. The words "DIE" are scrawled in the same red substance.

"Bloody fucking hell," I growl, my breath catching in my chest at the disturbing photo. I put it back in the envelope and close my eyes, but it's too late—the image is already etched in my brain. Rage starts to boil inside of me and I want to fucking destroy whomever is threatening to hurt my family.

"What do we do?" Robert asks anxiously.

"Unfortunately, death threats are common for celebrities, but I know what we need to do."

"Yeah, well it's not common for us poor ol' civilians," Robert sneers in sarcasm.

"My agent already has a contact with the FBI. Let me call him and see if we can meet with someone from the local bureau." I dial up Philip and update him on what's going on. He promises to have someone from their local offices call me within twenty-four hours.

The next phone call I make is to Chase to see if he's heard if anyone in his circle is talking about a threat against Jenna.

"No, no one has said a word, Cal. When the fuck are you going to get her a bodyguard?" he asks in frustration.

"I've sent a contract to one and am just waiting for him to sign it, but he was in Europe finishing up a job, so he might not be here until next week."

"Does Jenna know about the threat?"

"No, not yet. Robert just received it today and I told him not to tell her yet." I look up at Robert, who's looking at me with questions in his eyes. "I want to wait until after I talk to the FBI, which will hopefully be tomorrow."

"She needs to know, Cal," Chase warns and while I agree with him, I also don't want to scare her, which will be inevitable anyway. I'd rather have a plan in place to give her some peace of mind.

"She will," I assure him. "In the meantime, we need to keep a very close eye on her and not let her or Avery out of sight."

I hand the phone over to Robert so he can re-confirm with Chase her schedule this week. Once they're done, we hang up with Chase and go over both of our calendars. When I pull mine up, I groan out loud when I see I have late shoots the next three nights straight.

"I have night shoots the majority of this week, so I will be out of commission."

"I can stay here with them," Robert suggests but I shoot it down.

"Can you get me the name and number of the building manager? I can see if I can hire extra security around the perimeter of the building."

"I already know him. I will send you his number now." Robert vigorously types on his phone and texts me the information.

"I'm going to keep this." I hold up the envelope and he

shudders before nodding. I walk back into the living room and place the envelope in my bag, underneath my clothes. I sit down on the couch and lean my head back with a sigh.

Robert follows suit and joins me on the couch. "I'm scared to open the mail now," he admits, and I can't say I blame him.

"Let's hope we catch whomever it is before they can send another one."

ROBERT AND I tagged team the following week to make sure Jenna and Avery were never by themselves before bedtime. Any free time I had, I was with them, and Robert made up for the times that I wasn't. It isn't unusual for Robert to always be around, so Jenna never questioned anything.

No other death threats have been sent and when I submitted the photo to the local police and FBI, they told us the only fingerprints on it were Robert's. They questioned Robert, but because the photo was anonymously mailed to a P.O. Box and had no other fingerprints, they had nothing to go by. They gave the photo back to me and I increased security in and around Jenna's building to help, especially with the paparazzi. They're still being a nuisance and following her every move when she leaves her building. Chase reported that when Jenna met Layla for lunch two days ago, she couldn't even leave the restaurant due the number of paparazzi that were camped out front. The restaurant called the police and they escorted her to the car and followed her to make sure she got home safely.

"What's the status of the bodyguard, Cal?" Robert inquired when I was back again at Jenna's place helping him watch Avery while Jenna was at Jax's hockey game. It's the last game of his season and fortunately for me, they won't make the playoffs.

This means no more hockey games for her to attend by herself at nighttime, but I have yet to hear if Jax plans on staying in Chicago this summer or going back to Canada to visit his daughter.

*The fucker better go home.*

"He should be here any day now. Contract is signed but he just got back from Europe, so I agreed to give him a couple of days to go home and get what he needs. Fortunately, he lives here and used to work for some of the famous local basketball players."

"Good. When do you plan on telling Jenna?"

"The day before he arrives." I give Robert a knowing look and he shakes his head at me.

"Why do you want her mad at you?"

"I don't, but what other choice do I have? If I tell her now, she'll probably just concoct some scheme against it. Why give her time to think about it?"

Robert tilts his head to the side and thinks about it. "That's a good point."

"How's she been, Robert?" I ask softly, needing someone to tell me something about her. Layla is barely in town due to her job, so Robert is the only one who can give me any insight. "And please don't bullshit me. She's keeping me at arm's length and her wall is up. I'm genuinely concerned."

Robert studies me before sighing. "Truth? She's hanging on by a thread. Her relationship is in shambles and now she must question everyone's ulterior motives for getting involved with her—both personally and professionally. She has lost all privacy due to her association with you. She puts on a brave face, but I can tell everything is affecting her."

His words are tiny puncture wounds to my heart, and I hate that her association with me has consequences. "If she would just open up to me, I can try to help make things better."

"How would you make things better, Cal? And why should

she? Technically what happens in her personal and professional life is not your business."

"That will never be the case. Everything she does is my business."

Robert bursts out laughing. "God, you're so possessive. You sure you don't have a single, younger, long-lost, gay brother for me?"

I smile and am about to joke about cloning myself for him when we hear the lock on the front door turning. Jenna walks in and I'm relieved to see she is back with no Jax behind her, but one look at her face reveals she's been crying.

"Jenna, what's wrong?" Robert asks before I get the chance. We both jump off the couch and swiftly make our way toward her.

"Jax broke up with me tonight," she mumbles, not looking at either of us. "If you both will excuse me, I'm going to bed now. Please see yourselves out if you don't mind."

"I'm sorry, Jenna," I tell her sincerely, hating to see her hurting even though this is what I've been wishing for.

"Somehow, I quite doubt that," she says bitterly, and we watch her walk to her room and shut the door behind her.

Robert looks at me with raised eyebrows. "Well now, isn't that a game changer."

"I should go check on her." I start to turn but Robert grabs my arm.

"No, you shouldn't. If anyone should, it's me, but knowing Jenna, she needs to be alone right now."

I look back at her closed door with longing. "I hate seeing her so upset." *Maybe she did really love him and I just ruined it all?*

"Don't worry, she'll be okay. Even though I liked Jax, I think the relationship was going to run its course whether you were in the picture or not," he tells me with a sly grin. We walk toward her door and exit her apartment.

"Why do you say that?" I question while we walk the hallway toward the elevators, intrigued to hear his opinion.

"Jenna was never willing to meet Jax halfway on things and she certainly wasn't going to move to Canada. He has a daughter there and he didn't want to live here full-time. It was just a matter of time before one of them broke it off. Your arrival just sped up the process."

A slow, mischievous smile spreads across my face because now there's nothing standing in my way from pursuing Jenna.

Robert sees my grin and laughs. "Slow down, Romeo. She's not just going to fall at your feet. She's going to need some time before you start going all alpha male on her."

The elevator doors open, and we get in. "I'll give her all the time she needs because she's eventually going to be mine."

# CHAPTER 15

THE FOLLOWING EVENING, I'm sitting in my trailer going over my lines for the next scene we're about to shoot when I get a text from Jenna.

**Jenna: I just want to make you aware that I'm hiring a sitter for tonight.**

I frown at this. *Why does she need a sitter? Is she going out with Jax? Are they trying to reconcile?*

The fuck they are if I have a say in it.

**Me: Is Robert not available to watch her? Are you comfortable trusting a stranger?**

I know she'll get upset if I ask where she's going because in her mind, it's none of my business. I need to figure out how to find out her whereabouts for tonight and the only one who will tell me is Robert.

**Jenna: Robert will be with me tonight and this babysitter has been watching Avery since she was a baby. I trust her completely.**

Relief washes over me knowing she'll be with Robert and not Jax. Before responding back to her, I quickly call Robert for details. "Are you going out with Jenna tonight?"

"I was just about to call you. Yes, she called and said she

wanted to go to O'Malley's, which is our usual hangout that's only a couple of blocks from her place. Apparently, it's been a rough day for her."

"Why, because of Jax?"

"I'm sure that was part of it, but…" he pauses before continuing. "You know how she has a weekly segment at News Channel 3?"

"Yes." I respond and I already know what's coming next before he even says it.

"They dropped it effective immediately," he says, confirming my suspicions.

"Why?" I question with a low voice.

"You know why, Cal," he sighs, and I do. They dropped her because of the "scandal" with me.

"Shit," I mutter, pissed off because even if I called the producer to talk some sense into them, Jenna would get mad at me for meddling.

"So, she wants to blow off some steam. Both Layla and I will be with her tonight. She'll be fine."

"Okay," I tell him, but something doesn't sit right with me about this.

I hang up with Robert and send Chase a text, letting him know where and who she'll be with tonight. He confirms within seconds that he'll be there and I respond back to Jenna, thanking her for letting me know about the sitter.

I try to re-focus back on my script, but my mind keeps wandering back to her. Being associated with me is hurting her career and I don't know how to make that better. I just have to pray that the circus revolving around our story will die down soon and things will go back to normal for her.

"Mr. Harrington, there's a man named Chase Wilson outside claiming he has an emergency situation that needs your attention."

My heart starts to pound at the production assistant's words, and I bolt from talking to the director and run directly to the opening of the building. It's 11:30 at night and for Chase to show up at the set means something's happened tonight while Jenna was out. I see him in the distance, pacing back and forth and I yell out his name.

"Jenna was ambushed by the paparazzi on her way home from the bar. Physically, she's fine, but mentally she's traumatized."

"What the fuck?" I roar, my eyes almost bulging out of their sockets from my rage. "Where the hell were Robert and Layla? Where the hell were *you*?"

"Calm down and let me explain," he says, holding his hands up. "I was inside, watching them all night long. I ordered food and sat at the end of the bar so they couldn't see me. Jenna knows who I am, so I didn't want her to notice my presence. After a couple of hours, they all got up and it looked like they were going to leave together. I paid my bill and ran to the bathroom. By the time I got outside, I didn't see Robert and Layla anywhere and Jenna was by herself, surrounded by Danny Salari and his thugs. From what I could tell when I ran toward them, they had her surrounded and were blinding her with their flashes to the point that she was cowering on the ground, hiding her head underneath her arms. I pulled out my phone and took video while I ran to her so that you can have evidence to press charges."

"Where is she?" My mind visualizes what she must have looked like, how scared she had to have been and how I want to fucking kill Danny Salari.

"She's home, passed out in bed from the shock of it all. Robert must've been still inside the bar when Jenna initially left and saw the commotion as he was leaving because he came running over to help me get her home when he saw I was carrying her to her building. As soon as we got her safely inside, he called the police officer you guys were working with regarding the death threat. He's at Jenna's right now talking with him."

"Where was Layla?"

"Not sure."

"Follow me to my trailer so I can grab my things so we can get out of here," I order, both of us jogging to my trailer and I run in to grab my cell phone and clothes. When I look at my phone to see if Jenna has called me, I see I have missed calls from both Chase and Robert, but not her.

"Mr. Harrington!" I hear my name being yelled while walking out of my trailer. "Is everything okay?" The same assistant from earlier asks while running toward us.

"I need to leave and tend to a family emergency. Please tell James I won't be in tomorrow." He confirms that he will give my message to the director then Chase and I head to my car. I bark orders to my driver to take us to Jenna's and as soon as we get in the car, he speeds out of the lot.

"Where the fuck is her bodyguard, Harrington?" My jaw clenches at Chase's accusatory tone of voice and I give him a scowl.

"I've been working on it for fucking weeks now, Chase. There's no bloody bodyguard surplus store where I can just pluck one from a fucking rack," I sneer while I pull out my cell phone and dial Mason's number, Jenna's new bodyguard.

I keep calling him until he finally picks up. "I need you here tonight," I demand of him. "We had a situation with the paparazzi, and she needs protection *now*." I give him Jenna's address and tell him to meet me in the lobby of her building in one hour. After I hang up with him, I sit back and try to calm my fury.

"Why would Salari do this?" I question, not understanding his motives or what he thinks he would gain out of this.

"I honestly don't know. I've never seen him pull anything like he did tonight."

"Yeah, well he won't get away with it," I promise in a menacing voice. "Let me see the video."

Chase unlocks his phone, taps on his photos app and starts to play the video for me. My jaw clenches and the more I watch, the more I grind my teeth to the point I'm surprised I haven't cracked them. She was completely surrounded and on the ground like a wounded animal.

"There's one thing though," Chase comments as the video ends and he rewinds it to the beginning. "He never laid a hand on her. He will probably say she was drunk and fell because by the time I got to her, she was already on the ground."

"What are you saying? That you think he'll get away with this?" I ask incredulously because I will do everything in my damn power to make sure he pays.

"He might. Depends on how good his lawyer is."

"No fucking way," I snarl in disgust at the possibility of him getting off scott free.

"I've seen it happen before. Just trying to prepare you. You have enough evidence for a restraining order against him and all his cronies and that might be all you can get."

We pull into the circle of Jenna's building, and I don't even bother responding as I jump out of the car. I can see Robert talking to Detective Andrews through the glass windows.

"Why are you down here and not upstairs with Jenna?" I ask as soon as I reach them.

"Because Jenna and Avery are asleep, and we don't want to wake them." Robert responds in a tired voice. His hair is disheveled as if he's been pulling at it all night.

"I've got both yours and Mr. Wilson's statements recorded,

but tomorrow I will need to get Ms. Pruitt's," the detective tells Robert. He turns to me and shakes my hand. "Mr. Harrington, I'm hoping you'll persuade Ms. Pruitt to press charges?"

"Ab-so-fucking-lutely we are pressing charges," I confirm because there's no way I'm letting these bastards get away with what they did.

"Very good. Then I will see you both tomorrow." He nods at us and walks out.

"Why were you not with her when she left?" I demand, needing to know his side of the story.

He lets out a tired breath and rubs his eyes with his fists. "Jenna was ready to go before Layla and I were, but I was going to walk her home. She assured me that she was going to take a taxi and that she didn't need me, because normally, there are taxis waiting right outside for patrons. I checked outside first and saw plenty of taxis and no paparazzi. Jenna went to the bathroom during that time and when she came back, we parted ways. But she must have changed her mind as soon as she got outside and saw no one was around. I decided to leave ten minutes later and that is when I saw the commotion a couple blocks toward her place and ran over." He rakes his hand through his hair and when he glances back at me, it looks like he's fighting tears. "I'm sorry, Cal. She told me she was taking a cab. I should've made sure and walked her out and watched her."

I sigh out in frustration, put my hands behind my neck and look up at the ceiling before responding. "It's not your fault, Robert," I say in resignation, looking back down at him and lowering my arms. I know he feels like shit about it and is taking the blame. "You didn't know she was going to change her mind."

He swallows and nods but doesn't look convinced. "I've never seen her like that," he whispers and glances down at his hands. "She looked so small and fragile when Chase was carrying her. I've never seen her that scared in all the years I've known her."

I close my eyes and clench my jaw, my hands balling into fists wanting to punch something…preferably Danny Salari. As much as I want to hurt that man for what he did, me being behind bars is the last thing any of us needs right now.

"This will never happen again," I vow and look him dead set in the eyes. "Her bodyguard will be here any minute and I don't fucking care if she doesn't like it."

Robert nods and says, "Good, I'm glad he's finally coming."

"I'm still going to keep Chase on even with the bodyguard," I tell Robert, who looks uneasy at that news.

"Are you going to tell Jenna that she's purposely being followed?" he asks with a raised eyebrow.

"I will once she's used to Mason being around."

Robert shakes his head but doesn't say anything to that. "The babysitter went home, but I plan on sleeping in the guestroom tonight."

"I'll take the couch. I'm not leaving tonight. Not until I know she's okay." Robert nods his approval and we decide to sit down on the lobby's couches while we wait for Mason.

He shows up twenty minutes later with a duffle bag and I realize I hadn't even thought of his sleeping arrangements for tonight. I introduce him to Robert, who helps us get Mason on the guest list with the front desk. Jenna will have to give him final approval to be on the approved list.

We sit back down and update him on what happened tonight and what my expectations are for him while working for me and guarding the girls. We make sure he and Robert exchange phone numbers and then Robert helps me secure a hotel room for him at the closest hotel, which fortunately is only less than a mile away and has availability this late at night.

After saying goodbye to Mason, we go upstairs and silently enter the apartment. I first go check on Avery, who is laying horizontal on the bed and has covers everywhere but is sound asleep. I next check in on Jenna. She's laying on her back, fully clothed and remnants of her mascara are caked down her cheeks from crying. Even asleep, she's frowning and I pray she's not going to have nightmares over what happened.

I stand there staring at her, wishing everything was different because I know this wouldn't be happening if we were never separated all those years ago. Our relationship would've grown with my career, and she would know how to handle being with someone who's in the public eye. I know we would've been married by now with more kids. A wave of sadness suddenly crashes over me as I mourn what could've been our life together had I not let her slip away and let others interfere. But here we are today and my entrance into her private world has brought her chaos and uncertainty. I need to figure out how to make things better.

I *owe* it to her to make it better.

I look over her one last time with longing before exiting her room and shutting the door softly behind me. Having Mason here is the first step in making things right, but convincing Jenna is going to be a whole other story. She's going to think I'm trying to control her every move by having a bodyguard, which is why I can't tell her yet about Chase. If keeping Jenna safe is going to have her angry at me for a while, then so be it.

# Chapter 16

"Where's my mommy?"

I look up from my computer and see Avery standing in the doorway of her room, hair everywhere and sleepy eyed. It's 7:00 a.m. and I barely slept more than a couple of hours, my mind busy thinking of how I could make things better for Jenna but coming up empty.

"Good morning, sweetheart. Your mommy is still sleeping, and I think we should let her rest longer and not wake her up. How about we go get some donuts on our way to school?" Her face lights up and she's about to do her infamous squeal of delight when I hold up one finger and bring it to my mouth.

"If you stay quiet as a mouse, I will let you have two donuts. Let's see if you can go get ready for school without saying a word," I challenge and her eyes go wide, but she brings her fingers close to her mouth, pinches her index finger to her thumb and turns them as if she is locking her lips with a key. I bite the inside of my cheek from laughing and smile at her. She runs back in her room and shuts the door. I hear drawers being opened and closed and know she's getting ready.

I fucking love my kid.

Which reminds me, Jenna and I have yet to come up with a

plan on how we're going to reveal I'm her father. It's amazing the secret has been kept this long, but we just fell into a routine together that sometimes it doesn't even feel like she doesn't know yet, but the time is right. I'm hoping we can make it a priority after dealing with the incident from last night.

"Did I just hear Avery?" Robert comes out of the guest bedroom and looks around for her.

"Yes, she's getting ready for school. I bribed her with donuts for breakfast if she can be quiet in order not to wake up Jenna."

"She's still asleep?" he asks in surprise. I nod while closing my laptop and rising off the couch.

"Did you get any sleep?" I inquire, noticing the dark circles under his eyes.

"Barely, you?"

"Same. Mason will be here after I drop off Avery and we'll just wait for Jenna to wake up on her own. If she wakes up while I'm gone, please don't let her leave."

"Good luck with that. If that woman wants to leave, she's going to do it and there's nothing we can do to stop her. Unless you want to tie her to the bed." He smirks at me, and I chuckle, appreciating his sense of humor, especially because that's exactly what I would love to do.

"Future goals," I tell him with a wink. "But for now, I'll take her car instead to drop Avery at school."

"Oh, that will for sure piss her off," Robert comments with a laugh and proceeds to grab her keys for me off the wall hook.

Once Avery is ready to go, we head to the garage and get into Jenna's car. I find the closest donut shop in the car's navigation and head that way. Once we arrive there, it takes Avery only ten minutes to scarf down two donuts and a bottle of milk. She barely said one word while eating, completely consumed by the deliciousness of her sugary breakfast. I get her cleaned up and we leave to go to school.

I'm back in the condo within twenty minutes of dropping her off. Mason arrived for work while I was gone, and Robert was showing him around the condo when I walked in. I shake Mason's hand in greeting and Robert hands him a printout of Jenna's calendar for the month. We continue talking for another ten minutes when we hear Jenna's door open and turn around.

She's fully clothed in workout attire, her face unreadable. I wasn't expecting hysterics from Jenna, but I can feel the anger rolling off of her in waves. She looks between us and her gaze stops on Mason, eyeing him in suspicion.

"How are you feeling today?" Robert asks, breaking the silence.

"Fine," she tells him in a firm voice while walking over to Avery's room. "Where's Avery?"

"I took her to school already," I respond, watching her intently. "Jenna, I want you to meet Mason, your new bodyguard. He'll be with you at all times when you need to leave the house. We're extremely fortunate that he was available on such short notice." I nod at Mason with my gratitude. "I've reviewed his credentials and am 100 percent confident that he'll be able to keep you and Avery safe when out in public."

She stares at me, her eyes shooting daggers and if they were dipped in poison, I would be dead within seconds. She is furious and while I knew she was going to react this way, seeing it in person unnerves me.

She turns toward Mason with an extended hand and the fakest of smiles I've ever seen from her. "Nice to meet you. Do you have a last name, Mason?"

"You may call me Mason, ma'am," he tells her while shaking her hand and I can tell she doesn't like that he didn't answer her question by the way her smile falters.

"Well, Mason, I do appreciate you being here for my well-being, but you see, there seems to be a slight miscommunication as I was never asked whether or not I wanted you here and no offense to you personally, but I don't need a bodyguard. I'm sure Mr. Harrington is paying you generously to waste your pristine skills on babysitting me and my daughter. I apologize on his behalf and wish you the best of luck since I don't need your services." My blood boils at her words and I grab her forearm as she tries to turn away and leave.

"Mason, it seems Ms. Pruitt is ready for a morning run. Please feel free to get ready to join her by changing into your workout attire in the guest bathroom while I have a little chat with her," I tell him in a cold voice while staring at Jenna, daring her to defy me. She knows I'm becoming angry, but I don't give her a chance to respond as I pull her toward her bedroom to privately speak with her.

As soon as we walk in, she yanks her arm out of my grasp and walks straight to her window to look out. I shut the door behind me and start to pace, my frustration mounting at her stubbornness.

"Jenna, I know you're not stupid enough to believe that you don't need a bodyguard after last night's incident." The words are out of my mouth before I can even stop them. I don't mean to be so harsh or insult her intelligence, but I'm irritated with the way she's acting.

My words don't go over well as she turns to look at me, her hands balled into fists and her eyes narrow in displeasure. "Well, Cal, I guess in your eyes I'm stupid because I don't need a bodyguard! I feel that last night was an isolated incident and won't happen again since people will hopefully be appalled when they see the images once published."

I stop pacing, close my eyes and grip the bridge of my nose, mentally counting to ten to calm down. I did give Chase permission to post the video and publish any photos he has of them harassing her, hoping for public outrage but that doesn't mean things are going to change necessarily. "Unfortunately, that's not how it works in the paparazzi world. Last night just fueled their fire and they will be after you even more now."

She walks toward me and stops inches from my chest, her face stoic and her eyes determined. "I don't know the paparazzi world. I don't know your world. What I do know is that I don't want any part of their world. Just like I don't want any part of *your* world. You brought this into my life. You need to fix it by getting out of it."

I know she's mad at me, but her words stung and if she said them on purpose, then she hit her mark. I let her go, watching her turn on her heel, throw open her door and march straight across the living room to where Mason is standing at the front door. She says something to him as he opens the door for her. She walks past him, and he jerks his chin at me, following her lead and shutting the door behind him.

I slowly make my way out of her room and look at Robert, who's giving me a sympathetic gaze. I let out a slow breath of tension. "Help me understand why she's acting like I just ruined her life?"

"Well, let's see here." He taps his index finger against his lips and pretends to think. "You knocked her up and then your cunt of an ex-assistant pretended to be you and told her you wanted nothing to do with her or your baby, so she's hated you since. You come back into her life, and she finds out everything was a lie. Her personal life is all over the news. She has strange people following her every move. Her boyfriend dumps her and now her career is starting to suffer. She has lost all control of her very own life. Does that sum it up for you?"

His sarcastic tone darkens my mood even more. "Robert, if I could change the past, I would do so in a heartbeat, but I can't. I'm not the bad guy here and I'm trying my very best to fix things, but fuck if I don't know what the hell to do to make her trust me."

"Keeping secrets from her is not trying your best. You should have told her about the bodyguard the moment you were considering it."

"You're right, I should have, but I didn't and what's done is done."

"So do better. Tell her about the threat when she calms down and is in a better headspace. I guarantee she will start to warm up to the idea of having Mason around once she knows Avery's life has been threatened."

I nod at him, praying that he's right. He goes into Jenna's office to work, and I sit down on the couch and open my laptop to resume answering emails, the tension starting to leave my body at knowing she's safe with Mason.

Thirty minutes later, all that changes with a single phone call.

"I just fucking lost her! She ran right through oncoming traffic and caused a three-car accident! She purposely did this to try to get away from me. I need someone to come down here and take care of this situation so I can find her," Mason screams through the phone and hangs up, not even telling me where he is.

"*Fuck!*" I scream as loud as I can, tilting my head up to the ceiling. My fury causes Robert to come running out of the office.

"What's wrong?" Robert questions in a panic.

"Jenna ditched Mason and caused an accident. He's stuck there while she gets further away from him." I dial Jenna's number and we both look up at each other as we hear her phone ring in her bedroom. *Bloody hell, she didn't take her phone!*

"Let's takeover for Mason at the accident scene so he can look for her." Robert springs into action, grabbing his keys and running to the front door.

"Do you know her normal running route?" I inquire while following him out the front door and toward the elevator.

"She usually runs south along the Lake Front Trail to Grant

Park."

"Perfect, let me call Chase and have him follow that route to look for her."

I call Chase as we take Jenna's car to relieve Mason so he can continue on the path Jenna took before she disappeared. Because we aren't too far from the condo, Robert urges me to leave him and go look for Jenna with her car.

"I'll grab a taxi and start looking once I'm done." I agree to his plan and start driving within a fifteen-mile radius of the condo. I continuously drive in a square for two and a half hours, my hope of finding her diminishing with every ticking minute that I don't see her.

I call Avery's school and they confirm she's still there. Robert reported that both Layla and her parents have not heard from her. My anger starts to dissipate, and fear replaces it with the mental image of the death threat continuously flashing before my eyes.

I've never been a praying man, but I've prayed more in the last hour than I have my entire life.

*Please God, let her be okay!*

Mason, Chase, and Robert all have zero luck at finding her and Robert sends a group text that he's going back to the condo to see if she's there. I make one more final loop before pulling into her building and parking the car.

Once I get off the elevator, I run to her condo only to find Robert and Mason there, both shaking their heads in resignation.

"When do we call the police?" Robert asks, his voice shaking with worry.

"She's not considered a missing person for twenty-four hours," Mason responds, wiping the sweat off his face with a towel.

Robert pulls up a map on his laptop and we start going over the places we covered and the places we can go search when we receive a group text from Chase.

**Chase: Found her crying on Oak Street Beach.**

A photo comes through and it's Jenna curled into a sitting ball position in the sand with her head down, her arms hugging her knees.

**Chase: I will let her calm down before approaching her and walking her home. Give us another thirty minutes.**

"Ah, thank God!" Robert exclaims in relief, but I don't respond. The mixture of emotions has made me numb and I walk toward the window and stare out at the water of Lake Michigan. While I should've felt relief and happiness that she's okay, instead I'm back to being furious. I'm angry at her for recklessly putting her life in danger. I start to become a ticking time bomb and when I finally hear the door open announcing her arrival, I'm about to explode.

"I want everyone except for Jenna out of this apartment," I growl in a low voice and turn to look at her. My gaze drinks in her red, swollen eyes, puffy cheeks, disheveled hair and her clothes sticking to her body with sweat. The room is silent, and no one makes a move to leave.

She looks at me with wide eyes and swallows the lump of fear that's caught in her throat. "Cal, I—" she starts but I immediately cut her off. In three long strides I'm in front of her, my hands balled into fists from preventing myself from grabbing her and giving her a good shake.

"You little fool! Do you know what could have happened to you out there?" I yell, needing her to understand what she just put us through. Needing her to understand that what she did was anything but acceptable.

She winces and a tiny voice inside my head is telling me I need to calm down, but my emotions are like lava pouring out of an erupting volcano. Fast and furious.

"I'm sorry, really I am," she pleads and turns her gaze toward Mason. "Mason, I'm so sorry!" He nods his head in acknowledgment but doesn't say a word.

"What were you hoping to prove, Jenna? Did you know you caused a three-car pile-up with your little stunt?" She looks even more surprised, and her naivety enrages me. "Tell me, Jenna, what were you hoping to prove?" I shout and I watch her flinch at my harshness.

"C'mon Cal, she apologized. Jenna, you won't do that ever again, right?" Robert intervenes, but I'm past the point of no return, needing to get my point across.

"I promise, I won't ever do that again," she confirms with a nod of her head, but I'm not satisfied. Jenna needs to be shocked into understanding and I know the one thing that will do it.

"You're bloody right you'll never do that again because this is why you need a bodyguard, Jenna!" I back up to the table because I took out the envelope of her death threat earlier, trying to see if we could recognize any part of the city in the background in hopes we might find her in the same location, but their faces were too much of the focal point. I grab it off the table and walk to her.

"No, Cal! She's had enough for today!" Robert yells at me and tries to grab it from my hand, but I'm quicker. I shove it into her face and when her eyes focus on what she's seeing, she gasps.

She looks up and gazes between me and Robert, horrified at the image she sees.

"This," I growl in a menacing voice, shaking the photo in front of her. "This is why Mason is here! You could have gotten yourself killed today!"

"Stop, Cal! You've made your point!" Robert shouts out in frustration.

She stares at the photo and all color starts to drain from her face. She covers her mouth and runs for her bedroom. She slams the door and within two seconds, we hear another door slam. We can hear her throwing up and it's when she starts screaming and crying that I realized I've gone too far.

"Are you fucking happy now, asshole?" Robert looks at me with disgust. Mason just sits there in silence, his eyes averted downward.

My stomach drops and shame slams through me, vibrating from my head to my toes. Even though I made my point, I never should've handled it the way I did.

"Fuck," I mutter and walk slowly to her bedroom. I open the door and see she's still in the bathroom. I close it behind me and walk to the bathroom door. I stop and force myself to listen to her cry, each wail piercing my heart and making me throb with pain. It's pure torture hearing her like this, and I deserve to be tortured.

Because if it wasn't for me, she wouldn't be going through this.

If it wasn't for me, she wouldn't be receiving death threats.

If it wasn't for me, she wouldn't be chased by the paparazzi.

If it wasn't for me, she would have a normal life.

I slide down the side of her bed and sit in front of the door, accepting my punishment. *I don't deserve this woman.* The thought of leaving her and Avery alone briefly crosses my mind, but I know there's no way I can ever be without them again. That might be selfish on my part, but I know I'm the right man for her. I just have to prove that to her and include her in decisions that affect her and our daughter.

She eventually stops crying and I hear the water turn on from the sink. A few minutes later she comes out with her hair down, face puffy and eyes swollen from crying. She looks down at me and I stare up at her with remorse.

She slowly approaches and I hold out my hand for her, my gaze begging for her to take it. She reaches out to grasp it and in one swift move, I pull her down into my lap and hug her tightly.

I was expecting her to fight me, but instead she balls the fabric of my shirt in her hand and begins to sob into my chest. I close my eyes and let her tears soak through my shirt and stain my heart. I lift my hand and rub her back, encouraging her to let it all out. I hold onto her as tightly as I can and vow to myself that I will never let this happen again. I will never make Jenna cry and suffer like this because no one does this to the people they love.

And I fucking love Jenna Pruitt.

She's challenging and infuriating with her stubbornness, but I wouldn't change anything about her. I love her fiery spirit, her independence, and seeing her love for our child fills my chest with so much pride that it hurts. She's the woman of my dreams and I'll be the luckiest bastard in the world if at the end of all of this I can still get her to fall in love with me.

Her tears start to subside, and I gently rock her. She's so quiet that I look down to see if she's fallen asleep and my gaze is met with those beautiful brown eyes.

"I'm sorry, Jenna. I shouldn't have done that," I whisper in regret. "I was scared and angry when we couldn't find you and I needed you to understand the real reason why Mason was here. Last night's incident just moved up the process of him arriving sooner."

"Why didn't you tell me about the photo? When did we get it?" she questions softly and I know it's time for me to be honest and reveal the truth.

"It arrived in the mail last week. Robert found it and immediately called me. I went to the police, who got the FBI involved. They tested it for fingerprints, but it came up empty."

"Last week?" She lifts her head from my chest, her eyes filled with disbelief. "Cal, you can't keep these things from me!"

Disappointment at my actions consumes me and I grimace. "You're absolutely right, Jenna. But with everything that's been going on, I wanted to shield you from it and hope it wouldn't happen again. I know that was wrong," I admit, hoping she hears how sincere I am.

"You must communicate with me, Cal. I can't be left in the dark about something so serious, despite you wanting to protect me from it."

I nod, knowing I need to do better at telling her things instead of keeping things private in order to protect them. "Can we make a pact that we'll both work on communicating better with each other?" I ask with a raised eyebrow and she nods her agreement.

"Good." Without thinking, I lean down and kiss her forehead. She inhales sharply and my gaze is drawn to those lips. I watch her tongue slowly peek out and lick her lips, my dick throbbing at the memory of what it felt like to feel that tongue and those lips against mine. I look up and notice her eyes are dark and dilated and she's staring at me in hunger, just as I'm with her. Desire replaces her sadness and I bend my head, hypnotized with the need to kiss her. I'm inches away from her when a loud knock on the door stops me.

"Cal, your agent keeps calling you." Robert's muffled voice says.

"Be right there," I respond hoarsely, annoyed at the interruption. I sigh and lean my head back because I know Philip won't stop calling until he hears an update on Jenna. He called asking why I wasn't at work, so I had to update him on what was going on.

I look back down at her and smile. As badly as I want to kiss her, I know now's not the time. She's an emotional mess from the past forty-eight hours and just coming off a breakup. When I kiss Jenna, I want her to kiss me back with a clear head and heart. "Why don't you get freshened up and then come out so we can talk about how we are going to utilize Mason." She seems like she's in a daze and slowly nods her head. We untangle our arms and help each other up from the floor.

I exit her bedroom and close the door behind me for her to have some privacy. For the first time in hours, I smile, the feeling of hope back in my heart again because I know if we can survive this and come out together, then we will survive anything more that's thrown our way.

# Chapter 17

THINGS HAVE CALMED down since Jenna pressed charges against Danny Salari and his buddies a couple of weeks ago. He was arrested after Jenna gave her statement for harassment but posted bail a couple of hours later. She has a restraining order placed against him and that seems to have sent a message to the rest of the paparazzi. They have started to dwindle but not enough where she can venture out by herself without a bodyguard. Both girls have started getting used to Mason being around and even Avery was able to crack his stoic facade and gets him to smile more.

My schedule is still sporadic with the movie, but I try to maximize my time with the girls. I can tell Jenna is slowly starting to trust me more by her actions. We laugh more together, and I catch her watching me when she doesn't think I'm looking. As much as I'm ready to just dive right into our relationship and pick up where we left off from Vegas, Jenna isn't ready.

But she will be.

I LISTEN TO my agent talk on his cell phone, my mind racing as to what the real reasons are for him making a surprise appearance on set today. He barely ever visits me while I'm filming and if he does, he gives me notice when he's coming. I don't like surprises and him making a house call out of the blue doesn't sit well with me. He showed up when we were going on our lunch break and convinced the director to give me the rest of the day off so he could visit with me.

Something feels fishy about this whole setup.

He checked into the same hotel I'm staying at, but for only one night. We had lunch and now my driver is just circling around Chicago. He wraps up his phone call and hangs up.

"Sorry about that, Cal," he says while pocketing his cell phone.

"No problem. So, Philip, why are you here and why didn't you tell me you were coming?" No sense in beating around the bush anymore. I want answers.

He chuckles and says, "Can't I just come check on one of my most important clients?"

"Cut the bullshit, Philip. What's up?" I demand with a cold smile, not having the patience for his games.

"Nothing is up. I wanted to see how you're doing and finally meet Jenna and Avery. They're an important part of your life and therefore, important to me. I know this visit is sudden and I apologize but it was really the only time I had available the next couple of months and thought I could come out here, check on you and finally meet Jenna."

I know Philip is a family man, so I shouldn't be questioning his intentions on meeting my girls. It just seems odd to me that none of this was planned out. I have no idea what Jenna's plans are for today because I was supposed to be on set all day and wasn't planning on seeing them until the morning. I take out my cell phone and text Robert, asking if Jenna's home.

**Robert: Her and Mason went to the grocery store. Should be back shortly. Why?**

**Me: My agent is here and wants to meet her.**

**Robert: I'm at her place, so you can stop by now and wait for her.**

I send Jenna a text telling her about Philip and that we're making a quick appearance and instruct my driver to go to her house.

"Excellent, thanks for making this happen so quickly. Will Avery be home?" he asks.

"No, she's at school so you'll have to wait until next time."

He accepts my answer and within twenty minutes we are at Jenna's condo. Robert lets us in and I introduce the two men to each other. Robert's phone starts ringing and he excuses himself and leaves the condo. We sit down on the couch and start talking about the schedule for the press tour for my upcoming movie premiere.

"So, Cal, you know I'm always a straight shooter with you…" Philip starts, and my defenses are immediately up. "And well, the studio isn't really happy about your recent headlines in the news."

"As my agent, I would hope you've discussed with them the circumstances as to why."

"Of course I have, and they are very sympathetic to you and Jenna, but they feel there needs to be some damage control."

"Damage control?" I ask in confusion.

"Well, your image took a hit with that headline of being a deadbeat father and even though we know that isn't true and you've been here with your daughter for almost two months now, they are worried how your reputation will affect box office numbers."

I narrow my eyes at him, not liking where this conversation is going. "And what are they suggesting we do?"

"They want Jenna to accompany you to the premieres and portray yourselves as a happy, in love couple."

"No," I state firmly with a shake of my head and zero hesitation. "Absolutely not." I will not allow Jenna to be a pawn in their game.

"But it's not that far-fetched," he argues with urgency. "You are hoping to get back together with her."

"That will be on our terms—not theirs. My personal relationship is none of their fucking business and it certainly will not be used to sell tickets. The fact remains that Jenna and I are currently not together, and I will never ask her to lie for me just to appease the studio."

"Cal, you need to think about this..."

"End of discussion, Philip," I command in a stern voice. "Now if you don't have any more business to discuss, then we're leaving."

"But I haven't met Jenna yet."

"Not sure I want you to anymore."

"Oh c'mon, Cal! You know I only have your best interest at heart. I'm sorry this made you angry. Just forget I mentioned it and let's talk about what projects I've heard about that I think you need to consider."

He changes the subject and for the next fifteen minutes I tell him what interests me and what doesn't on his list of potential projects when the front door opens, and Jenna and Mason walk in carrying groceries.

Her eyes widen and she looks between me and Philip in surprise, making me question if she ever read the text I sent her.

"There she is! The woman who's been causing all the uproar," Philip greets her when she steps forward and I want to punch him in the fucking face. Jenna gives me a quizzical look and plasters a fake smile on her face.

"Jenna, this is my agent, Philip Logan. We had a break from

shooting and Philip wanted to meet you."

They shake hands and Jenna seems genuinely happy to meet him. "Nice to meet you, but I could have met you on set or at your hotel. What are you both doing here in my apartment? Where's Robert?" she inquires, looking around for him.

"What a lovely home this is too—the view is spectacular! Cal, did you buy this place for her?" Philip interrupts and my annoyance with him is mounting. *What kind of stupid question is that?*

Jenna's mouth drops open in shock and I can tell she's insulted. "No, I bought this place with the money I make in prostitution," she retorts sarcastically and my lips twitch with a smile. *That's my girl.* "Why are you both here again?" she demands in annoyance as Philip seems to have worn out his welcome already.

Philip, now realizing she was joking, starts to laugh awkwardly. "You are a sassy little thing! I love that!"

Jenna doesn't look amused at his compliment, and she turns around when we hear Robert walk back in. He smiles hesitantly at us, sensing the tension in the air and he decides to help Mason unload the groceries.

"Let's sit down, Jenna, and make ourselves comfortable," Philip suggests and sits back down on the couch. Jenna gives me an exasperated look before joining us. "Besides coming into town to check in on Cal and discuss business, I wanted to meet you in person because, well, we need your help."

*Oh, he better not be doing what I think he's about to fucking do.*

"I told you no, Philip," I tell him with a firm voice. "Leave it alone."

"My help? With what?" Jenna questions, looking confused.

"Nothing, Jenna," I respond, shooting Philip a warning look that he better not continue with this conversation.

Philip moves his body so he's completely facing her and ignoring me. "Cal's movie that he shot last year is releasing in two weeks and well, the studio is concerned over the recent headlines that paint Cal in a negative light."

"No, Philip!" I command, raising my voice. Jenna looks even more perplexed, her gaze going back and forth between us.

"The recent photos of you guys together around town looking like a happy family have been great for publicity and repairing Cal's reputation, but the studio is requesting a little more from you."

"Philip, I don't fucking care what the studio thinks!" I yell, losing my patience with him since he keeps defying me.

"Cal, this is one of the biggest studios in Hollywood, they can crush your career. If you want any kind of future as an a director, we need to comply with them," he pleads with me and I continue to shake my head, not giving two shits what the bloody studio wants. I'm so busy engaging with Philip that I fail to notice Jenna's change in demeanor.

"All this time here with us has been for publicity?" she whispers, and I see the hurt flash in her eyes before she becomes angry.

And just like that, all the progress that I've made within these last couple of weeks with her has vanished.

*Fuck!*

"Do you really think that of me, Jenna?" My stomach starts churning at the thought of her even thinking this was all a publicity stunt. We stare at each other and I'm silently begging her to believe me. To trust in me.

She breaks our eye contact and looks over at Philip. "What does the studio want from me?" She continues to ask questions and I feel like this is going to be a losing battle.

"The studio requests that you attend both the Los Angeles and New York premieres of his new movie, walking the red carpet with him and continuing to look like you're trying to work things out."

"Why?" she questions.

"The studio thinks that Cal will regain the female fan audience if they see you supporting him and that will increase ticket sales," Philip says, looking uncomfortably at her.

She starts to laugh, and the sound is bitter and mocking. She shakes her head and looks at Philip in disgust. "You guys are unbelievable," she mumbles, and I grab her hand, forcing her to look at me.

"Jenna, I don't want you to even consider this," I tell her, my eyes pleading with her. "I will be perfectly fine without the studio's support."

"And if I say no?" She ignores me and looks at Philip for the answer.

"Cal signed a multi-million-dollar contract with them for a three movie franchise series. They could pull out and demand the money they already paid him."

I drop her hand and turn to Philip. "I will gladly give back the fucking money to avoid this bullshit!"

"It isn't just the money, it will affect his career and whether other studios will want him in their future movies," he tells her, not even looking at me.

She raises a questioning eyebrow and I shake my head. "Don't do it, Jenna," I warn because I don't want her to feel obligated in any way that she has to do this. She has nothing to gain from doing this and she already despises my industry.

"Everything will be taken care of for you, Jenna. We'll fly Cal's stylist in to take your measurements and provide a wardrobe for you. His publicist can coach you through what to do the day of each premiere. It'll be easy and maybe even fun for you." Philip tells her with a smile, a smile that I want to slap right off of his face.

"Do I have time to think about it?" she asks, and I throw my hands up in the air in defeat and walk toward the window.

"Unfortunately, no. They want an answer today. I'm sorry, Jenna."

The room grows silent as Jenna contemplates what to do. I close my eyes and know what she's going to say. She's one of the most selfless people I've ever met in my entire life. She's mad at me, yet she doesn't want to see my career suffer. She would subject herself to more public scrutiny if it would save my career. I open my eyes and realization hits me: Jenna does care for me, because if she didn't, she wouldn't agree to this. I bite my cheek to hold in my smile.

She's been mine this whole time…she just doesn't realize it yet.

I turn back around when I hear her sigh with resignation and she stands up from the couch. "I'll do it," she tells Philip with a firm nod. "But don't ever ask me to do anything like this again." I watch her walk toward her front door, my heart swelling with pride.

She tells Mason she's going to work out upstairs alone and walks out. He looks at me in question and I shake my head, letting her be alone since the gym is secure inside the building. I turn toward Philip and my smile quickly vanishes. I stride toward him with a scowl and point my finger right in his face. "Pull that shit ever again and I'll make sure all of your clients drop you."

"Cal, I'm sorry but you were being unreasonable. There was no harm in asking her and she even agreed," he tries to justify his actions, but I'll never forget him defying me.

"Get the fuck out of here and don't talk to me until I see you in Los Angeles." His apologies fall on deaf ears while I walk toward the door and leave Jenna's condo.

Even though I'm mad at Philip and the studio for orchestrating this, it will give me time alone with Jenna away from Chicago.

I smile as I enter the elevator, excitement brewing inside me that this trip to Los Angeles might be the turning point in our relationship.

# Chapter 18

THE DIRECTOR DECIDED to work our asses off the week leading up to my departure for Los Angeles since production will be shut down while I'm gone and they will work on other things that don't require the actors. With a grueling schedule, I've not seen the girls all week except via FaceTime, but today is my first day off and I'm making the most of it. I woke up early and stopped at the donut shop to bring over breakfast. We then dropped off Avery at school and I ran back to my hotel to pack for the trip. I head out first thing in the morning to California and I hate that Jenna and I aren't flying out there together, but she refused to spend more than two days away from Avery. She made it crystal clear that she only wants to fly in for the two premieres and quickly get back home. I'm disappointed that I won't have more time with her, but a press tour is hardly a vacation. We do interviews more than eight hours a day, so my time alone with Jenna will be limited regardless. Because the first couple of days are for the press junket, Jenna won't join me for the premiere for another couple of days.

True to his word, Philip has made sure Jenna's wardrobe for each event was taken care of. My sister had my team of stylists fly out to Chicago and grab her measurements and show her dress designs for approval. All her travel arrangements have been made and my driver will take her to and from the airport. A car will be waiting for her when she lands in Los Angeles, and she will be with me and the rest of my team when we land in New York.

"Does Jenna have her own hotel room?" Robert asks while we grocery shop. I wanted to make the girls a home cooked meal tonight and asked Robert to accompany me so I can learn more about what they like to eat.

I turn to look at him and he wiggles his eyebrows, causing me to chuckle. "Of course she does. I'm trying hard not to give her any more reasons to be mad at me, so making her share a room when she's not ready for that would definitely not help my cause."

"Good point," he says with a laugh. "Things seem better between the two of you, don't you think?"

"I do," I tell him in agreement, but leave out the part that I wish it was going faster. Lately she will stay on the phone with me after I'm done talking with Avery and we make small talk. When I ask her about her day, her answers are more than just one word and she gives me glimpses into her day-to-day activities that don't just involve Avery. I'm starting to feel included in her world and it's a small victory that I'll gladly take.

I grow silent in my thoughts and ask him the question I've been wondering about. "Is she excited at all about this trip?"

He sighs and gives me a pitiful smile. "While most women would be ecstatic about attending multiple Hollywood premieres with one of the hottest actors on the planet, our girl is the total opposite. She's nervous and on edge, Cal. You know she hates any attention to herself."

I know she does and that's one of the things I love about her. "Everything is taken care of for her. All she needs to do is just show up and I'll try to be with her as much as I can. She's there for such a short amount of time that it will fly by."

"Yes, but she's never been away from Avery before in this kind of capacity. Sure, her parents have watched her overnight for Jenna before, but she's never been on a trip without her, so she might be in a mood the whole time she's there."

"Thanks for the warning," I mutter and try to make it my mission for her to have some fun at least while she's away.

We wrap up grocery shopping and return back to Jenna's condo. The rest of the time flies by with getting Avery from school and making dinner. Jenna seemed genuinely surprised at my cooking skills and devoured her lasagna with garlic bread. I do the dishes while she gives Avery a bath and then once it was story time, she joined us and sat at the edge of the bed to hear my storytelling.

"Can you please read me one more story, Cal?" Avery requests after I finish the first one and when I look up at Jenna for approval, I catch her staring at my mouth. Her gaze drifts back up to mine and we look at each other, the air getting so thick with our sexual tension that I sharply inhale.

"Sure," she stutters and I smirk at her. She immediately gets flustered and stands up to head out of the room.

"Mommy, stay here with us," Avery demands of her, and Jenna stops, turns around and sits down on one of Avery's bean bags.

I read one last story and once done, declared it's bedtime. Jenna and I kiss her goodnight and we're about to leave her room when she calls out to me.

"Cal, are you my daddy?" she asks softly while looking down and fidgeting with her blanket.

Jenna gasps and I freeze in my place, my heart pounding in my chest. I swallow and look at Jenna on how she wants me to answer. We still haven't discussed how to broach the subject so for Avery to bring it up has caught us completely off-guard.

"What makes you think that, honey?" she gently asks Avery.

"We have the same eyes, silly," she says in her miss-know-it-all-voice and I chuckle at how astute she is.

It feels like a weight has been lifted off my shoulders now that Avery finally knows. I kneel down next to her bed and grab her little hand. "Yes, sweetheart, I'm your daddy," I confirm, my eyes watering and my voice gruff with emotion.

Her eyes shine with love and it renders me speechless. She gives me the brightest smile and says, "I knew you would come back one day," she whispers, and I reach for her and take her in my arms. I hug her tightly and stick my nose in the crook of her neck, inhaling her scent.

I loosen my arms and lay her back against the pillows. "I'll never be away from you for long periods of time again," I promise, and I hear Jenna sigh behind me.

"Will you sleep with me?" Avery asks, giving me those puppy dog eyes that I can't resist.

"I'll stay with you until you go to sleep." I look over my shoulder at Jenna, who is wiping a tear away from her cheek and she nods. She leaves the bedroom and I lay down next to Avery and wait for her to drift off into dreamland.

Thirty minutes later, I quietly walk out of Avery's room and shut the door. I look over at the kitchen counter to see an empty bottle of white wine. Jenna is sitting on the couch with a wine glass in her hand. She looks up at me, places the glass on the coffee table, stands up and walks toward me. She looks angry and I'm baffled as to why considering what just occurred in Avery's bedroom.

"If you break her heart, I will personally kill you," she hisses in a low whisper. I see what's happening with her: Jenna is in her head, my promise to Avery that I'll never leave her for long periods again is eating at her from our experience. She thinks I'm going to break my promise. I know Jenna is still having trust issues stemming as far back as her failed marriage and she's especially still traumatized from what happened with us. It's going to take time—and actions from me—for her to move on and let go. But this protective mama bear that is raging out of her right now is hot as fuck and I'm done for.

Before she can even continue her rant, I grab her biceps and bring my lips crashing down to hers. I walk her backwards toward the wall and pin her against it, my mouth never once breaking our kiss. She gasps against me, and I swoop my tongue between her parted lips, moaning at how fucking amazing she tastes. My hips start grinding into her, my dick aching to be inside of her.

"Stop," she weakly protests and tries to push me away, but then grips my shirt and pulls me closer. She breaks our kiss and moves her head to the side, giving my mouth access to her neck. I lick and suck my way up until I reach the lobe of her ear and gently nip at it.

Her soft moans are driving me wild and I need more from her. "When are you going to stop ignoring this, Jenna?" I growl in her ear, my hands untangling hers from my shirt. I lace our fingers together and hold our hands against the wall, needing to feel her completely flushed against me. "You want me just as much as I want you. I see it in your eyes and feel it with your body."

My hips start pumping against her covered core and if one of us doesn't stop, I will fuck her against this wall. My need for her is all-consuming and it feels so damn good to be touching her again. I start kissing across her clavicle, my hands itching to rip off her shirt so I can feel her flesh.

"No," she cries and pushes hard against me. I immediately stop in concern and look at her. "I want nothing to do with you," she pants out in a non-convincing tone. I know she's lying to herself, but I see the fear in her eyes.

The fear of wanting me, only to be left again.

"I'll go to these premieres with you and continue a charade of being a perfect little family, but when we return, we'll start your visitation rights. No more popping into my apartment whenever you feel like it. You don't need me around anymore when you visit her."

She's believing her own lies and I will let her…for tonight anyway. I know her body is vibrating with need from our chemistry and soon she won't be able to deny it any longer.

I lean in close and give her a wicked grin. "I see your wall is up again, but let me tell you something, Jenna. I look forward to burning it down." I steal one more kiss and abruptly let her go. I walk to the door, open it and turn around to look at her one more time. "I'll see you in Los Angeles." Then I turn away and close the door softly behind me.

I stand outside her door and I hear her lock it behind me. My fingers graze my lips and I smile in anticipation for my time with her in California.

# Chapter 19

I PACE BACK and forth in my suite's living room and look at my watch for the umpteenth time. It's almost five o'clock and Jenna has been here since this morning, but I've yet to see her. I've been in interviews all morning and when she arrived, she was whisked away to her own suite by my team of stylists to prepare her for tonight. I made sure she was in a beautiful two-bedroom suite with food and drinks at her fingertips and a bouquet of fresh flowers from me to welcome her. I know she's uncomfortable being away from Avery, so I want to take as much stress off her plate as possible and make her feel pampered.

I've missed her and Avery terribly while I've been gone. I don't like not having them with me and I know this is going to be an issue with my next movie when it's in a different location. I don't even want to think about how Jenna is going to react to that news. She's had her guard up with me since our kiss and it's been hard to crack that icy exterior of hers over the phone. Now that I get to see her in person, I'm eager to have some alone time with her so we can talk.

A knock on my door halts my pacing and I walk over to open it. Sean is there, looking dapper in his black suit with a white collared button down underneath. "Time to go, loverboy," he teases as he walks in. He looks around and walks to the bedroom but comes back out with a puzzled frown.

"Where's Jenna?" he asks in confusion.

"In her own suite," I respond in amusement.

He wrinkles up his nose in disgust. "But why?"

I sigh, annoyed that I have to explain to him. "Because we aren't 'officially' together yet and I wanted to be respectful and make her comfortable by having her own room."

"Well, that's fucking dumb," he responds, and I roll my eyes at his lack of sensitivity.

"And this is why you're still single. That and your horrible taste in women." He punches my arm at my jab, and I chuckle at his scowl.

"Fuck you and hear me out on this, mate. Jenna's been single for over a month now, not even crying over the ex-boyfriend anymore and you haven't made your move yet?"

"Well…yes and no."

He blinks at me, even more confused than before. "What the bloody hell does that mean?"

"It means I'm trying to regain her trust by taking things slow. We've kissed, but she's still weary of me and our situation." I give him the Cliff Notes version because I don't have time to get into specifics and frankly, Sean Lindsey is not the best man to give relationship advice. He goes through women like water and the one woman he wants to be serious with doesn't reciprocate his feelings.

"Cal, rip the Band-Aid off already. Tell her how you feel and stop giving her options. You want her, she wants you, blah blah blah. It's just semantics." He shrugs as if it's really that easy and already I feel a headache coming on from his speech. "Stop walking around on eggshells and just fucking be with her already."

"Thank you, Dr. Ruth," I comment sarcastically, and

fortunately, a knock on my door saves me from having to continue this conversation. My publicist, Liz, and Cora, walk in, and I try to hide my surprise at seeing the latter. I haven't spoken to her since the award show, so I was unaware that she would be at tonight's premiere. She probably pressured Sean into inviting her and unfortunately, he has no willpower when it comes to her. She gives me a hesitant smile, and I politely smile back at her, having no desire to exchange pleasantries.

"Limo is waiting for us downstairs, and Kellan called saying Jenna is ready," Liz announces, and my adrenaline starts to pump at the mere mention of her name. Kellan is my main stylist and I informed him that Jenna is the priority whenever she's with me. I've been doing this long enough that I can dress myself. He dropped off my suit this morning and spent the remainder of the day with her.

"Let's grab Jenna so we can leave." Everyone exits my suite and I shut the door behind me. We walk toward the end of the hall where Jenna's suite is located and knock on her door. It doesn't take long for one of the stylists to open it and let us in.

We greet Kellan, Morgan and the rest of the team and thank them again for everything. Sean is the first one to see Jenna and goes to hug her. It gives me a chance to stand back and appreciate the vision that she is. She looks like a Greek goddess in a teal Grecian style gown that simply takes my breath away. I drink her beauty in, and I want nothing more than to demand that everyone leaves us so we can stay in this suite for the next forty-eight hours with no interruptions, no distractions. Just her and I, talking out our feelings, our hopes for our future together and exploring each other's bodies.

I walk toward her, my body craving to always be near her whenever she's around. Cora steps up next to me and we both stop in front of Jenna. I let Cora introduce herself and I can tell it's taking all her strength to be nice to Jenna. Jealousy is radiating off her and I glare at Sean for even bringing her.

"It's nice to meet you," Jenna tells her with a cordial smile.

"It's a pleasure," Cora responds in a husky voice. "Cal has told us so much about you." I stiffen as she slides her arm around my waste and squeezes. Jenna watches with a bemused smile at Cora's antics. I push Cora's arm off me and move to stand in front of her so that Jenna is finally looking at me and only me.

I see her breath hitch as she looks me up and down and I can tell Jenna likes what she sees. Her gaze rests where the top two buttons of my shirt are undone, revealing a peak of my chest. She licks her lips and I swear to God if we didn't have an audience with us, I would be taking her right now. She finally looks up at me and our eyes lock. I know she feels my hunger for her smoldering from my stare and it starts to affect her as I watch her eyes slowly start to dilate from her own desire.

"All right everyone, let's go. Limo is waiting downstairs," Meg announces, breaking our trance.

I give Jenna a sexy smile and wink before gesturing for her to go ahead of me. My politeness gives Cora the perfect opportunity to snake her arm through mine. I look at Sean and motion for him to follow Jenna while I have a little chat with Cora.

"What are you doing, Cora?" I hiss in a low whisper, not wanting to cause a scene in front of the team of stylists who are packing everything up so it's ready to board the plane to New York.

"I'm just walking with my friend," she says in a childlike voice. "I've missed you, Cal. I hope you're not still mad at me?" She raises her eyes feigning innocence, but I don't fall for her old tricks. We walk out of the suite and down the hallway together, but before joining the others, I stop us and turn to face her.

"Understand something, Cora, I'm here with Jenna. Jenna is my future and if you want to remain friends, then you will respect her, respect my daughter, and respect my relationship.

Got it?" My voice is harsh, but I don't care. I'm done playing her games and if she's any friend at all, she'll be happy that I've found someone.

"Of course, Cal! I would never do anything intentional to hurt you or your sweet little family. I can't wait to get to know them better," she smiles smoothly at me and pats my arm before untangling herself from mine and joining the others. I need to watch that one like a hawk because my gut tells me that I still can't trust her.

---

THIS EVENING HAS already been exhausting and all I want to do is take Jenna and get the fuck out of here.

When we arrived at the theater, we took our mandatory photos at the step and repeat, some by myself, some with Jenna, and then the rest with the whole cast of the movie. I could tell Jenna was completely uncomfortable by how tight she stood next to me, but she plastered a smile for the cameras and made it through. Once photographs were done, Liz whisked Jenna away so she wouldn't be bothered by the reporters, and I continued answering questions for those who were given permission to be on the red carpet.

Sean and I introduced the movie to the audience who was in attendance but decided to skip watching it with them. We normally don't watch our own movies on premiere day, and we headed straight to the afterparty. Jenna was already there waiting for me, but as soon as I arrived, I was surrounded by people wanting to congratulate us and talk business.

"Where's Jenna?" I asked Liz before another studio executive made their way up to me.

"I put her at the bar, in a private corner so she wouldn't be bothered by anyone."

I nodded my approval, but I hate that she's by herself. I plastered a smile on my face as the next person stopped me and I tried to inch my way closer to the bar. By the time I took photos with people and made it through the crowd, over an hour had gone by.

I walk around the bar, trying to locate Jenna, but it seems she has moved. I'm walking behind one of the drapes to the lounge area when I hear my name being called behind me. I turn around and my heart stops at the sight of Valerie cautiously walking toward me.

*What in the hell is she doing here?* She's wearing a formal gown, her hair and make-up done so she must be here with her husband, who has ties to the studio.

The closer she gets, the more volatile I become and I'm mentally not prepared to have this conversation right now. There's nothing she can say that will take back what she's done to me.

"You," I growl in a low voice. "You've got a lot of nerve trying to talk to me."

"Cal, please," she pleads, and I hold up my hand for her to stop but she doesn't listen and continues walking until she's just a couple of feet away from me. "Please let me just explain."

"Explain?" I sneer in a mocking voice. "You told the woman I love lies and kept me from my child for four years. What the fuck is there to explain?"

"I didn't know she was that important to you, Cal. I thought she was just a fling! I'm sorry. *I'm so sorry.* I was blind with jealousy, and I know I should've never kept her pregnancy from you."

"You had years to tell me! *Years!"* I scream in her face and she starts crying. Her whole body is shaking to the point that she's having trouble breathing. "If it wasn't for some goddamn stranger who wanted to make a buck off my name, I still to this day wouldn't know about her!"

"I know," she gasps out when she has enough oxygen to talk. "I didn't realize the severity of what I've done until I found out I was pregnant with my own child." She cradles her belly and it's then I notice the small bump.

Black tears from her mascara start zig zagging down her cheeks as she continues to cry and repeats her apologies over and over again. I can't stand to look at her anymore, nor do I want to hear her pathetic excuses. I just want to be done with her and never see her for the rest of my remaining days.

"Stay the fuck away from me and my family, you hear me?" She nods her head and I turn to leave and that's when I see her husband walking toward us.

"What's going on here?" he questions in a suspicious tone, his gaze moving between me and his wife.

"Ask your wife, but I bet it won't even be the truth." I walk away in disgust and go straight to the bar, needing a stiff drink. I need to get the hell out of here. I need to get away from these fake as fuck people and take the one person that matters the most to me here and leave.

The music has gotten louder, and the crowd has thickened. After I get served at the bar, I grab my drink and try to find Jenna. I see Cora watching something with a sour look on her face. I walk over to her to ask if she's seen Jenna and that's when a movement on the dance floor catches my attention. Sean is dancing with Jenna, holding her way too close and everyone is watching them, whispering in fascination. He looks over at me and winks.

*I'm going to fucking punch him.*

"Seems Sean is really taking a liking to Jenna. Maybe a little too much. Such a scandal this will cause," Cora comments and I tune her nonsense out while I stare at them, my jaw clenched in anger. Sean is whispering something into Jenna's ear, his lips looking like they are making contact with her skin.

I continue to watch them dance but focus on Jenna's facial expression. They try to keep their fake smiles in place, but soon they start engaging in some sort of battle of words. Sean's smile fades all together and as the music ends, he abruptly dips Jenna and kisses her full on the lips in front of everyone.

*Red*. All I see is fucking red.

"Don't make a scene, Cal," Cora warns, placing her hand on my forearm to prevent me from murdering my best friend. *What the fuck is he thinking?* I know he would never go after Jenna for himself. Knowing Sean, this is a game he's playing to make Cora jealous and using Jenna as his pawn.

Judging by the sly smile that's on Cora's face, the only one it seems to have worked on is me.

Sean forces Jenna to take a bow at the applause of the crowd and walks her over here with his arm around her waist. Jenna is whispering harshly at him and his only saving grace right now from me not knocking him out is that everyone is watching us.

"She's all yours," Sean says with a smirk and grabs my drink from out of my hand and downs the rest of it before stalking over to the bar.

"We're leaving now!" I announce in an angry voice and grab Jenna's hand. She tries to remove it from my grasp as we maneuver our way through the crowd to the exit, but I grip her tighter and pull her faster.

"You're hurting me," she complains when we get outside. I let go of her hand when I see our limo and I tell the driver to take us back to the hotel. I open the door for her and get in after her, slamming the door shut.

"What the fuck was that?" I snarl at her after the partition is closed so the driver can't hear our conversation. Rage is making me incoherent and blind with jealousy. I was already in a bad mood from seeing Valerie, but what I just witnessed on the dance floor has taken me to another level.

"If you're referring to Sean kissing me, you need to ask him. He's the one who kissed *me* and wanted to dance," she explains, but I'm seething that she agreed to dance with him. People will be talking tomorrow about their kiss, and it makes me furious that they are going to assume the worst. I can just see the headlines now from the tabloids about a love triangle.

"I don't give a fuck about Sean, it's your reputation I care about!" I snap and run my fingers through my hair in aggravation.

"My reputation? I thought the whole point in me being here tonight was to save your precious reputation," she counters back, and it makes me feel even worse that she came here because of me. Any hit her reputation takes tonight due to that kiss was because of me. If anyone took videos or photos and uploads them to social media, it's going to be plastered everywhere and hurt her career even more. Why did she not think of this before dancing with him?

"I'm not the one who looked like a slut kissing another man!"

The words are out of my mouth before I can even stop them, and I know I just made a grave mistake. I didn't mean to imply she was a slut, and I should've never used that term. I was angry that she wasn't thinking of what people were going to say seeing her dancing with him when she was at the premiere with me. Hollywood is ruthless and always looking for a scandal and unfortunately, they just gave them one on a silver platter. My anger should be directed at Sean, not Jenna since she's the innocent bystander who didn't know any better.

I'm a fucking asshole.

She stares at me in shock for a split second before she cries out in anger and starts hitting me. I let her take her fists to my arms because I deserve this. I deserve her wrath and I want her to let it out before I apologize.

"You asshole! I hate you!" she screams, and the tears start rolling down her cheeks. I can't handle a crying Jenna. All I want to do is hold her and ask for forgiveness. I wish I could take back everything I just said, but the damage is done. I grab her wrist to try to get her to stop hitting me, but she starts to struggle harder. I don't want to hurt her, so I loosen my grip and that's when she takes me off guard by getting on top of me to try to get her hands free. The feeling of her body so close to mine and her hips pressing into my cock undoes me. I haul her against my chest and seal her mouth with my lips.

She freezes in surprise and as soon as I feel her softening against me, I sweep my tongue across her lips and when she opens for me, I invade her mouth. She kisses me back, matching every stroke of my tongue and I moan at the pure, sweet ecstasy of it. *Yes*, my body screams and I let go of her hands to grab her hips. She plunges her hands into my hair and tries to bring me closer. We are as close as we can physically get, but it doesn't feel like enough. Every stroke of her tongue is like a spark being lit, swallowing me up in flames of passion.

I break our kiss and start trailing my tongue down her neck, sucking on her most sensitive points that make her pant out my name. She tugs at my jacket, trying to get it off my shoulders and I move forward so she can push it down my arms. I manage to free myself from the sleeves just as she rips open my shirt, the buttons popping off and flying everywhere. She spreads it open, leans forward and kisses a trail along my neck, making a path of hot destruction down my chest where she starts sucking on one of my nipples.

"Jenna," I groan out in desire. I yearn to feel her bare flesh, so I trail my hands down her back and when my fingers reach her zipper, I quickly unzip the top portion of her dress. She kisses her way up my chest and goes straight back to my mouth. She nips at my bottom lip before slipping her tongue inside.

I start to pull down one of her shoulder straps then my hands cup her bare breasts. I squeeze her nipple gently between my fingers, and she moans against my lips. I pull away from her mouth and start sucking on her sweet, sensitive bud. She grips my hair in between her hands and whimpers in desire. She's moving her core against my throbbing erection, the friction making her gasp. I can only imagine how wet that sweet pussy of hers is and I growl, needing to be inside of her. Jenna must feel the same way because her hands go to my belt and start unbuckling my pants. I feel the zipper being pulled down and I lean my head back and moan out in pleasure when she finds my cock and wraps both hands around me. She starts moving her hands up and down, her thumb grazing against my tip.

"Jenna, you're going to make me come if you continue doing that," I pant, and she starts rubbing my pre-cum around the head. Her hand disappears inside the slit of her dress and before I can blink out of my haze of desire, she's engulfs me in her tight, wet core. I moan loudly at how goddamn amazing she feels. I've been fucking my fist for years now with the fantasy of her and it can't even compare to the intensity of what reality feels like.

She moves down slowly and once I'm deep inside of her, she wraps her hands around my neck and brings her lips to mine. Her mouth opens and I thrust my tongue inside, deepening our kiss. She slowly starts to ride me but soon the pent-up hunger inside of her takes over and she bounces faster on top of me, her head thrown back in bliss.

Her core muscles start tightening around me and I moan louder, not caring if the driver can hear us anymore. "Fuck, Jenna, you're just like how I remembered. You're still so tight," I murmur while cupping her breast and squeezing it. Her core starts gripping me tighter and I know we're both going to come soon. Jenna deserves more than a quick fuck in the back of the limo, but we're past the point of no return.

I wrap my arms around her and maneuver us to the carpet. Her legs wrap around my hips, and I thrust hard inside of her. I feel her nails dig into my ass and she grips me as I pound into her. "Fuck, I'm coming Jenna," and as soon as the words are out of my mouth, she screams out my name and comes hard against me. My release explodes inside of her, and I collapse on top of her, my body shuddering from the intensity of my orgasm.

I smile into the nape of her neck, slowly coming down from my high. Sex with Jenna had always left me feeling like I was in another stratosphere. No one has ever come close to making me feel the way she does. She was meant for me and there's no way I'm ever giving her up.

I turn my head and notice out the window that the car isn't moving. We must already be back at the hotel. I move my head back toward her neck to kiss her when I feel her hands slide between us and push against my chest.

"Get up," she demands, her voice anxious and upset.

I slowly lift up and look at her with concern. "Jenna, what's—"

"Get off of me!" she yells and I'm in complete shock over this change in her mood. *What the fuck?* I lift off her and watch as she hastily sits up, grips her dress to her chest, grabs her purse and crawls over to the door. As soon as she opens it, she bolts out of the limousine. I quickly pull up my pants and button them, throw my jacket on and follow her out.

"Jenna, stop!" I call out her name multiple times, but she just runs faster away from me. She makes a beeline for the stairs and I head straight to the elevators, praying that I beat her up to our floor and can try to calm her down to find out why she's so upset. Unfortunately, the elevator was the wrong choice because it made multiple stops along the way up since people were taking it up to the rooftop pool. Because I'm personally paying for her room, I have a key card to it. I let myself in to see if she's arrived, and I quickly see her slamming the bedroom door.

I stride toward it and start banging on it.

"Jenna, let me in! We need to talk!" I bang so hard on the door that the picture frames on the wall begin to rattle.

"There's nothing to talk about! That was a mistake and will never happen again!" she shouts through the door, and I'm hurt that she called what happened between us a mistake.

"Open this door, Jenna!" I yell louder, getting angrier that she keeps shutting me out. There's no way in hell that the passion I felt from her was a mistake. She wanted me just as badly as I wanted her, and we need to talk about what's making her doubt us surviving as a couple.

"No! Please go away, Cal!"

My emotions start taking over and as usual when it comes to Jenna, I start to think unclearly. She needs to understand that she'll never be able to shut me out of her life. She's mine and I won't let her ruin us because of the ghosts of our past.

From the sounds of her muffled voice, I know she isn't close to the door. I start kicking at the doorknob and after a few hard thwacks, the door swings open and I enter her room. I see her standing in the doorway of her bathroom, looking at me as if I'm the craziest person she's ever seen. I feel fucking crazy right now.

"If I want you, Jenna, no goddamn locked door will stop me," I declare in a low, menacing voice. I look at her disheveled appearance and wild-eyed disbelief over my actions. I know talking tonight is not going to happen. Tonight was a lot for her and she's an emotional mess running on barely any sleep. She needs to rest so she can be level-headed when we hash out what's going on in the beautiful head of hers. "Go to sleep. We'll discuss this in the morning."

I don't bother looking back at her as I leave her suite and shut the door behind me. I feel defeated but refuse to lose hope even though every time we take three steps forward, it feels like something forces us a thousand steps back.

# Chapter 20

MY ALARM GOES off at five in the morning and I groan while reaching to turn it off. I barely slept more than three hours, my mind replaying everything that happened last night. When I left Jenna's room, I had to call Philip to let him know we wouldn't be making our flight to New York because Jenna "didn't feel well." Fortunately, Philip said the studio agreed to fly their jet back to Los Angeles after dropping off the crew who did make last night's flight. Kellan stayed and made sure mine and Jenna's outfit for the NYC premiere was pulled from the plane before last night's takeoff. Because it takes at least five hours to fly there plus with a three-hour time change, Kellan will get us ready on the plane so when we land, we get in the car and go straight to the event.

When Jenna and I didn't show up for the flight, Sean came back to the hotel to check on us because I kept ignoring his calls. I told him if he ever pulled a stunt like that again, we won't be friends anymore. He apologized and admitted he didn't think about the ramifications dancing with Jenna would have, not to mention the kiss at the end. I accepted his apology and we stayed up with a nightcap talking and I told him about my encounter with Valerie.

I sigh with tiredness and get out of bed to take a shower. Once that's done, I pack up my things and send Jenna a text that we need to be downstairs in one hour. I would've asked her to join me for breakfast, but when I checked on her before I went to bed last night, she was out cold, still wearing her dress and makeup. I know she'll be on edge when she sees me this morning but somehow, we need to have a private conversation. And it needs to happen today.

I leave my room and am about to go to check on her when I see Kellan knocking on her door. I hear him telling her it's time to wake up to catch our flight. I know she's a little bit of a grump in the morning before she has her coffee so, I made sure room service would deliver food and coffee to her room. It's probably better that she doesn't see me right away after what transpired last night. I decide to go downstairs and meet Sean for breakfast instead to give her some time. Once we are done eating, we go to our designated car and wait for Jenna and Kellan. I watch out the car window as she walks outside and looks around. She has a scowl on her face, and I chuckle at how crabby she probably is from lack of sleep. Kellan points toward our car and they walk over.

"There she is, my beautiful dance partner. Did you sleep well, sweetheart?" Sean smiles at her as she enters the car and I'm glad I have my sunglasses on so no one sees my eyes roll at his sarcastic comment. Jenna gives Sean an annoyed glance, takes her sunglasses off the top of her head and pushes them up the bridge of her nose with her middle finger. Sean starts to laugh, and I bite the inside of my cheek to keep from smirking.

She stares out the window for most of the ride to the airport, giving me access to watch all the emotions playing out on her face. About ten minutes in, she realizes something and it makes her gasp. Kellan asks if she's okay, and she quickly recovers and tells him she's fine. I wonder if she now remembers that we never used a condom last night. Whatever she's thinking blackens her mood and it stays that way until we get to the plane, where she asks Kellan to sit next to her so they can go through how he plans on styling her tonight. I know this is her way to avoid sitting next to me and I go along with it.

The studio's plane is incredible with large leather seats, leather couches, a large screen television and a master bedroom with a bathroom in it. I purposely choose to sit across from Jenna as a reminder to her that she can't ignore me forever. She continues to pretend I don't exist well after takeoff while concentrating on whatever Kellan is telling her about tonight's attire. Sean hands me a script he wants me to consider for a future movie with him, and I get so lost in the storytelling that I don't realize Jenna has fallen asleep until I hear Kellan tell her to go to sleep in the back bedroom.

She agrees in a daze and walks back to the bedroom, closing the door behind her. I stare at the door, debating whether I should go in there so we can talk.

"Stop bloody overthinking it and go in there," Sean grumbles, not even looking up at me from his script.

I chuckle and decide he's right, there's no better time than right now to go talk to her. Once we land in New York, we will be busy with doing press at the premiere, interviews, and then heading back to the airport where we will part ways and won't get to see each other for another week. I don't want us leaving things like this.

I stand up and go to the bedroom. I open the door slowly to see she's asleep on the bed, on top of the covers. I close the door softly behind me and lay down next to her. She doesn't even move when the bed dips under my weight and I stare at her, memorizing this moment of how peaceful she looks. We've been through so much together in these last couple of months that I have to believe that things are only going to get better once we discuss our feelings. I continue watching her, but exhaustion takes over and I don't realize I dozed off for a couple of hours until I feel her stirring next to me.

I open my eyes and look at her. I bring my fingertips to her cheek and gently brush the strands of hair that are sticking to it. She moves into me, wrapping her arms around my torso and sighing in contentment. I gently place my arms around her and close my eyes, never wanting to let this woman go. I hear her breathing start to pick up and open my eyes to look at her.

I can tell she's awake because her head starts to move against the fabric of my shirt covering my chest. She jerks her chin up and looks straight into my eyes. She looks confused as to how we got in this position, and I smile. I swallow the lump that has formed in my throat and tell her in a low, husky voice, "We need to talk." She nods in agreement and I'm relieved to see that she's ready to listen to my feelings.

"I understand how hard it is for you to trust me, given the circumstances you have been placed in. I probably would feel the same way if I were in your shoes. But while you've hated me for all these years, I've never stopped thinking about you. Anytime I saw someone who remotely resembled you, I always wondered if you were happy. And I can't help but feel that we were given a second chance to try to be together because of Avery."

"People shouldn't be together just for children," she interrupts, and I can see that her eyes are getting watery from holding back tears.

I'm taken aback by her words and frown. "Do you really think I want to be with you just because of Avery? Do you really believe that my desire for you is an act? You're the most infuriating woman I have ever met, yet no woman has ever made me feel the way I do when I'm with you." I turn us so that we're facing each other, and I lift her chin so she can look into my eyes to see how serious I am.

"I want a chance, Jenna! I want you to give me a chance to prove to you that we belong together. That my feelings for you and Avery are very, very real." Tears start to stream down her cheeks, and I try to wipe them away with the pads of my thumbs. "I want us to start over. I want to properly date you. I want to make you laugh. I want to go on adventures with you. I want to hold you in my arms every night and wake up with you every morning. I deserve a second chance, Jenna," I whisper fiercely because I fucking do. I deserve a second chance to show her what life together could be like.

A knock on the door interrupts me from continuing. "Cal, I need to start getting Jenna ready." Kellan's muffled voice is heard through the door.

"I'll be right out," I say back, sighing in frustration. I gently caress her cheek, my gaze never wavering from hers. "Please, Jenna…will you please think about it?" I plead, my eyes begging for a chance. "If you don't feel the same way for me after some time together, then I'll leave you alone and just co-parent Avery with you."

She smiles softly at me and cups my cheek with her hand. "I'll think about it," she whispers and relief spreads through me like wildfire. I'm so fucking happy that I can't stop smiling at her.

"Thank you," I whisper before claiming her lips in a quick kiss. I don't want this to end and I can feel her lips starting to part, giving me full access in. I reluctantly pull back, knowing we need to start getting ready or this is going to lead to another quick fuck. The next time I'm intimate with Jenna, I want to worship her body with a night filled with making love.

"I promise you; you won't regret giving me a second chance."

And I pray to God I don't fuck up my promise.

# Chapter 21

*Two Months Later.*

IT'S BEEN THE best two fucking months of my life.

It was hard leaving Jenna after the New York premiere knowing she was going to give me a chance. I was so worried she was going to get back into her head and let her fears take over while I was gone that I made every effort in showing her that even apart, she can still trust me and know that I think about her every minute of the day. Any free moment I got, I was calling or texting her. I had flowers delivered every day that I was gone.

"Cal, as much as I love flowers, I beg you to stop." She laughed while we were on the phone the night before I was scheduled to arrive home. "They're not necessary, you know. All I want is you," she shyly told me. She couldn't see it, but I had to place my hand over my chest where my rapidly beating heart was because I was so damn happy with her revelation.

"You have me, sweetheart," I told her. "You and Avery are all I think about, all the time. I can't wait to come home and show you how agonizing it is to be away from you." And when I arrived home twenty-four hours later, I did exactly that by making slow, passionate love to her that left her useless the following day.

Jenna has opened up more about her fears and insecurities regarding us. Some of it is from dating a Hollywood actor, but most of it stems from her prick of an ex-husband—that I'll grow bored with her, fall in love with one of my co-stars or I would prefer working over being with my family. While I reassured her I would never get bored of her or cheat on her and that my family will always be my number one priority, I fear my grueling work schedule is going to be the biggest test yet for us. She needs to be willing to pick up and go with me when I have international shoots and that's something she's never had to do before with anyone. I know I'll survive it, but the question remains if Jenna is going to be willing to put the work in when it gets hard, and she doesn't see me for weeks on end. In my eyes, she has no choice. She's mine for eternity, but I also don't want her miserably unhappy that she becomes bitter. I decided I can't worry about what the future brings and that I need to focus on the present and shower her with unconditional love until she sees for herself that I'm hers.

I practically moved in with her and Avery the same week I arrived back home because staying in the hotel was pointless. I kept my suite to conduct meetings with Chase and use it as an office, especially since Jenna and Robert work out of her condo most days. I strategically started bringing things over with me every day, little by little. I didn't want Jenna scared that we were moving too fast, because in my mind, we needed to play catch up, but she never said a word and made room for my things in her closet.

To our good fortune, there was no press about Sean and Jenna at the Los Angeles premiere, but now that Jenna is officially my girlfriend, there are still false stories and negative press about her. Robert still handles being the "anonymous source" and calls the press when something is inaccurate or he gives them a positive story about her and our relationship. I'm hopeful that things will calm down and we won't be newsworthy for much longer. Jenna will always have people trying to take her photograph as long as she's with me, but the number of paparazzi outside her building has started to dwindle.

As the weeks started flying by, our life as a family was falling into place and when I wasn't working, I spent all my time with my girls. Jenna's parents have had us over for dinner during my days off and it's been nice getting to know them better. I love watching Avery interact with her grandparents and it makes me eager to take her and Jenna over to England to meet my whole family.

My movie finally wrapped last week and we took our first vacation as a family up to Wisconsin for a quick weekend getaway. I've never seen that part of the United States before and the more time I spend in the Northern Midwest, the more I love it. I know a house on Lake Michigan will be in our future.

Today I'm being a lazy bastard and working on my laptop in bed. Jenna should be home soon after taking Avery to school and was meeting Robert for a morning work appointment with a current client. I debate whether I should go workout when my cell phone starts to ring. Bridget is calling and I had forgotten that she texted me last night saying we needed to discuss business.

"Where's your bloody shirt?" she asks as soon as I answer her FaceTime.

"Why do I need a shirt if I'm in bed?" I question her with a cocky grin.

"Look at you, you lazy twat who doesn't need to work," she jokes and I roll my eyes with an exasperated sigh.

"I just worked almost four months straight with numerous twelve to fourteen hour days. I think I deserve to lay in bed and do nothing. Besides, I was checking my emails when you called."

"I'm assuming then that Jenna is not in bed with you, and we can discuss your upcoming schedule?"

"Unfortunately, she's not and yes, we can discuss my schedule."

"Brilliant, but do me a favor though? Put a shirt on. I'm your sister, after all, and I don't need to see all of that." She waves her finger around, pointing at my chest, and I laugh at her ridiculousness.

"You're so demanding," I tease and get out of bed to get a shirt. We make small talk about the family back home, her giving me an update on everyone first. We then transition into work and go through business emails together. She helps me decide what business engagements I should keep and what I can decline. The last topic of discussion is my upcoming movie that starts production in the next couple of months.

"We got the preliminary production schedule and they will start off in Dubai first, so we will need to get your travel arranged."

"Dubai?" I question in disbelief, my stomach dropping at the thought of being so far from my girls. "But that's halfway around the world."

"Glad to see you know your geography." She laughs at her own sarcasm but when she sees I'm not happy, her smile fades. "What's the matter? I hear it's lovely there. Hot, but beautiful."

"How long are they predicting we're there for?" I ask, ignoring her question.

"Two to four weeks minimum, but you know that can vary. Then you go back to Thailand for another two weeks." She pauses and looks at me in concern when she sees my frown. "Won't Jenna and Avery go with you?"

"Fuck," I mutter, not happy at all with this schedule. "I don't know. Jenna runs her own business and this is all so new for her…and for Avery." I'm not sure how Jenna is going to handle this news and I'm predicting it's not going to go well.

"We can try to make it a holiday for when they are there. Myself, Mum, and Dad can come and meet you guys in Dubai and keep them occupied while you work," she offers and I nod, liking the idea but it won't solve the problem of feeding into Jenna's fears.

"Thanks for the offer. Let me talk with Jenna first before we make any plans." I rake my hands through my hair in frustration. "I also need to talk with Philip. I can't do these back-to-back movies any longer."

"Your life has changed a lot since you signed those contracts, Cal," she gently reminds me and I know she's right, but I don't need to be working so hard anymore. That's what I've done for the last five years and it has paid off, but my priorities are shifted now with Jenna and Avery in my life.

"Yes, but the discussion needs to happen sooner rather than later."

We wrap up our conversation and I leave the bedroom, wondering when the best time to broach the subject with Jenna will be when I come to a halt seeing her looking out the window in the living room.

"Dubai, huh?" She says in a soft voice, her gaze still looking over Lake Michigan.

Fuck, she heard everything.

I walk over to her and wrap my arms around her waist, pulling her flushed against me. "Are you up for an adventure?"

She turns around in my arms, places her hands against my chest and looks up. Her eyes are watery, and my heart begins to ache at seeing the sadness that she's trying to hide. "I can't go to Dubai for long periods of time, Cal," she whispers with a small shake of her head and looks down at her hands.

A ping of disappointments hits me, but I push it aside. I cup her face with my hands and gently lift her head up to look at me. "We'll make it work, Jenna." I lean in and kiss her softly on the lips, not wanting her to worry about this now. We've been doing so good that I can't have this becoming a dark cloud over us. "Please trust me."

I kiss her again and again and soon, we're clinging to each other. We start taking each other's clothes off, leaving a trail on the floor as we move swiftly to the bedroom. She sits on the bed and leans back to take off her thong, but I push her hands away and do it for her. As soon as they are off, I'm all over her, my mouth salivating thinking about tasting her. My hands spread her legs wide and my lips land straight on her core. I spend the next few minutes licking, sucking, and going in and out of her, her little moans of pleasure making my cock hurt with need.

"Fuck, I love this pussy of yours," I murmur before diving my tongue right back into her. Eating her out can make me come almost as hard as when I'm inside of her, but right now, I want more. I can tell when she's almost at her breaking point by how hard she grabs my hair and when she starts to move against my face. I ease up and stop what I'm doing, rubbing my hands up and down the insides of her thighs.

"Get on all fours," I command, and she obeys, her eyes hooded with desire. She scoots to the middle of the bed and flips over to her knees and gets up. She looks over her shoulder at me in anticipation and I swear to God I almost orgasm from just her looking like that.

I get behind her and start kissing her back, making a trail of wetness with my tongue down to her ass, giving each succulent cheek the attention it deserves. My dick is throbbing to be inside of her, and I know I'll need to end the foreplay soon when an idea comes to mind.

"Do you have any toys, darling?" I inquire in a husky voice, not expecting her to say yes.

"Top drawer in my nightstand," she rasps out and my fingers find her folds and start playing with her clit. I'm ecstatic to hear that my girl has no problems taking care of herself when she needs it. I inch closer to her nightstand while my left hand continues to play with her and my right tries to open her drawer. At first, I don't see anything, but then in the back to the right is a wooden box. I open it to find two toys: a clitoris stimulator and a pink rabbit vibrator.

"Hmm, my little minx likes to get naughty," I murmur, pulling out both toys and laying them on the bed next to her. I grab the vibrator first and turn it on. I adjust it to medium speed and start to lightly rub it against the back of her thighs, then over her ass cheeks and finally teasing it up to her clit. She starts rocking against it, moaning out my name and the sound is one of the sweetest fucking sounds I love to hear.

"You like that, sweetheart," I coo, moving the vibrator back and forth against her, but not inserting it inside of her. "You don't like it better than my cock, do you?" She shakes her head no and I smile. I turn off the toy and replace it with my hand. "That's enough of that because the only dick allowed inside of you is mine," I tell her before throwing the toy to the ground, grabbing a hold of her hips, and plunging inside of her.

"Cal," she cries out, and I clench my jaw in ecstasy at how wet and tight she is. I start pumping into her slowly at first but when I see her grab the clit stimulator and start using it on herself, I start fucking her like a dog in heat. I can feel the vibrations inside of her and it causes her to squeeze around me tighter and tighter. The combination of the vibration and her gripping around my dick is so powerful that we both don't last long and scream out our releases at the same time.

My body is convulsing like it's never done before and I see stars. We both collapse on the bed, and I'm so overcome with emotion that I start kissing her back while still inside her. "I fucking love you so much, Jenna," I pant out in between kisses. Her body tenses at the words and when I finally catch my breath, I realize she's shaking and it's not from the afterglow of her intense orgasm. I move to my side and bring her with me, wrapping my arms around her waist.

I peer over her shoulder to see she is crying and my stomach drops. I'm not sure if it's tears of joy or tears of despair, but I hold her tighter and let her cry it out. When she calms down and stops crying, I continue to hold her and in minutes, she's fallen asleep.

"I love you, Jenna, and it's okay if you're not ready to say it back," I whisper despite her not being awake. As confident as I am that she does love me, I hope she doesn't wait too long to say the words.

# CHAPTER 22

*Another Two Months Later*

THE DAYS FLEW into weeks, which in turn flew into months, and Jenna still hasn't said the words I didn't realize I was yearning to hear. At first, it didn't bother me because her actions screamed that she loved me, but every time I said those three little words, it seemed to completely change her demeanor from happy to sad. Her eyes always tear up and I know the words are on the tip of her tongue, but she refuses to say them. When I asked her why she cries every time, she shook her head and told me it was because she was so happy. That answer sufficed for a little while, but soon it wasn't enough. I need to hear her say she loves me back.

One day I told her I loved her right before she went to drop Avery off at school and when she only smiled at me and gave me a kiss goodbye, it completely ruined my day. I tried to get my aggression out on the boxing bag in the gym, but my mind played that scene repeatedly, torturing me with doubt about us. When I left the gym not feeling any better, I decided to call the one person who's refused to help me with Jenna the whole time I've been here

"Tell me why she won't tell me she loves me, Layla? Help me

understand," I barked into the phone as soon as she picked up.

"Not my problem you can't understand her," she retorted back, which made me want to smash my phone against the concrete.

"Layla," I said in a strained voice, "I'm trying my hardest to make your best friend happy. She's my sunshine on her happiest of days and my darkest of clouds on the days she's mad or sad. I've told her countless times how much I loved her, how I feel fucking insane with the need I have for her and yet I somehow still feel like I'm failing her. I try to be supportive of her career, I try to be an equal partner, and I'm trying to be patient with her fears and insecurities. But obviously, I'm still missing the bigger picture here because I can't for the life of me understand why she won't say it back."

"It's not always about you, asshole," she mocked, but her voice was softer and not filled with so much animosity toward me. I knew she didn't approve of Robert working with me behind Jenna's back, despite it being for Jenna's own safety, but she's kept it a secret.

"Please Layla," I beg of her in a tired, pleading voice. "Help me."

She was silent for a few seconds and then she sighed. "She loves you. She's just scared to say it out loud because telling you gives you complete control to shatter her heart into a million pieces if you change your mind about the relationship. She was a mess after her first divorce, but somehow, you affect her more than her ex-husband ever did."

"But I'm not him," I growled in frustration. "When is she going to stop comparing?"

"When she's ready!" she yelled into the phone, her patience with me gone. "Why can't you just be happy she's accepted you back into her life? You've turned her whole world upside down in such a short amount of time. Let her get used to her new 'normal'. Let her understand what it's like dating someone like you. She'll tell you when she's ready…unless you push her away with your demanding, alpha-asshole ways."

And with that, she hung up on me and darkened my mood even more.

I went back home and called Chase, telling him I'm keeping him employed until I return from overseas. I was considering letting him go since Jenna has Mason and things have quieted down with the paparazzi, but for my own sanity while I'm gone, I want him to stay on.

When Jenna came home with Avery later that day, I stayed quiet and put my focus into playing with our daughter. I took her to the indoor swimming pool, but dinner together was a somber affair and Jenna noticed the change in my mood.

"You're angry today. Did something happen?" she asked once Avery was asleep and we were in the privacy of our bedroom. She approached me and wrapped her arms around my waist, concern streaming from her gaze. Layla's words echoed through my mind as I stared down at Jenna and although I knew she was right, I was beyond the point of being in a logical mood. I was feeling angry, possessive, and irrational and Jenna was now in the line of my wrath.

I grabbed hold of her biceps and leaned down into her face. "I. Love. You," I told her with gritted teeth, my frustration lashing out at her from my eyes. "Stop comparing me to him!"

Her eyes widened in shock, and she knew right away what I meant. "Cal—" she started to talk, but I cut her off with my mouth. I don't want to hear any excuses. The only thing I want to hear back is her love. My kisses were bruising, but she didn't protest and accepted my roughness.

"I want you," I snarled, tugging off her clothes roughly. "I want *all* of you, Jenna. Your body, your mind, your soul, and *your heart*." My words come out menacing and my grip on her is firm, but she never told me to stop. She wrapped those legs around my waist and surrendered herself to me. I've never angry fucked her before, but I was out of control with my emotions and needed to be inside of her quickly. When I was done and we both climaxed, I rolled away from her, ashamed of how I handled myself. We laid there in silence and just when I was about to fall asleep, I felt her lips on my shoulder and her arm snaked around my waist.

"Please don't give up on me," she whispered against my back. I covered her hands with mine and squeezed, showing her I appreciated her words.

But as we got closer to my departure date, sex with Jenna started to change. Her appetite was insatiable, and she acted like it had to be urgent, and I was a willing participant because I felt the same way she did, as if our time was ticking away. Even during the times I tried to make love to her and savor her body, she would turn the tables on me and start sucking me off. She knew she could have me whenever she wanted because when it came to her, I was always ravenous. She occupied my thoughts during the day, and I made sure to occupy her body at night. It didn't matter anymore that she wasn't saying the words; she was giving me her body over and over again.

And I prayed her heart would soon follow.

TOMORROW, I DEPART for Dubai, and it's been a busy week trying to get ready and being present for my girls. Jenna took the week off from work and kept Avery home so I could maximize every second with them before leaving. We agreed that I would go there first by myself to get settled in and then her and Avery would join me two weeks later with the hopes to not be apart for more than a few weeks at a time. This isn't going to be easy to maintain, especially being on the other side of the world. I can't always rely on Jenna traveling to me with an almost five-year-old and she knows work won't let me take that much time off during filming to come to them. We both know this, but we've agreed we'll cross that bridge when we come to it.

Today, we let Avery dictate what our plans were, and she decided we were playing in the park, swimming and eating lots of ice cream. She didn't have her usual smiles and giggles and I know it's because she's sad about me leaving and can feel the undercurrent of tension between Jenna and me.

Tonight, I'm taking Jenna on a formal date to one of Chicago's finest restaurants. I had Kellan ship a special dress to me for her and I left it on the bed before I went to go drop Avery off at Jenna's parents' house for the night. I'm now getting ready back at my hotel so I can formally pick Jenna up from the condo. I finish getting dressed and walk toward the mirror to check out my appearance. I'm wearing the same pinstripe suit I wore when I took Jenna out on our first official date back in Las Vegas. While we've been on many dates since getting back together, tonight marks the anniversary of that said date and while I know Jenna only keeps track of the date we met, our first date holds a special place in my heart. Satisfied with the way I look, I glance down at my watch to see it's time to go pick her up. I leave my room and take the elevator downstairs to where my driver is waiting for me.

We arrive at Jenna's within fifteen minutes, and I grab the bouquet of flowers I have for her and go inside to take the elevators up to her floor. I knock on the door, despite having my own key, and wait for her. When a couple of minutes go by without her opening it, I chalk it up to her still getting ready. I let myself in and call out her name, but I'm greeted with silence. I put the bouquet down on the kitchen counter and walk back to the bedroom. A pit in my stomach starts to form when I see the dress she was supposed to wear tonight laying out on the bed still. I take my cell phone out of my pocket and call her number, but it goes straight to voicemail. Fear slithers inside of my veins and I walk out of the bedroom and go into her office. Her desk is clean and the only thing on the second desk that Robert uses when he's here is his laptop. I walk back out of the office and call Mason.

"Are you with Jenna?" I demand as soon as he picks up.

"No, you gave me the night off, remember?" he asks in confused hesitation. "What's going on?"

"I'm supposed to be taking her on a date right now, but when I arrived home, she wasn't here and the dress I wanted her to wear is still on the bed. I called her cell phone, but it went straight to voicemail."

"Check the parking garage to see if her car is still there and if it is, call the front desk and ask if they've seen her walk out tonight. I'm on my way in," Mason orders and hangs up before I can respond.

I do as he instructed and go to the garage to find her car is still here. I call the front desk, who says they have not seen her, but they did change staff over an hour ago and will pull security footage and call me back. I go back to apartment and look around for her purse and keys and notice both are gone, so she must've gone out, but why is her cell phone turned off?

The next person I call is Robert, who confirms that he hasn't seen or heard from her and tells me he is coming to the condo. I text Layla and while waiting for her response, I call Chase.

"Has anyone mentioned seeing Jenna out alone right now?" I ask him when he picks up my call.

"No, but I can ask. Is Mason not with her today?"

I repeat my story of what was supposed to happen tonight, and he reassures me he will ask around, and in the meantime, go out and see if he can find her at her usual spots.

I start to pace back and forth, not knowing what to do. I keep calling and texting her, but everything goes to voicemail and the texts remain unresponsive. Layla texts back and says Robert already called her and they're going to go out looking for her as well. I text Mason and tell him to call Robert so they can divvy up places to search. I decide to stay at the condo in case she comes back.

I feel fucking hopeless and scared out of my mind. Security at the front desk finally calls back and said footage shows Jenna briskly walking out of the lobby over an hour ago and into an awaiting taxi that drove off. I asked if they could read the phone number off the side of the taxi and fortunately, they were able to and gave me the number. I then call the taxi company and ask if they could track down which taxis were at our condo because I'm looking for a missing person. The manager said it will take some time, but he can radio all his drivers and see who was recently here and will call me back.

The minutes seem to tick by at a snail's pace before I hear back from anyone. I tell my driver to go home since I can use Jenna's car if I need to go anywhere. My mind races with the worst thoughts and I have to shake them all away and trust that there's a logical explanation.

Thirty minutes later, Robert finally calls with news. "Layla just got a call from the bartender at O'Malley's. Jenna came in two hours ago and seemed upset. She's drunk and he's cut her off and has given her food. We're on our way there."

"I'll meet you there," I tell him and run out the door as fast as I can. Because I'm not thinking straight anymore and just want to see Jenna, I take the elevator down to the lobby and run to O'Malley's since it's only a couple of blocks away. Before I can even reach there, the paparazzi see me and start following, asking questions along the way. I don't answer them, my focus solely on getting to Jenna. I'm confused and angry as to why she's drunk at a bar when we were supposed to be together for my last night home.

The paps follow me to the front door of the bar but have to stop since it's a private establishment and they aren't allowed in. I pull the door open and immediately start looking around for her. I walk around the bar to the corner and finally see the backs of Robert and Layla, who are trying to help Jenna walk. She's having trouble walking due to her inebriation and her face is red and blotchy from crying. She looks up just as I approach and her eyes are filled with anger. I don't know what she's so angry about, but I'm starting to get pissed that she didn't talk to me first about whatever has her furious enough to want to get drunk and not be found. It was foolish on her part to go out alone, despite the restraining order we have against Danny Salari.

"Jenna, it's time to come home. We can discuss whatever you think is going on in private." I grab her arm to help her, but she yanks it out of my grasp.

"It's *my* home! I want you packed up and gone from it. We are done!"

"And why is that?" I ask calmly, but I'm seething on the inside that she's trying to throw away our relationship.

"Why? Because I can't trust you! I found everything out, the stories you planted about me, how you pay Chase to follow me! How could you, Cal? Why would you?" She starts crying and I feel like a fucking bastard. I look over at Robert, who shakes his head at me, indicating he was not the one who told her. I don't know how she found out, but it doesn't matter. She should have found out from me in the first place.

"Everything I've done has been in your best interest," I tell her, trying to quickly explain in hopes she willingly comes home with me so we can talk more in private. "I had Chase follow you to make sure you were safe before we got Mason and I asked

Robert to plant those stories because you were getting shredded in the press. You say you don't care about your reputation, but it would have affected your business and how people treated Avery. I couldn't watch that happen."

She shakes her head as the tears continue to silently fall and I can tell she doesn't believe me. I stare at her, my blood starting to boil at her unreasonableness. I grab her chin and force her to look deep into my eyes.

"I will not apologize for my actions, Jenna. The only thing I will apologize for is not telling you sooner. Now let's get out of here," I softly growl, not wanting to cause any more of a scene as I let go of her chin.

"How many more things are there that you haven't told me about that were done in my 'best interest,' Cal? I'm sorry, but I can't do this anymore," she cries, and my chest feels like it's about to explode from the pain her words have just caused. I know she's drunk and irrational right now, but I'm fucking pissed that she didn't come to me first when she found out and that she's the one deciding we're done.

"So that's it? You're going to cast me away for one mistake? I think you're just grasping for any excuse in order to protect yourself because you are too scared to feel anything. You want me gone? So be it," I say out of spite because that's how I feel right now. "Help me get her home," I bark out to Layla and Robert and turn around to shield her from the crowd that has formed.

Robert stands next to me and Layla holds Jenna up to steady her. We slowly make our way to the front door and once it's opened, we're blinded by the flashing lights from the cameras of the paparazzi. There's no way we can walk back to her apartment so Robert runs ahead, secures a taxi and then comes back to help. They start shouting questions at us, and I hear Layla tell Jenna to keep her eyes covered and she'll guide her to the cab.

"Here, let me help you with her." I see Chase emerge from the crowd and try to shield Jenna with his jacket.

"Ah, well if it isn't my own personal watch dog. You failed at your job miserably tonight, by the way. I think Cal should deduct from your wages," Jenna says to him and my jaw clenches in anger at my stupidity for not telling her sooner.

"Jenna, I can explain—" Chase starts but gets cut off by Layla.

"It's you! Get the hell away from her!" Layla screams and I turn around just in time to see her push Chase away.

I frown in concern, surprised by Layla's reaction to Chase. "What's wrong?"

"This is the guy!" She points a finger at Chase, and I look at her in confusion.

"Yeah, it's Canadian Chase. He's the one Cal is paying to follow me," Jenna sneers, giving me a look.

Layla looks at Jenna in shock, her blue eyes starting to blaze in anger. "He's the guy who I told your story to in Las Vegas."

My blood runs cold and I look at Chase in disbelief. All this time it was him who leaked the original story and he never said a word? He played dumb when I told him I didn't know who it was. "*What?*" I don't even think of the consequences my actions are going to cause, and I punch him in the face for deceiving me. He stumbles back and covers his eye.

"You bastard, you never told me that!" I roar and lunge for him when I'm restrained by Robert.

"Cal, get in the cab!" Robert pushes me toward the taxi as the paparazzi have a field day with what's transpiring. I know this is going to be all over the news within the hour, but I don't fucking care anymore. My hand is throbbing from hitting Chase, and all I want is to get Jenna home.

We reach the cab, and Robert gets into the passenger seat while Layla pulls Jenna into the back of the cab. Chase is trying to talk to Jenna, but I slam the door in his face and flip him off as we drive away.

The cab is silent until Jenna starts laughing uncontrollably, the sound manic and not at all like her. Robert, Layla, and I look at each other, not understanding how she could find anything funny with what just happened.

"I can't believe this is so funny to you," I mutter, shaking my head in disbelief.

"Oh, c'mon now, the irony of the puppet master getting played by one of his puppets is very funny." She looks at me with disdain and her words make the blood in my veins run cold.

"Cal, she doesn't mean it, she's upset and drunk," Robert says, a pleading look on his face when I gaze at him.

"That's right, traitor! I may be drunk and beyond hurt, but I'm not stupid. I'm done with all of you!" She slurs, slashing her hand through the air and almost hitting Layla in the face. "I'm also done with this smell. What *is* that awful smell?" she asks, looking around the taxi for the source and all of our eyes land on the small box of pizza that is sitting in the driver's lap.

"Oh god," Jenna mutters and she starts to dry heave. "Sir, whatever you do, do not open that box!"

The taxicab driver looks at Jenna in his rearview mirror with a confused smile. "It's my dinner. You should probably have a slice to help soak up that alcohol."

"Please no! If you open that box, I'm going to throw up," Jenna warns before burping.

"C'mon, it's just pizza. Here, have a slice." The driver opens the box with one hand, grabs a slice and starts handing it to Jenna. I watch her color rapidly change and I start screaming at him when she pukes all over herself and the pizza and then proceeds to slump over.

"Fuck," I shout and the driver screams, almost side swiping another vehicle.

"My car!" he wails and immediately starts to roll down the

windows.

Thank fuck Jenna's building is ahead of us, and we can get out here because the smell is making all of us want to throw up. "See that opening over there?" I point to the garage door for the residents of Jenna's building. "Go there instead of the front."

He pulls in and Layla gets out to type in the garage code. As soon as the doors lift open, he pulls in and I guide him to Jenna's floor. Robert navigates him up and we have him stop where Jenna's car is.

Layla helps me maneuver Jenna out of the cab and I tell her and Robert to get her into the condo while I pay the cab driver. I give him five hundred dollars, asking him to keep this incident private. Robert must have texted Mason while we were driving back because he runs over to the cab with cleaning supplies and a trash bag.

"Go help out with Jenna. I'll help him," Mason tells me, and I jerk my chin up at him in acknowledgement. I thank the driver and sprint to Jenna's condo.

Jenna can barely keep her eyes open, but we manage to get her clothes off her and I hold her up while Layla and I try to give her a quick shower. I swiftly get clothes on her and Layla tries to brush her teeth as best as Jenna allows her. Once she's done, I carry Jenna to the bedroom and tuck her in. Layla leaves the bedroom, and I glance one more time at Jenna before exiting and closing the door behind me.

Exhausted and feeling defeated, I walk into the kitchen and pour myself a straight shot of whiskey. I down it in one gulp and pour myself another one.

"I figured out how Jenna found out," Robert starts and I look at him in curiosity. "I called her earlier this afternoon needing a file off of my work computer because I needed to work on it at home, and I left my USB here. I asked her to email the file from my laptop. She must've seen something that peaked her interest to go snooping around and found the emails. I'm sorry, Cal," he says with remorse and I just shake my head at him.

"None of this is your fault, Robert. I take full responsibility. I should've never kept it from her. I just wish she would've confronted me first instead of handling it the way she did."

"She felt betrayed. I probably would've done the same thing," Layla responds with a sigh. "I can stay the night to help out." She offers and Robert nods, offering as well.

"Thanks, but we need to be alone." I throw back the other shot, wincing as the liquid burns down my throat.

"She didn't mean any of it, Cal," Robert says, referring to Jenna breaking up with me.

"Oh, but I think she did," I tell him with a sad smile. "Now if you'll excuse me, I'm going to shower. Thank you both for your help." I nod at them and walk back to the bedroom, knowing that they can show themselves out. I want to get out of these clothes, get cleaned up, and be alone to think about what I'm going to do about Jenna.

# Chapter 23

I watch Jenna sleep for hours, not knowing if this will be the last time I get to do so. I had to walk out of the bedroom a couple times to take calls from Philip, my publicist, and my sister. Since they have Google alerts set on me, they were notified right away when the first news article hit about tonight's activities.

"This is a PR nightmare, Cal," Liz whined after we all got on a conference call together. "You better pray Chase Wilson doesn't press charges against you."

"He won't," I tell them with confidence, because they don't know the truth about Chase and that bastard now owes me.

"How are we spinning this, Cal?" Philip questioned and I needed a couple of minutes to think before I figured it out.

"He said something inappropriate about Jenna and I was defending her honor."

"Okay, we can go with that but how do we explain Jenna being at the bar drunk?" Liz had me stumped there, because I didn't know what we could say to explain it without revealing the truth and there was no fucking way that was happening.

"No comment. I'm hoping reporters are too intrigued as to why I punched Chase and not on Jenna being there in the first place."

"Cal, is everything okay?" Bridget quietly interjected and my stomach started to feel queasy at the implication regarding the status of my relationship.

"No, it's not, but I'm hopeful that it will be." I changed the subject, not wanting to talk about Jenna anymore.

"It might be best if you left earlier tomorrow to avoid the media circus," Philip suggested. "The plane is there already and can leave whenever you're ready."

"I'll think about it," I muttered. "I'm going to try to get some sleep. I'll talk to you all tomorrow." I hung up with them and came back into the bedroom to try to get some rest.

It's now almost five in the morning and my mind won't shut off, replaying everything Jenna said to me. I don't know how we're going to recover from this if she can't learn to trust me. Even though not telling her was wrong, I don't regret hiring Chase and having Robert help me behind her back. I would do it all over again if it meant keeping her safe and protecting her reputation. But I'm hurt that Jenna doesn't want to fight for us. To me, this is just another bump in the road that we need time to work through, but unfortunately, time is not on our side. Maybe this trip comes at the perfect time. Maybe Jenna needs a break and even though that thought slashes my heart, it might just be for the best. It's not that I don't want to fight for us—I do—but I need a willing partner who wants to fight for us too.

And as of last night, Jenna doesn't want to be that partner.

Sleep evades me so I decide to take Philip's advice and leave early. I make the necessary calls to my pilot and driver and text Robert and Mason about my earlier departure. After everyone who needs to know has been notified, I get ready to leave. Once I'm dressed and ready, I stare at Jenna one more time while she sleeps. I lean down, kiss her forehead and whisper, "I love you," in her ear. She doesn't even stir, and I don't bother waking her up. I can only pray she soon sees my good intentions behind everything I kept from her and forgives me. I exit the bedroom and look around one more time with deep regret, wishing things were different, but I can't change the past. I can only live in the present and try for a better future. I grab my suitcase and the stuffed animal Avery wanted me to take along and leave half of my heart in that condo.

"I NEED YOUR passport please, Mr. Harrington," the flight attendant requests as she fills out the immigration paperwork for the flight. I reach into my travel bag and the pocket I keep it in is empty. I start to rummage through my bag, taking everything out, only to come up empty.

"Shit," I mutter in disbelief. "Seems like I've left my passport at home."

She winces and I can tell we're not going anywhere now. "I'm sorry, sir, but we can't enter Dubai without it."

"I understand. Let me call my driver and I will run home to get it." The flight attendant walks to the cockpit to inform the pilots of the delay and I call my driver, Marco, to come and get me.

"For fuck's sake," I mumble to myself in annoyance. I can't believe I forgot one of the most important things I would need for an international flight, but with everything that happened last night, I'm not surprised.

Marco arrives within thirty minutes and whisks me back to the condo. It's been two hours since I've left Jenna and I'm unsure if she's awake or not. I pull out my phone and text Robert, telling him about needing to come back to get my passport and asking if Jenna's awake.

**Robert: I haven't heard from her so not sure if she's**

**awake or if I'm even still employed by her.**

I frown at this because I would hope that Jenna wouldn't fire him. He was just trying to protect her as much as I was. She might have trust issues for a little while with him, but I pray she doesn't do anything rash. She needs him just like he needs her. I start responding back to him when he sends me another message.

**Robert: By the way, I had to tell her parents what happened because the local news covered the story about you punching Chase. They are still Team Cal…just like we all are. I'll be at the pool with Avery if you want to come say goodbye to her again.**

I smile at his words about being Team Cal and I definitely agree to get one more hug from my daughter before I take off again. We arrive within twenty minutes and Marco pulls up to the front circle of the building. I hop out, enter the building, and get in the elevator to head up.

My heart starts racing with adrenaline at the thought of seeing Jenna again. If she's awake, I'm not sure what I'll be walking into. She's either up and will ignore me; awake and want to talk or will still be asleep. Part of me hopes she wants to talk things out before I leave, but another part doesn't think I can handle her telling me again that we're done, and she wants the remainder of my stuff packed up and sent to the hotel. The thought of her telling me that is a real possibility, and I can already feel a tidal wave of sadness wash over me.

The elevator stops and opens up on her floor. I walk out, each step I take filling me with dread as I get closer to her door. As soon as I'm in front of it, I take a deep breath and shield my heart, preparing for the worst.

I quietly unlock the door and slowly open it. I hear her voice and my body immediately reacts to the sound of her. I walk through the doorway and come to a halt. She's on the phone talking to someone, but when she turns around and sees me, she freezes and the phone slips out of her hands. Tears spring to her eyes and before I can react, she launches herself at me. I stumble back in surprise while she wraps her arms around my torso and squeezes.

"You came back! Thank God, you came back!" Her voice is muffled by my chest and I'm so caught off guard by her response that I just stand there. I don't know what to believe or how to act because this Jenna is a complete 180° from last night's Jenna. My heart can't handle being played like a fiddle any longer.

"I came back because I forgot my passport," I mutter with zero emotion left in my voice.

She looks up at me with watery eyes and my chest aches to the point that it's hard to breathe. "I'm so sorry for last night, Cal. I know I said some hurtful things but learning that you hired Chase to follow me felt like you didn't trust me, that you were trying to control me and I realize that isn't the case now. You were only trying to protect me, and I was too stubborn to listen," she says rapidly, and my brain is trying to digest her words.

It's exactly what I want to hear, but I still feel tormented. I can't handle the yo-yo of emotions anymore. I gently grab her arms and move her to the side, trying to find where I left my passport because I can't look at her right now while I think. I see it sitting on the entryway console and I grab it, placing it in my back pant pocket. I turn around and stand in front of her, taking a shaky breath before gazing down at her. I want this woman so fucking badly, but I need her to be all in. I need her to stop doubting me—to stop doubting us—and I just don't know if she's capable of that.

I stare at her with longing before smiling sadly and shaking my head. "I don't have enough love for the both of us, Jenna," I quietly tell her and I turn toward the door, my heart feeling like it's going to explode into a thousand pieces.

She grabs my arm to prevent me from leaving, forcing me to stop. "I do love you, Cal. I'm so in love with you that…that I was just scared! Scared I was going to get hurt again."

I close my eyes as she finally says the words I've been needing to hear, but I'm fucking struggling with my emotions. I'm bothered that this is coming out now when I'm leaving and not before last night. Is this genuine or is she just too scared? She barely trusts me.

"Please Cal, please don't give up on me!" she cries out in anguish, and I open my eyes to look at her. "I promise this will never happen again."

"How can you love me when you don't even trust me, Jenna? We have nothing without trust!" I say harshly and I still have reservations about believing her because trust has been one of our issues all along. How can she just flip a switch so suddenly? Has the thought of losing me forever finally been her breakthrough?

"I do trust you, Cal, I do!" She smiles at me through her tears, and she can see how I'm still struggling with my feelings.

I narrow my eyes at her and reach for her hands, needing to feel her touch. I want to fucking believe her so badly, but I still have doubts. "You really trust me, Jenna?"

"Yes, Cal, I really do," she says with conviction, squeezing my hands in reassurance.

She needs to prove herself to me in order for me to believe this. I think for a moment and then realize what I need from her. "Then come to Dubai with me now. You and me for two weeks by ourselves. I'll take care of all the arrangements."

She gasps and lets go of my hands, causing the balloon of hope that started to grow to immediately be punctured and deflated. I can see from her facial expressions that she's having an internal battle with herself, and I start to get angry. "Why do you even hesitate?" I question, my voice rising with irritation.

She's struggling to find the words to explain and is grasping for excuses. In my mind, she should fucking have none and I get more furious while she continues to stall. This just proves to me she still doesn't trust me and isn't ready.

"We'll take great care of Avery, Jenna," Pamela Pruitt's voice interrupts and I didn't even realize Jenna's mother was here. Her confirming that they will take care of Avery for us fuels my fire even more.

"What are you so scared of, Jenna? Avery will be fine with your parents! Robert can handle your business. Why can't you just say yes?" I ask in harshness, losing my patience with her. I need a fucking answer. I need to understand why she just can't say yes and be with me.

"I…I don't know." Her words stumble out and she looks just as confused with herself as I am.

"Trust me, Jenna!" I yell out in frustration while throwing my arms up in the air. "I'm not your goddamn ex-husband. Why won't you just take a chance on me? Haven't I proven my love for you?" I say the last question in anguish, which causes her to suck in her breath. I know she can see how hurt I am, can feel the pain that is radiating off of me from her lack of action. She knows this is it for me, that I need more from her in order for this relationship to survive. Although I'm a man who knows his worth, I have feelings too. I need love and validation just like she does.

I grab her arms and lean into her, needing her to see I'm done with this game. "Take the goddamn risk of letting go of your control, letting yourself feel, regardless of how you may think the end is going to turn out. I know how it's going to turn out if you take that chance on me." I let her go and my arms fall away from her, and I gaze at her with sadness. "I would be your forever."

Her tears are silently streaming down her face, and I feel emotionally spent. I'm defeated with a broken heart, and I need to get out of here. I start walking away from her and open the door, but something stops me from leaving.

*Give her one more chance to come with and if she says no, you're done.*

I turn back around and hold out my hand while staring intensely at her. "Last chance, Jenna. What's it going to be?" Her eyes are pleading at me, begging me not to do this but I will not waiver. Either she comes with me now or that is the end of us.

I watch her squeeze her eyes shut and I'm assuming it's to not watch me walk away. I decide to count to five. If she doesn't agree in five seconds, I'm leaving.

*One*: She inhales a deep, body shaking breath.

*Two*: She opens her eyes and love is shining so brightly back at me that my breath catches in my throat.

*Three*: She takes a step forward.

*Four*: She places her hand in mine.

*Five*: She's fucking mine and I crush her to my chest, my lips searing hers in a burning kiss that sets my soul on fire. We slowly break away from our kiss and I rest my forehead against hers. I open my eyes and stare at the woman who's had my heart from the first moment I met her in first class on that airplane to Las Vegas.

"Go grab your passport. Don't bother packing. We'll buy you everything you need when we arrive in Dubai," I tell her, giving her an encouraging smile to get moving.

She nods at me with happy tears and runs to her office where her safe is holding her passport. I turn to look at her mother, tears of joy running down her face and I mouth "Thank you" to her, because without her stepping up and encouraging her daughter to go, she might not be coming with me right now.

Jenna comes out of her office with her passport and stuffs it in her purse. She runs to her mother and gives her a tight hug, thanking her for watching our daughter. She turns back to me with the biggest smile on her face and I'm so fucking relieved to see there's no hesitation and no regrets about the decision she just made. We say goodbye to her mother and walk out of the condo hand in hand.

"Are you ready for our next adventure, sweetheart?" I ask her while we stride briskly toward the elevator.

"I'm ready for a lifetime of adventures with you, my love," she tells me with love beaming at me from her eyes. The elevator doors open, and I pin her to the wall, hit the down button with my finger and then ravish those lips of hers.

Jenna Pruitt is ready to be mine forever and now we can live in happiness, without fear or excuses, and have unwavering trust.

# EPILOGUE

*14 Months Later*

I STARE IN awe at the long lashes on his closed eyelids, mesmerized by their length. My gaze travels to his tiny, button nose and those small, red lips that are parted while he sleeps. I run a gentle hand over the thick, shiny brown hair that covers his little head. The emotions of today start to bubble over and tears spring to life in my eyes as I fall completely head over heels in love with my newborn son.

Brooks Charles Harrington came screaming into this world twenty minutes ago and I feel like the luckiest bastard all over again. I gaze at him while he's cradled in my arms, swaddled in the blanket my mother crochet for him. I memorize this moment—this feeling—because I know how quickly time will take it away from me.

"You know, it would be nice if I got to hold him for more than just a second since he came out of my vagina and all," Jenna complains from her hospital bed, and I snort at her humor. I shake my head at her, not ready to give up my son.

"You've carried him for almost ten months, it's my turn now."

"Great, so are you going to grow breast milk and feed him

for the next ten months straight too?" I chuckle and give her a playful grin. The adrenaline coursing through her veins from giving birth must be the explanation for sassy Jenna right now and I fucking love it.

"You know how fucking sexy you are to me when you're feisty, so keep it up over there and I'll put another baby in you in exactly six weeks." She throws Brooks's tiny hat at me, and I laugh.

"Language, Cal. His first words don't need to be fuck or any variation of it."

I shrug at her, completely disagreeing. "Oh, I don't know about that. It would make him very cultured if it was."

"Of course you would think that," she says sarcastically with a laugh.

"Just give me a couple more minutes with him," I say to appease her and continue staring at my son. He's a beautiful baby, and I wonder if he looks like Avery when she was born. The thought makes me frown and I swallow back my sadness at not being around when she was born.

"Don't go there, Cal," Jenna softly warns, and I look up to see her watching me with a sympathetic smile. She must have seen my demeanor change and I love that she knows me well enough to know what I'm thinking. She's right—I can't go there because the past is the past and I can't dwell on it. I'm just so grateful to have been given a second chance with her and Avery.

Everything changed the day Jenna put her trust in me and came to Dubai. We needed those two weeks alone to reconnect both mentally and physically. Watching her leave gutted me and I vowed to not agree to any more international projects without her consent. We tried our hardest to see each other every two weeks, but it started to become impossible with my work schedule and delays with production. We went one month without seeing each other and it was the ultimate test for our relationship, but Jenna handled it better than I could've imagined. When production moved to Thailand and we were getting closer to wrapping up, I had my whole family come out for a vacation. After the last day of shooting, I proposed to Jenna on the beaches of Phuket where she said yes without hesitation.

I wanted to move her and Avery into a bigger home and when another death threat appeared, it moved the process up faster. This time, I didn't hide the threat from Jenna and showed it to her as soon as it arrived. She trusted that I would protect her and our daughter and agreed to the move and a second bodyguard. We found the perfect home on Lake Michigan in a gated community that was closer to her parents' house and only twenty minutes north from her condo, which Layla is staying in for the time being.

Career wise, things couldn't be better. I won what every actor covets—an Academy Award. Since winning, I have taken a much-needed break from work, which came at the perfect time during Jenna's pregnancy. I loved being there for every doctor's appointment and watching her body transform each month while giving our child life. My priority is my family and I have no plans to make another movie until everyone is ready and whenever that time comes, I demand that they come with me no matter where the location is.

I stand up and bring Brooks back to my soon-to-be wife. I take my cell phone out of my pocket and start snapping photos of the two and send them to family and friends who've been anxiously waiting to hear the news. I get a text from Jenna's mom letting me know she's here with Avery.

"Your mum is on her way up with Avery," I tell Jenna and I'm excited for Avery to meet her new baby brother. I watch Jenna kiss our son's forehead and my chest tightens with love. Her engagement ring catches my eye, and it reminds me that we need to discuss wedding plans.

"Now that you've had the baby, when can we get married?" I inquire and Jenna looks up and scowls at me. We were supposed to get married last fall, but she postponed it once she found out she was expecting.

"Cal, I look like a pregnant gorilla right now. I need time, please." I shake my head at her negative comments about herself because Jenna being pregnant lit me on fire—on a whole different level. I couldn't keep my hands off of her and that's usually the case when she isn't pregnant. But this was different—I wanted to touch and kiss every part of her while she was growing our child.

"I can go get the justice of the peace and we can get married as soon as your mum arrives," I offer with a mischievous smile. She looks at me as if I've gone mad and I chuckle. I know Jenna would never say yes to that, but she also knows that if she did, I would make it happen with the snap of my fingers. I don't need a big fancy wedding and even though I know she's mine, I still want that damn piece of paper legally binding her to me for all eternity.

"Your parents would kill us if we got married without them." She's right, they would, and they fell in love with Jenna as soon as they met her just like I knew they would. Her and my sisters are best friends and sometimes I think they call more frequently just to talk to her over me.

"Eh, they would get over it. We hold all the power now because we can keep their grandchildren hostage until they stop being mad at us." She laughs and the sound wakes up Brooks, who starts to cry.

I take the baby from her and walk around the room to help calm him down. Just when he's about to doze back to sleep, Avery comes barreling into the room with excitement, the sound startling him awake again. Jenna's parents follow behind her and walk straight to me to see their new grandson.

"Mommy!" she screams and races toward the bed. She climbs on top of it, and Jenna embraces her in a tight hug before kissing her on the head.

"I've missed you, my Avery Boo. Are you ready to meet your new baby brother?" Jenna asks and Avery looks at her with wide eyes and nods.

Jenna moves over so Avery can sit right next to her, and I walk a crying Brooks slowly over to them. "Sweetheart, do you think you are strong enough to hold your new brother?" I ask and she gazes at the baby with trepidation while he continues to cry. She looks up at me and I see that she's scared.

"Don't worry, honey. I bet he will stop crying once you hold him," Jenna reassures her and that gives Avery the confidence she needs.

"I'm ready, Daddy, and I promise I won't drop him." We all laugh at her words, and I gently place him in the crook of her arms. I sit on the other side of her and wrap my arm around her back so that my hand can help hold up his head.

He continues crying while I adjust him into her arms, but soon he stops and opens his eyes. He looks up at Avery and they stare at each other. I glance over at Jenna and see she has tears in her eyes. As if sensing I'm watching her, she looks up at me and smiles. "I love you," she whispers as the tears stream down her face.

"I love you," I tell her and my gaze shifts to our beautiful children. "Thank you for continuing to make me the happiest man in the world."

I lean over the top of Avery's head and bring my lips to Jenna's, savoring this moment with her, with our family and praying for a long, healthy, and happy future for us all.

Is this your first time reading about Jenna and Cal? Want to know how they meet in the first place? Want to know why Jenna felt the way she did? Check out their full story from Jenna's POV in Heartbreak Warfare (https://books2read.com/HeartbreakWarfare). Turn the page to read the first couple of chapters.

Cal and Jenna also appear in:

Perfectly Lonely (Let Me In, Book 2)

Edge of Desire (Let Me In, Book 3)

Shopping For Love (A Standalone Novel)

# Prologue

EVERYONE HAS DAYS in their lives that will never leave them. Days of happiness, days of experiences, days of sorrows. Today is one of those days for me. A day I thought would never happen to me. When you're writing the story of your life, this day isn't in your happily ever after.

Today is the day my marriage officially ended.

Today is the day my husband told me he no longer loves me. Correction—no longer is *in* love with me. He says he'll always love me, but I deserve to be with someone who is in love with me. He promises there's no one else but after eight months of therapy, he doesn't see his feelings changing, and it's unfair to me for him to stay in something that's dead.

I pretend not to hear him as I continue typing on my keyboard, but of course I heard him. I can't look at him. My breath is caught in my throat—words can't get past the giant lump that has now formed. He knows I heard him; he sees the tears streaming down my cheeks. His words will forever resonate with me. Gone are the happy memories we once had. Now when I think of him, this will be that moment.

*Fuck you* my head's screaming as he walks toward the door. I wish I could say those two words and their significance of how I feel. But the moment is gone. Instead there's silence that's filled with anger, defeat, and pain. I won't chase him. I won't beg for him to reconsider. I'm done being the only one fighting to save us. If he isn't in love with me anymore, then I shouldn't want him to stay. What I don't understand is where and when did he fall out of love with me?

We just had what seems like our millionth fight. Of course, it was over something stupid—aren't most fights over something stupid? Simple things that could have simple resolutions. Our war with each other has been me wanting his time and him not willing to give it to me anymore. I used to be his number one priority. Now I'm more like his mistress and work is his wife. Once upon a time, I *was* his life.

We met while working for the same sports agency firm. I was Assistant Director of Corporate Events and he was the Vice President of Corporate Sponsorship. He was charming, smart, funny, and good-looking. He knew how to use his looks and charm to land sales, especially if he was pitching to the female clientele. Each time he got our company a new corporate sponsor; I threw a lavish event in their honor. We had to work closely together, so we became fast friends. It was hard not to have a little crush on him, but I was professional and enjoyed his friendship, so I assumed that's what we were only ever going to be. I didn't think I was his type in the looks department either. He seemed to always gravitate towards blonde, blue-eyed women. Women who looked exactly like him, the complete opposite of me. Imagine my surprise one night when we were working late and he kissed me. We spent the next three hours kissing instead of working. I was head over heels in love with him and thought I found the perfect man.

We were married two years later and I was in complete bliss, both personally and professionally. After our one-year anniversary, we talked about having a baby. But another year passed, and we still had not conceived. My doctors did more testing, and we found out that I had an abnormal uterus. The doctor said it would be "tough" getting pregnant.

I was devastated.

I felt like a complete failure as a woman and wife. I started questioning why my husband would want to stay married to me if I couldn't give him a family. He thought I was being ridiculous and told me it didn't matter to him if we didn't have a baby. That all he needed was me. My intuition didn't believe him, and a woman's intuition is usually right. As the months moved on, I would catch him looking at other people's children with longing in his eyes. I knew my depression was affecting us, and I vowed to try to go back to being that bubbly, positive girl that he married. When I suggested we try using a surrogate, the light immediately came back in his eyes and we started making plans. He was about to accept a new position as Director of Corporate Sales for a Fortune 500 company, so with the extra income coming in, we were going to be able to afford a surrogate by the following year.

The love for my job was lost once he left the agency for his new position. I hadn't realized how much I relied on him professionally, as well as personally. I started feeling like maybe I had lost my identity. Sure, I was someone's wife, but I was still *me* and needed to do things that made me happy. With his blessing, I quit my job and started my own event planning business, with a specialty in children's parties. This required me to learn more about social media, including starting my own blog. I loved absorbing all this new information and I was back feeling like I could conquer the world with the best husband by my side supporting me. But as I engrossed myself more into my new business, I failed to notice the newfound changes in my husband.

His new job required that he traveled more, which at first I had no issues with since it gave me the time to devote to growing my business. His travels went from once a month to every week.

He was traveling to land the big accounts, and with those big accounts, came big commission checks. Money was always important, but it now was an obsession to him. It became a game–how much money can he make in a short amount of time. All he wanted to do was make more and more. Even when he was home, he was still always on his computer or taking phone calls late at night. His tastes started to become expensive. Our cozy apartment turned into a cold, modern looking museum from all the remodeling he had done. He always was generous with buying me little gifts here and there. Before it would be a new book that I wanted or a gift card to my favorite coffee shop. Now my gifts were lingerie from La Perla and jewelry from Ippolita. The gifts just felt like he was buying my forgiveness for his lack of attention.

Maybe some women are fine with that. For me, it was unacceptable, so I demanded we seek couples therapy. At first, he was reluctant to go. He didn't believe that outsiders should know the business of our marriage. But when the fights continued, he finally agreed.

Therapy bored him. He was physically present, but mentally unavailable. Even the easy suggestions of weekly dates seemed difficult for him. I was ecstatic when he suggested we go on a vacation. But in those weeks leading up to our vacation, he was busier than ever and hardly around. Once our vacation arrived, we were walking on eggshells around each other. He felt like a complete stranger to me. Even the sex felt cold and distant. I still never gave up hope though. I knew in my heart that the man I married was still in there, and he wasn't going to give up on me either. I was the same girl he married. Physically, I hadn't changed much, give or take five pounds or so. I was always his biggest cheerleader. I always put his needs before mine. We were constantly having sex up until he preferred work over me. But he did give up. He gave up on me. He gave up on us.

*Why did he give up on me?*

I'm trying to concentrate on my daily blog post, but I can barely see through the tears. The keyboard becomes saturated with their wetness, my fingers slipping as I try to type. The post has become more of a journal of my emotions in this moment than an article on a Valentine's Day party. Memories are flooding though my brain like waves during high tide. It's as if my mind wants to wash them right out in order to stop the pain that is throbbing through my heart. The music selection on Pandora Radio is only making things worse, playing every single sad song known to man. It's like she knows what's going on and wants to break me even more.

*Pandora, you're a bitch!*

I can't take it. Between the music, the memories, and the realization of what's actually happening, I need to find refuge. I run to my room and throw myself on what used to be our bed and cry.

I cry for the girl who thought she got her happily ever after.

I cry for the lost man that used to be my husband.

I cry for the children we will never have.

I cry at the realization that I'm now alone.

In my misery of the demise of my marriage, I conveniently don't recall hitting publish on a blog post that talks more about my failed marriage than of a themed party. I unconsciously just committed career suicide.

Or so I thought.

# Chapter 1

"Oh my, I think I just wet my panties!"

I roll my eyes at my assistant's favorite saying when he sees something he likes, which can range from articles of clothing to a human being. We are sitting in JFK International Airport, waiting for our respective flights. He's people watching while I'm trying to write some thank you emails. We just came from speaking at a three-day bloggers workshop, and now I'm on my way to Las Vegas for another speaking engagement at a women's entrepreneur convention. Robert, my fabulous, fun-loving, always cursing, gay assistant and friend, goes back home to Chicago to man the office.

When I accidentally published my emotional blog post over a year ago, never did I think thousands upon thousands of women would share it with their friends and would skyrocket me to success. The advice, sympathy, and support I received from strangers was indescribable. It took us two days to go through all the emails and comments. I tried to write everyone back, but ended up just writing a long thank you post instead. Never underestimate the power of women who band together to support each other when you are down or up.

"Jenna, stop what you are doing and look at this fine specimen of a man!" Robert demands loud enough for the entire waiting area to hear him.

"Robert, can you stop talking about wetting your panties so

loudly in public?" I chide while continuing to type on my laptop. "Anyone listening can be current or future clients and might not like your choice wording." I try to get my point across delicately since I don't want to hurt his feelings, nor do I want him to feel he can't be himself around me.

"If people don't like me for me, then we don't want them for clients anyway."

"Robert…" I warn, giving him a stern look that says that's the wrong attitude to have.

"Fine, next time I'll whisper it in your ear. Now will you please check this guy out!"

Sighing, I look up to appease him. The object of his lustfulness is talking to the lady at the ticket counter. With his back to me, I notice that he's very tall with curly brown hair peeking out from underneath his baseball cap, and has a very fine, round, hard ass.

"Tall and a fine backside... right up your alley, Robert!" I go back to typing out my email, not wanting to waste any more time staring at the stranger.

"That isn't just a butt, Jenna, that is a USDA Grade A Ass!" He laughs boisterously at his own joke, causing me to shake my head at him.

"You are seriously worse than a straight guy checking out women at Hooters," I respond, despite the fact that I do find his comment humorous.

"Oh, lighten up, Jenna! Did you sign away your sense of humor in those divorce papers too?" I immediately stiffen at his poor choice of words, the ink on the papers still a fresh new wound on my heart.

Robert knows how devastating my divorce has been for me. His first day on the job was the day after my infamous blog post. He showed up sharply dressed and ready to impress. He didn't anticipate having his boss answering the door in hysterics and looking like a zombie. At that time, I didn't realize I had thousands of emails waiting for me in my inbox, and I dumped it all on him that first day. I had no idea how to deal with it, ashamed that I'd made my personal life so public. I was an emotional wreck; a horrible example of the kind of boss you want to be working for. He left me alone the remainder of that day, but decided I was worth sticking around for. Even today, I can't believe he hasn't quit to look for something, or someone, more stable.

I can tell Robert realizes he has gone too far. His constant chatter has stopped and he's fidgeting in his seat. I ignore him while I finish my emails. He clears his throat, expecting me to look at him or ask if he's okay, but I refuse to acknowledge him.

"Um, Jenna, I'm really sorry. That was uncalled for. Please accept my apology?"

I give him a tight smile and nod my head. It's hard for me to stay mad at him because he's right. I have changed since my divorce. When I hired Robert, I was this wide-eyed, excited, energetic new business owner who thought she was the luckiest girl in the world to be her own boss. I was aware of my marriage problems, but to me, life was still good. I still loved my husband and thought we could get through our problems, no matter how bad they got. But that girl left with her ex-husband. That girl has been replaced with an insecure, wounded shell of her former self, who struggles to get out of bed every day and not be depressed when I realize that I'm alone. My heart has a wall of ice around it with cautionary tape. Work is the only thing that keeps me going. I'm the only one who pays the bills now and I have people who rely on me in order for them to pay their own bills. I've got to succeed, so I've thrown myself into work. I work twelve-hour days on new party concepts, updating all of our social media outlets with the latest trends in parties. I also try to continue inspiring women to keep going, to better themselves, and that we *are* worth it. I travel more now that I'm in demand to do public speaking engagements. I couldn't have done any of it without Robert and my best friend, Layla. They helped nurse me back to reality and put me in my place when I start getting depressed.

"I'm working on trying to lighten up more and have fun. I thought I did a good job while we've been here in New York."

"Oh yes, I was very proud that you stayed up past midnight," he jokes with a wink.

After our last seminar, everyone that we were networking with wanted to go out. Not wanting to lose the chance at making new relationships, we went bar hopping and ended up at one of the gay bars, dancing until four in the morning. I had so much fun and for a split second, I did feel like my old self. But that vanished as soon as I got back into my hotel room and reality came crashing in. I'm about to tell Robert that I'll continue to work more on bettering myself when he starts pawing at my arm in excitement.

"Jenna, look, he turned around… quick, before he walks away from us!"

The only thing I can see is a strong, chiseled jaw, and a very broad chest. His hat is pulled down so low over his face that I can't make out his features. He's wearing a brown leather jacket that is open to reveal a gray t-shirt that clings to his muscled chest and jeans that hug his hips very nicely. He seems to be concentrating on whatever his ticket says before he turns to make a beeline for the chairs near the entrance of the gate.

"Holy balls, do you *know* who that is? That's Cal Harrington!" Robert says with glee, his hazel eyes wide with astonishment at seeing a celebrity. I must have a blank stare on my face, because his expression turns to shock.

"You don't know who Cal Harrington is? The guy who plays Erik in the TV series 'Wrath of The Vikings'?"

"Nope, can't say I know who he is since I don't watch

television and when I do, it's all of the Real Housewives series because you live and breathe BravoTV."

"Girl, Cal Harrington is this hot up-and-coming actor who's currently on one of the highest rated television shows. His character is so hot on that show. You might not recognize him because he wears a long blond wig. He has gorgeous blue eyes and he's mostly bare chested in every episode. And the sex scenes," he says with a heavy sigh. "Let's just say I masturbate to them all the time."

I hear someone laugh and look over my shoulder at a young lady who's listening to our conversation. She quickly looks away and I turn my attention back to Robert.

"Robert, *please* lower your voice!" I whisper, but he has peaked my curiosity. "So, the sex scenes are man on man?"

"Oh honey, do I wish, but alas, he's banging hot Viking chicks. I just take them out of the equation and insert myself."

We continue to watch Cal Harrington as he proceeds to disappear in the crowd. "*Oh my lawd*, what if he's on your flight to Las Vegas? I bet you he is. You lucky bitch! If you're sitting next to him, you better kiss him full on the lips with tongue and get his autograph for me."

"Highly unlikely since a) I would probably get arrested for kissing him when he shouts that a stranger sexually assaulted him and b) he's probably in first class while I'm in coach."

"Jenna, did you not look at your ticket? You *are* in first class!"

Confused at what he's telling me since I never fly first class, I look at my ticket and sure enough, I'm in seat 3B, which usually is first class.

"Robert, you know I can't afford first class! Why would you do this?" I demand, getting angry just thinking about how much a first class ticket from New York City to Las Vegas is going to cost me.

"Have a little faith in me, Jenna. You have a gazillion frequent flyer miles, so I used some of your points to upgrade you. I knew it was going to be a long flight and figured maybe you would use your time on the flight to rest, even though I know you'll work the whole time."

Now I'm speechless because that's one of the nicest things anyone has ever done for me. With no rebuttal, I just give him a hug and whisper thank you in his ear for always taking care of me.

"You're welcome. I better get going. My flight back home is going to board soon." He grabs his laptop bag, and I stand up to give him another hug.

"Call me when you land," he says before walking away to his gate.

"I will and have a safe flight back home!" I yell after him.

I finish a couple of more emails and put my laptop away. One of my favorite pastimes at an airport is to people watch, so I sit back and entertain myself with the viewings. A few minutes later, the announcement is made that my flight will be boarding, starting with first class. I make my way to the entrance of the gate. I hand the lady at the counter my ticket to scan, trying to act calm, cool, and collected, when inside, I'm giddy as a kid in a candy shop to be in first class. I get inside the plane and notice there are four rows of first class, with two seats on each side. Someone has boarded the plane ahead of us, and I recognize the baseball hat immediately.

It's Cal Harrington...and he's sitting in the seat right next to mine.

# Chapter 2

If Robert only knew I was going to be sitting next to the object of his desire for a five-hour flight, he really would wet his panties. I'm not one of those people who freaks out when in the presence of a celebrity and since I've never seen any of Cal Harrington's work, I couldn't care less about who he is. To me, he's just a regular stranger.

I place my jacket in the overhead bin and sit down in my seat. I look at him from under my lashes while he plays on his phone. I still can't get a good look at his face or see his eyes because of how low his baseball hat is sitting on his head. What doesn't escape me is how large his build is. Even in first class with the bigger seats, he looks like he's cramped against the window. *I wonder why he isn't flying private?* Maybe he isn't as famous as Robert says he is.

I start into my pre-flight ritual of taking all the things I want to use during the flight out of my ridiculously oversized purse, and place everything in the seat pocket in front of me. This includes my laptop, a book, and some magazines. As I struggle to get everything into the now overflowing seat pocket, my purse slips off my lap and spills all of its contents right onto his feet.

*Shit, now I have to talk to him.*

I start apologizing profusely for my clumsiness while trying to get everything off of his feet and the floor. He leans down next to me and graciously starts to help. I'm suddenly overwhelmed by the most enticing, delicious smell my nose has ever had the pleasure of inhaling. I close my eyes, take another deep breath and smile. The mix of his natural scent with whatever cologne he's wearing can make any woman orgasm without even a physical touch. I'm basking in his manly aroma when I open up my eyes to see the most incredible blue eyes staring back at me. I immediately turn beet red, realizing that I was just caught inhaling him. I sit back up and wait for him to finish handing back my stuff. As he finally sits upright, I'm about to issue another apology when the words are caught in my throat.

He's holding one of my tampons with a charming smile on his face.

Not only am I speechless because he's holding my tampon, but I also finally have a view of his face.

He's one of the most magnificent looking men I have ever seen.

Chiseled high cheek bones with a straight, strong nose. Full kissable lips cover sparkling white teeth. But it's his eyes that have me mesmerized. They are the color of aquamarine and are the most beautiful shade of blue I have ever seen. His gaze is intense, making me feel raw and I struggle not to squirm in my seat.

"You know, you can do some really evil things with these," he says about my tampon, waving it around in the air like a wand, as if he's Harry Potter about to cast a spell.

Again, something that should be embarrassing isn't holding my attention—his strong, masculine, British accent is.

"Hey, are you okay?" he kindly asks.

"Excuse me, but what did you just say?" I ask as I shake my head, trying to snap out of my trance.

"I asked if you're okay?"

"Oh yes, thank you, but before then?" I try to get the tampon out of his hand, but it's conveniently out of my reach.

"I said you can do evil things with these. I used to pull pranks on my sisters all the time with their tampons." He flashes a smile that I can tell has him fondly recalling those memories.

"That's quite evil of you, and I hope they got you back with something equally humiliating," I say, finally being able to snatch the tampon out of his hand.

His laughter is deep and husky. The sound vibrates through my core, making me clamp my legs together. My body's reaction to him is foreign to me, leaving me speechless. I really don't know what to say to him. What do you say to some hot man who was holding your tampon hostage?

"Right, so, um, thank you for your help." I mumble in embarrassment and refusing to look at him.

"You're welcome, and it's Acqua di Gio," he says with a smirk.

"Excuse me?" I ask, looking at him in confusion.

"My cologne—it's called Acqua di Gio by Giorgio Armani. I noticed that you enjoyed the scent. Just thought you might want to know so you can buy it for your significant other," he responds, his smile deepening and then he winks at me.

*Oh god, can I be even more embarrassed?*

"Yes, well, thank you for that information," I stammer, turning very red again.

He throws his head back and laughs. I stare at him, completely transfixed by his laughter. *Why is he laughing at me? How can I get him to laugh again?*

Beautiful eyes, handsome face, tall, muscular body, and a scent that makes me want to lick every inch of him. Yup, I'm totally not talking to him the rest of this flight.

What the hell is wrong with me? *Get a grip, Jenna!* He's probably used to this adolescent behavior from psychotic fans. I'm a grown, professional woman, and can handle sitting next to a gorgeous man.

“My name is Cal, by the way.” He holds out his hand for me to shake.

“Jenna, and thanks again for the help,” I say as I reluctantly shake his hand back.

I knew there was a reason why I didn’t want to shake it. His hands are firm, warm, and the contact with them sends sparks tingling all over my body. This is absolutely absurd that some hot stranger’s touch is making me feel this way. Robert’s right—I need to get rid of this pent up sexual tension I have caused myself. I might have to go shopping for the perfect battery-operated boyfriend while in Las Vegas.

“No worries. Are you going to Las Vegas for business or pleasure?”

“Business, although, I do have a couple of days off for some down time. You?”

“Same. Relaxation before business begins.”

I was just about to ask if he frequents Las Vegas often when the most obnoxious, high-pitched voice rudely interrupts me.

“It’s *you*! *Oh my god! Oh my god! Oh my god!*”

Cal and I look up to see a platinum blonde, middle-aged woman with bright pink lipstick, and hair as big as the state of Texas hovering over our seat. Her heavily made up green eyes are bright with excitement at discovering him on the same flight as her.

“Oh, I just love you! You sure are a good actor. You turn this old woman on every week!” She says with a laugh. “Oh, but I’m sorry, I don’t mean to say anything disrespectful in front of your girlfriend.”

She looks at me when she mentions the word “girlfriend” and I’m actually flattered she thinks I would be. I smile at her, despite feeling mortified for him that she just revealed he gets her all hot and bothered.

“Thanks, but I’m not his girlfriend,” I tell her.

"I didn't think so, because I just read in a magazine that said he was single, but I didn't want to be rude."

Before I could ask if she believes everything she reads about him, she leans down to my ear and whispers, "If I give you a hundred dollars, would you trade seats with me? I know my seat isn't as fancy as yours since it isn't first class, but please, he's my favorite actor!"

I quickly glance at him to see his reaction, but he looks as if he didn't hear her request as he continues to smile at her. I, on the other hand, cannot believe that this lady has the balls to ask me to trade my beloved first-class seat for her economy seat.

"I'm sorry, ma'am, but I work hard at my job to be able to afford a first-class seat, so the answer is no, I will not be giving up my seat." She doesn't need to know that I used points to upgrade to first class.

"Well, there's no reason to be rude about it," she huffs.

"I'm sorry, but I wasn't being rude about it," I counter back, annoyed that she called me rude.

"You're holding up the line, lady!" an agitated passenger shouts behind her.

"Good gracious, I've never been so insulted! Enjoy your flight, Cal, and I'm sorry you are sitting next to such a bitch," she declares, and stomps off toward her seat.

My mouth falls open in shock. *Big head just called me a bitch?* I turn to look at Cal, who's biting his sexy lip to keep from laughing. "Oh my god, are all of your fans like that? She calls me a bitch for not giving up my seat for one hundred dollars? That's *crazy*!"

Not being able to contain it any longer, he lets out a deep bellow of laughter. "The expression on your face when she called you a bitch was brilliant," he says, laughing. "And no, not all of my fans are as, hmm, how should we describe her… protective of me as she is. I'm sorry she called you a bitch."

“No need to apologize for her. I’m sorry if I came across that way. I wouldn’t want you to lose fans because of how I reacted.”

“I don’t think I need to worry about losing her as a fan,” he laughs. “I’m very appreciative of fans like her, even if they can sometimes become overzealous. It’s the ones who try to get into your personal business, or talk to you as if you are your character, that scare me.” He looks at me with a devilish grin and says, “Let’s be honest, for all I know, you could be one of my stalkers.”

“You would only be so lucky if I was your stalker,” I joke with some sass. ”In all seriousness, I must confess that I haven’t seen any of your work. I’m sorry, I just don’t watch television or get to go to the movies very often.”

He stares at me, showing no emotion. I hope I didn’t just offend him, but then that would be very egotistical if he did feel that way. *Maybe he doesn’t believe me?* I’m sure there have been female fans who have said that just to play it cool. How do I convince him that I’m telling the truth?

*Why do you even care if he believes you or not?*

“I like that you haven’t seen my work,” he says, staring straight into my eyes. His intense gaze stirs something within me. Blushing, I break our eye contact and look down at my hands. I don’t like this feeling of butterflies in my stomach that his gaze is giving me.

The captain of the airplane conveniently gets on the intercom to announce we will be taking off momentarily, and to expect turbulence for most of our ascent to 35,000 feet. Once we reach 35,000 feet, the air will be calm and the flight attendants will start inflight drink service. I dread this news as I’m not the best flyer. I’m very uneasy with take-off, but add turbulence to the mix, and I’m going to be a hot mess.

*Wait, why would we have turbulence during take-off?* It was beautiful out when we arrived at the airport. I look out past Cal at the window and sure enough, ugly, mean looking gray clouds surround the airport.

I must have moaned while grabbing my noise cancellation head phones, because Cal asked if I was okay. "Yeah, I just hate hearing about turbulence. I'm not the best flyer, but I shouldn't do anything embarrassing that would make you regret sitting next to me. I keep my turmoil on the inside." *Oh my god, stop rambling, Jenna!*

"I understand about not liking to fly. I find distracting yourself to be the best way to handle it. I can tell you some naughty stories to keep your mind off of the bumpy ride," he says with a wicked smile.

His looks are already causing turbulence inside my body. "Maybe you can tell me the stories for the rest of the flight. For take-off, I just like to put my headphones on, close my eyes and hug myself." I reveal, laughing at how pathetic that sounds.

"That actually sounds really sad. But okay, if you change your mind, you know where I sit," he jokes.

I say thank you and settle into my seat. The plane is just waiting for the control tower to give us the okay for take-off. The cabin is silent, almost like the calm before the storm. We must've received the go-ahead, because the jet engines start to roar and we start to move, accelerating faster toward taking off. I start my ritual take-off prayer/chant in my head as I feel the plane lifting off the ground.

*Please God, safe flight.*

*Please God, safe flight.*

I'm not a religious person, but for some reason, saying this over and over inside my head makes me feel better. Soon I start emphasizing the *please* and the *God*, with every bump, shake, and tilt of the plane as it gets worse. Despite wearing noise cancellation headphones, I can hear the engines working at top speed, the gasps of the other passengers as the plane turns at an uneven angle. My arms are crossed over my stomach, my hands gripping the arm rails, holding myself down into my seat. My head is permanently settled back into the head rest. My eyes are squeezed shut, and I'm pushing my feet as hard as I can into the floor to prevent my body from matching the jerking movements of the plane.

I barely hear the first ding signifying we have reached 10,000 feet. Not that it matters, because with the way the plane is jerking all over the place, the flight attendants can't get out of their seats to announce the use of portable electronic devices. You can feel the plane flying with ferocious velocity, the captain trying to get out of this horrible weather to the promise land of clear skies above the dark clouds and swirling air.

Suddenly, the plane drops and our bodies are momentarily suspended in the air, our seat belts preventing us from hitting the roof of the plane. We come crashing back into our seats as the plane continues its journey up. My headphones can't cancel out the crying and screaming of other passengers. I feel something rubbing my hand and I quickly open my eyes, look down, and see Cal's hand over mine. I look up at his face to see his jaw muscles clenched, his head motioning down to his open hand for me to take. With that encouragement, I raise up the arm rest, grab his right hand with mine and launch myself onto him. My hand grips his right arm and smothers it into my chest while I bury my head into his armpit. It doesn't matter that I just threw myself onto a complete stranger. It doesn't seem like I can grip him hard enough to prevent the feeling of falling. His left arm comes around to bring me closer to him, trying to shield me from this nightmare. This would be the perfect time to appreciate feeling his hard body, but the plane takes another dip and I'm lost again in my prayer.

*Please God, safe flight.*

*Please God, stop this turbulence.*

*Please God, I am not ready to die.*

*Please God, please God... please listen.*

I hear him then. Not God, but Cal, softly repeating to me, "It's going to be okay." And I start to believe him. I secure my grip on him and focus on his voice, his words. More time passes and I feel the plane evening out, the bumps getting fewer and far between. I stop praying and try to enjoy the feeling of his arms, his chest, and how good it feels to be held by someone. It has been so long since I have been held by a man that I realize I miss it. I'm reflecting on my loneliness when the captain comes on the intercom.

"Folks, I apologize for the scariness of the last five minutes. If anyone has been injured, please press the help button to notify the flight attendants. Flight attendants, please do not leave your seats yet. If there are any injuries, we will be landing at the closest airport away from the storm. I'm happy to report that we are out of the storm, but please keep your seatbelts fasten for the next five minutes to make sure we don't experience any unexpected rough air."

I keep my eyes closed, waiting to feel another dip in the plane. I'm also listening for any call buttons being pushed, signifying the need for help. Five minutes comes and goes and nothing happens.

"Flight attendants, it's safe to move about the cabin," the captain says, and the whole plane erupts into applause. I open my eyes and feel Cal's left arm still wrapped around me. I'm enjoying being held in his arms when I look down at our adjoining hands and suck in my breath. Our hands are conveniently located in my lap, only a few inches from my crotch, and I have completely nestled his arm in between my breasts. I quickly pull out of his arms only to bang my head on his chin. We both say, "Ouch" at the same time and look at each other—him rubbing his chin, while I rub my head. We can't contain the burst of laughter that bubbles out of both of us.

"Holy fucking shit, that was scary!"

"Oh my god, I thought we were going to die!"

We continue laughing, letting the therapy of laughter ease the tension out of our bodies.

# Chapter 3

I'M NOT ONE to indulge on flights for work, but a cocktail is definitely in order after what seemed like a near death experience. The flight attendants start their inflight beverage services, and we're more than happy to receive the free champagne. Personally, I feel the whole flight deserves some champagne and not just first class. The attendant brings us our drinks and without realizing what I'm doing, I gulp my drink down.

"Well, I was going to toast to us being alive, but now I see you have started the fun without me," Cal jokes, nodding towards my empty glass.

"Sorry," I say, grimacing from the taste of the not so great quality champagne. "I just needed something quick to calm my nerves and let's not jinx ourselves, the flight isn't over yet."

"This is true. Let's get you another drink." He attempts to get the flight attendant's attention, but I stop him before he can hit the help button.

"No, that's all right. I usually don't drink on flights, and I have a bottle of water in my bag that will be just fine." I grab the water from my bag underneath the seat in front of me. He holds out his drink to me and toasts, "To a quiet, calm, and easy remaining flight."

We clink our drinks together—his champagne to my water bottle—and drink, our eyes locked together as we enjoy the cool liquid going down our dry throats. His eyes move to my lips as a drop of water escapes from the tip of the water bottle and runs down my chin. Blushing, I wipe the back of my hand against my mouth and chin, breaking the intense gaze he has captured over me. Drinking water just turned *very* sensual as thoughts of him licking the water off me enter my mind. I need to start doing some work to get my mind off of what this man would be like in bed. I reach down to retrieve my laptop to start working on some more theme party ideas for my blog.

"Please don't tell me you are going to ignore me for the rest of the flight after our delightful groping session," he teases while I place my laptop in front of me. Of course, I don't want to work, but I'm afraid that I will make a fool out of myself if I keep talking to him.

"I wasn't necessarily going to ignore you, I was just going to try to do some work in between our conversations," I respond back with a grin.

"Good answer, but what exactly do you do for a living that makes working right now so important?"

"I own an event planning business, my specialty being children theme parties. I create the parties, and then showcase them on my blog. We also sell the products that we use on our website." I pull up a design board of saved pictures from our recent photo shoot of a country fair birthday party to show him.

"My assistant and I will create a party, design it with products from the vendors we use, then set it up for a photo shoot. Afterwards, we upload the photos and create a blog post on that party. Sometimes clients want the type of parties we already feature on the blog or we have a meeting with them and custom design a party. Children's parties are my favorite, but our bread and butter are the corporate parties."

"I had no idea that children's parties can get so detailed. Very impressive. This makes you enough money for it to be your full-time job?" He pins me with a skeptical look, one eyebrow arched higher than the other.

“Yes, Dad, I make enough money to support myself and pay an assistant,” I joke, noting that he sounds just like my father did when I first told him my business idea. “People who have lots of money want to have fabulous and unique parties. We understand that the average person is on a budget and might not be able to afford to hire an event planner, so we also give advice on our blog on how you can do the party yourself on a budget.”

“What made you get into this kind of business? Do you have children of your own?”

“No, no kids, and I just fell out of love doing only corporate business meetings and parties. I still enjoy planning corporate parties, but for me, there’s nothing better than seeing the pure joy on a child’s face when they see their birthday party for the very first time. I like to create that imaginary world for them.”

There’s no need to tell him that creating these parties for other people’s children fills the void and ache I feel for not having my own. He’s probably so far removed from having kids, let alone a serious relationship.

“No kids and I don’t see a ring on your finger?” It isn’t a statement, but more of a question. It’s a simple answer really, but one that stills makes me swallow down the lump in my throat.

“I’m divorced,” I say quietly, not giving any more detail.

“Divorce is painful and I’m sorry you went through that, but I must admit, I’m a bit relieved to know that I don’t have to feel guilty flirting with you.”

“Yes, but do I need to feel guilty flirting with you?” I smile with a questioning look.

“If what you have been doing is flirting, then you need a better teacher,” he responds back with a devilish smirk.

Shocked, I just stare at him with an incredulous look on my face, not believing that he actually insulted me. But now that I think of it, he’s probably right. I have become cold and probably so dull and boring compared to other women who he's encountered. *Am I trying too hard to be calm and play it cool around him while he is making my insides turn into jelly?* He makes me want to behave like a high school girl, twirling their hair while talking to their crush. If high school girls even do that anymore. I'm just an uncool, divorced, fuddy-duddy who has cobwebs on her vagina from the lack of sex.

He throws back his head and laughs. "You're so brilliantly fun to mess with." He rubs his hands together as if he has more insults up his sleeve. I can't help but chuckle at him, and I can now relax knowing he's joking with me.

The flight goes quickly as we continue asking questions about each other, laughing, and flirting. I feel like I'm on a first date, the giddiness of getting to know someone new for the very first time should feel awkward, but comes easily with him. I learn that besides being single, he has two sisters, is from Broadstairs, England, and lives in London when he isn't shooting his TV series or a film. He got into acting because a scouting agent approached him while he was on break from school and asked if he was interested in becoming an actor.

"I truly believe that fate played a role that day because the agent not only chose me, but also my two best mates, and we were the only ones out of our group of school friends who were on break together hired to be in a commercial. All these years later and all three of us are still acting. It just feels like it was meant to be."

"That's pretty amazing that all three of you got chosen and are still acting," I agree, wondering who his friends are, but don't want to ask.

"My friend, Sean, is the one who has the biggest career out of all of us. You might have heard of him if you at least go to the movies - Sean Lindsey?"

My mouth drops open. Of course, *I* even know who Sean

Lindsey is. He's a huge movie star, especially with romantic comedies. Rumor is he might be the next James Bond.

"Yes, I know of him. Who is your other friend?"

"Cora Gregory."

Cora Gregory is every male species object of wet dreams. One look at her and men probably blow a load in their pants. She's gorgeous, with green cat-like eyes and long, black hair. In photos, she either has resting bitch face or is making love to the camera with those hypnotizing eyes that make men bend to her will.

"Wow, Cora Gregory, huh? She's beautiful. Why aren't you dating her?" The question slips out of my mouth before I could keep my curiosity at bay.

"Everyone asks me that because we attend events together, but to be quite honest, she's more like family to me. I just don't have those type of feelings for her."

My face must have shown my utter disbelief at his statement because he laughs. "Why does everyone think that's bullshit coming out of my mouth? I'm well aware of her beauty. I wouldn't be a man if I didn't notice it, but even to this day, I only see her as one of my sisters. I have known her since she was a lanky, skinny young girl who had a horrible home life. Sean and I decided we were going to protect her at school from all of the wankers and mean girls. That's all it has ever been for me."

I silently ponder what he just said. As we sit in compatible silence for once, the captain choses this time to announce that we will be making our descent into Las Vegas and for the flight attendants to prepare for landing. Cal and I smile at each other as I pack up my carry-on bag with my items, being very careful to make sure it doesn't fall on his feet again.

As I place the bag underneath the seat in front of me and wait for us to land, I realize that this has been one of the best flights I have ever been on, despite the turbulence from take-off. Not because I am sitting next to a man who is physically gorgeous, but because I am sitting next to a human being who cared enough about my well-being and was curious as to the type of person I am. He engaged with me the whole flight, and genuinely listened to everything I said. I would expect actors to stay recluse and speak to the stranger sitting next to them unless spoken to first.

"Are you okay? Do you need to hold on to me for landing?" His face shows genuine concern as the plane is about to touch down.

"I actually like landing," I say with a laugh.

"Really? That's the most dangerous part!"

"I know, silly isn't it? But to me, landing signifies that we have arrived and that makes me happy."

"Well, I get scared at landings and you owe me some emotional support, so hold my hand." He grabs my hand and rests them on his very tight thigh.

"I find it *very* hard to believe that you are scared of landing." I laugh back at him.

"Men can be as sensitive as women, just in different departments," he says, holding my eye contact. I blush at the dirty thoughts that enter my brain. *Get your mind out of the gutter, Jenna!*

"Thank you for helping me," I say softly, not wanting to say anything more, but hoping he can see my sincerity and gratitude in my eyes.

"The pleasure has been all mine," he says sincerely as the plane touches down with a small bump. I smile at him and pat his hand, breaking the contact.

We reach for our phones, turning them on while the flight attendant welcomes us to Las Vegas and ask that we stay seated until we safely stop at the gate. I scroll through my text messages from Robert and Layla, trying to stay focused and busy, while realizing I will probably never see him again. A reality that is surprisingly disappointing.

We reach the gate and as soon as the plane comes to a stop, the clicks of seatbelts unbuckling fill the air. I suddenly feel shy, like I have no idea how to say goodbye to him. I decide to stand up and stretch my legs instead. Since we're in first class, we really don't have a long wait to depart the plane. I turn and notice he has decided to stand as well.

"Thank you again, and I truly hope you have a wonderful time here."

"Thank you, I hope you do too. When does your conference start?"

"It officially starts Wednesday morning, but I have some prep work I have to do before then," I say, moving out onto the aisle to depart.

"*Cal! Cal!* Can you please wait so I can get a picture with you?" We turn to look down the aisle to see Big Head frantically trying to make her way past people to get to the front. He gives her a thumbs up and we continue to walk out of the airplane.

"Mr. Harrington, would you mind stepping aside and taking some photos with our flight crew real quick?" one of the flight attendants asks him as well.

"I don't mind at all," he says, smiling at them. I feel this is the perfect opportunity to just walk away and stop feeling so awkward about saying goodbye.

"Best of luck, Cal Harrington." I wave and without waiting for a response back, I turn and walk up the jetway.

# Acknowledgments

It takes a village to publish a book and I want to thank the following people:

My husband, kids and immediate family, who gives me the support and encouragement every day to keep going. I'm the luckiest girl in the world to call you all my family.

To my team who personally worked on this book with me: Najla Qamber, Tracey Vuolo, Dorothy Bircher, Brittany Holland, Barbara Hoover, Emina Ross, CP Smith and Stevie Schneider. You girls are my rockstars. Thank you for your support, encouragement, honesty, and putting up with me when I whine about imposter syndrome.

To all of the readers, bloggers, bookstagrammers and BookTok friends: Thank you for your continuous support and sharing how much you love my books. There are not enough words to truly express how grateful I am for every kind word and review.

# Also by Jessica Marin

***The Let Me In Series***

Heartbreak Warfare (Let Me In, Book 1)

Half of My Heart - Cal's POV

Perfectly Lonely (Let Me In, Book 2)

Edge of Desire (Let Me In, Book 3)

***Bear Creek Rodeo***

The Irish Cowboy

The Celtic Cowboy

***Standalone Novels***

Love At The Bluebird

Until Valerie: Happily Ever Alpha World

Shopping For Love

# About the Author

Jessica Marin began her love affair with books at a young age from the encouragement of her Grandma Shirley. She has always dreamed of being an author and finally made her dreams of writing happily ever after stories a reality. She currently resides in Tennessee with her husband, children and fur babies.

CPSIA information can be obtained
at www.ICGtesting.com
Printed in the USA
JSHW021536090622
26816JS00001B/35

9 781736 376645